# Other Mysteries by Martha Kemm Landes

Framed Fur Murder

Upcycled to Death

Pity the Movie Lover (1)

Pity the Garage Sale Addict (2)

Pity the Reluctant Fan (4)

# PITY THE
# STRANDED TOURIST

by

Martha Kemm Landes

Elemar Publishing

# Dedication

To our parents, Jim and Betty Kemm, thank you
for instilling in us the love of travel.

To my husband, Dan, and my sister, Kathy,
thank you for being the perfect travel partners.

To my wonderful daughters who joined me on an amazing
trip and ended up stranded in Switzerland,
I'm sorry I jinxed you by starting this book early.

This novel is also dedicated to fellow travelers everywhere.
Each trip is a gift for the senses with new sights, sounds,
and tastes to explore. Whether traveling in the U.S. or abroad,
our view of the world broadens with each new culture
and tradition we encounter.

May your luggage gather no dust.

# Pity the Stranded Tourist

Martha Kemm Landes

# Travel Tip #1

*Choose the perfect traveling companion.*

I stared at the article and blinked several times. "Lauren, is this print out-of-focus?"

Ren gave a sigh as she came in from the kitchen with a glass of water. She set her glass down and stuck her head over my shoulder. "It looks fine to me."

"You can read that?" Of course she could. She was only 17. I held the magazine closer to my face, which made it worse. I pushed it farther away as I had seen my dad do years ago and surprisingly, that worked. How in the world could the print get clearer by moving it away? That just seemed counterproductive.

My flexible daughter plopped down on the floor and stretched. With her head upside down, her voice was muffled, "You probably need glasses."

I sucked in a horrified breath and stared at her. "No, Lauren. My vision has always been 20/20. The last time I went to the eye doctor my eyesight was 20/15, which is even better than perfect."

She pushed herself up into a backbend, a feat I hadn't accomplished since age ten, and asked, "When was the last time you saw an eye doctor? I mean you are getting old."

I scoffed. "I am not old. Forty-five is the new twenty-five." At least I was pretty sure I heard that somewhere.

I held up the magazine again, squeezed my eyes tight, and blinked a few more times. Relieved, I said, "Ahh. Never mind. I can read it now." I studied the magazine article further and turned my head upside down so I could see Ren's face. "Anyway, old or not, I have as good a chance to win as the other contestants!"

She lay down on the carpet and shook her head. "But you've never even driven a Greco. Why would they choose you?"

I looked at her in disbelief. "Because I am going to write the best jingle they have ever heard. That's why."

Ree entered the room and picked up an ornament that had fallen from the Christmas tree. She hung it back up and said, "A jingle?"

Ren answered, "You know—a catchy tune to advertise a product."

To demonstrate, I sang, "Like a good neighbor—"

My youngest, officially named Marie, rolled her eyes. "I'm not stupid. I know what a jingle is. I want to know why Mom wants to write one."

Ren shrugged. "Oh, she thinks she's going to win a contest by writing a jingle for a new style of Greco sports car."

I sat up straighter. "Yes. It's called the Macchina Forte. I looked up the Italian word Macchina and it means machine, or Automobile."

Before I could tell them what Forte meant, my 13-year-old sat beside me on the couch and said, "So it means strong or loud car? I mean, you taught us that's what forte means in music."

So, Ree *did* remember something from my music classes.

I smiled. "I guess either strong or loud could work for a car."

Ree pushed a strand of long blond hair behind her ear. "Have you ever even seen a Greco car, Mom?"

"Well, no. But they don't need to know that. I just must come up with something so clever that everyone will want the new model."

She lifted the corner of the magazine I held and made a face. "Since when do you read *Car and Driver* magazine?"

"It's Mike's. He gave it to me so I could check out the contest."

She nodded. "What's the prize? A new car?" She perked up.

I smiled at the thought of that prize but said, "No, but the winner gets to fly to Rome for the unveiling of the new Macchina Forte where the jingle will be performed live!"

Ree sucked in a breath. "Oooh! If you win, can we go with you?"

I frowned. "Well, no. I can only take one guest to Italy and that person must be at least 18. Sorry, girls."

Ren's eyes widened. "When is the trip? I'll be 18 in June!"

Her sister pounded on the couch cushion. "That's not fair if she gets to go and I don't."

Attempting to thwart a full-on fight, I jumped in, "Hold your horses, girls. Let me look." I squinted and traced the fine print with my finger. "Okay, it says here 'All entries must be received by December 25th and finalists will be announced on New Year's Day!'" I looked up and shook my head. "Wow, that's a fast turnaround. Those poor judges will have to work during the holiday."

Ren tapped her toe. "But when is the trip?"

"I'm getting to that." I read silently. "Oh here. The vacation of a lifetime will be February 12th to the 16th."

As soon as the words came out, I knew I would hear grumbling from both girls. And it came – in stereo.

Ree gasped, "That's right before my birthday. You had better be back for it."

Ren said, "Well, that's just great – four months before I turn 18." She was silent for a minute then her eyes narrowed. "Couldn't you just fudge on my age? I *look* 18."

I studied my olive-skinned teen. She would easily pass for 18 or even 21. I shook my head. "I'm pretty sure that wouldn't work, Lauren."

"But you lied about my age so I could go to ski school."

I smirked. "Yes, but that was different. You had to be three to join the bunny class. You were an advanced talker and never had accidents, so we told them you were three. Nobody noticed you were only two and a half." I smiled as I remembered my adorable toddler in her bright pink snowsuit gliding down that bunny slope on super short skis.

She said, "So, how is this different?"

I cleared my throat. "I'm sorry to say it but there are these things called passports, and you would have to have one and show it around – a lot. No fudging there, girl." She frowned, but thinking of passports reminded me mine should still be good. I had gotten one a few years ago for a trip to Mexico with my bestie from high school, Lis.

Ree pouted. "I can't believe you would leave me and go to another country right before my big birthday."

I wasn't exactly sure how 14 qualified as a big birthday, but I pulled her into my arms and whispered, "If I do win, I'd be back in time and would get you something very special in Italy for your 'big' birthday."

She raised an eyebrow "It has to be better than pasta sauce."

I chuckled, then noticed her expression change. Her wheels were now turning, and she tried a different bargaining chip, "Mom, you don't have to get me anything if you will take me to the Francesca concert." She clasped her hands together. "She's on tour and will be only four hours away in Dallas. That's all I want for Christmas and my birthday combined!"

I had wanted to treat Marie to a special birthday weekend in Dallas to see Francesca and stay a night in a hotel. But it wasn't to be. I frowned "Honey, I tried, but the concert was sold out within 20 minutes of going on sale. I'm so sorry."

She looked so defeated that I felt awful.

Ren pulled up her phone calendar, "Well, at least you won't miss the state swim meet. It's the following Saturday and you I've already qualified, so you better be there." She turned to her little sister and smirked. "I bet Mom takes Mike along to Italy since it's over Valentine's Day."

"Probably." Ree was still pouting but nodded.

Just the thought of an exotic vacation alongside the clever man with sparkly chameleon eyes gave me a tingle of excitement. I pictured us holding hands as we walked along romantic cobblestone streets eating cannoli and drinking Italian wine. Then, of course, we would take a selfie standing in front of the Colosseum and possibly one of us standing beside the shiny new Greco Macchina Forte.

When one of the girls cleared her throat, I snapped out of my reverie to find them staring at me.

I stammered, "Oh, Mike and I aren't ready for a big trip together like that. I mean we've only been dating since October."

I didn't know where our relationship was going and sure didn't want to discuss it with my daughters. After pushing the handsome policeman out of my mind, I considered other companion options: My best friend, Lin? She was single, and we would have a blast. Or Lis from Texas? But, of course, duh, I would take my sister, Kim. She was my favorite travel buddy. I couldn't even consider taking anyone else.

I shook my head and said, "Why are we discussing who I will take? I doubt I'll even have time to write a decent jingle in the next two weeks. Do you realize what I still have to do before the holidays?" I counted on my fingers: "Prepare for my winter program at school, write Christmas cards, buy and wrap presents and bake cookies. And don't forget Aunt Kay is coming for Christmas. It will be difficult enough to get all that done without creating an award-winning jingle."

Ren smirked. "Okay Miss Multitasker-of-the-Year, since when has an overload of plans ever stopped you?"

True. The more I piled on my plate, the more I got done. And really, I had already taught the classes their songs and it was more of a concert than a big production. Since I started Christmas shopping last January, I already had a stash of presents. Maybe I could find the time.

I stood up. "Well, I'd better do some research on Greco Motors, or I won't have enough data to write a jingle. I'm going upstairs now to do some Googling and Wikipediaing."

Ren said, "I'm not sure Wikipediaing is a word, but good luck."

Ree called out as I left the room, "Hey Mom, which kids will Aunt Kay bring?"

I stopped at the foot of the stairs. "Just Cara and Jon, since Jess and Jer are celebrating with their spouses."

I left the two to discuss the arrival of their California cousins and climbed the steps to our multipurpose room.

At my computer, I reread the rules and information about the contest, then typed in Greco Motors to read about its history. The assembly plant was in Rome. I smiled to see the familiar vintage black and white photo of the woman, Isabella Greco, known worldwide as Signora Greco. The image was as recognizable as the Gerber baby since her face had appeared in every Greco ad. I read that in 1964, as a young woman, she got a job designing vehicles. When that company went under in 1966, she started Greco Motors, and ran it until just a few years ago when her three children took over. What an amazing woman.

Greco's sporty vehicles had been very popular all these years but according to the stats they took a dip in sales since Isabella transferred the company to her heirs.

Never having been remotely interested in cars, my eyes glazed over as soon as the information morphed from Italian car makers to the mechanics of automobiles. I shook my head to wake up before closing my laptop.

Maybe I would get inspired while making a giant star? Costuming was just an example of odd things an elementary music teacher did. I kneeled on the carpet and drew a large star on foamboard with a Sharpie. I called Kim as I slid out the blade of my X-acto knife. "So, Kim…do you want to go to Italy with me in February?"

"Uh, of course. But how? And why February?"

I put the phone on speaker and explained the contest while slicing the outer points of the star. I smiled to hear Kim's excitement as she relayed each piece of my story to her husband.

When R.A.'s voice boomed through the phone speaker, my blade went off course and cut off one whole point. I frowned at the rounded shape. He said, "Pity, how are you going to write a jingle about a car? You don't even know the difference between a sedan and a coupe."

He had me there. "Ok, so it's a stretch for me, but I have to try."

"If you want someone to carry your bags in Rome, I'll volunteer."

"That would be so cool, R.A., but if I win, I can only take one guest. Sorry. And keep in mind, I haven't written anything yet."

I should stop telling people about the contest until I have at least sent in an entry. Everyone was just getting excited about nothing.

Kim came back on the phone. "You can do it, Pity."

I frowned. "But R.A. is right. I started researching Greco Motors and within five minutes I was bored stiff with all the car information."

Kim chuckled while I cut a hole for a fifth grader's face. She asked, "So are you excited Kay is coming for Christmas?"

I perked up. "Of course! It will be great to have the whole family together again for a holiday."

She said, "Yeah. It will be a fun crowd. Twelve this year!"

I said, "Actually, a baker's dozen for Christmas Eve dinner. Mom said to invite Mike as long as he understands the oyster stew rule."

"Haha. Have you told him yet?"

"No, but I will."

"I hope he can handle it because we all like Mike. Now get started on that jingle. I'm beyond excited."

After hanging up, I had too much stuff to carry downstairs, so I stuck my arms through the elastic straps and poked my head through the face hole so I could also carry the tarp, glue, and a jar of glitter.

"Well, now that's an interesting look." Ren looked up from the dining table where she sat working on her homework.

"Wait until you see me dressed as a candy cane!" I winked.

I opened the door and Harriet met me in the backyard with her big fluffy tail wagging. Hmm. Maybe glue and glitter near a shaggy sheepdog wasn't a good idea. I turned around and yelled into the house, "Ree, wanna help me with a project in the front yard?"

Always ready for a craft, Marie bounded out of her room and shook her head. "Mom, you're not a star. You didn't win yet."

After the big star was sufficiently glittered, we left it on the front porch to dry. I turned to Ree. "I have nine more ornaments to make. Tomorrow, I'll get foamboard and we can start on them after school."

Ree's eyes lit up. "I'll ask Caitlyn to help." She grabbed her phone.

I said, "Call her after homework or you'll never stop talking to finish."

She nodded and put it back in her pocket.

. . .

The next morning, I entered Arrowstar Elementary School, my home away from home. Unfortunately, I was met by the world's worst principal, Dr. Barry Love.

He stood, arms folded, and said in his whiny voice, "Ms. Kole, I need to speak to you before you go to your classroom."

When Melanie, our sweet secretary frowned and shook her head, I knew the news would be bad.

I followed the scrawny man into his stark office and set my school bag, purse, coffee mug, and giant gold star beside the chair and sat down. Where had he found such an uncomfortable chair to go with his uninviting office?

I tried not to stare at the man's comb-over hair, his thick glasses, or his worn 1990's suit and tie. "Is everything okay Dr. Love?"

Instead of sitting behind his foreboding desk as he normally did, he paced the small room tapping his fingers together like a supervillain.

He squeaked, "We have a problem."

My eyes widened as my imagination ran wild. Before I had time to ask if there had been a break-in or a fire in my room, he spat, "I believe I told you NOT to have a Christmas program this year."

I relaxed. My room was fine. "Oh, right." I nodded. "Yes, you did and that's why I renamed it a "Winter" program. You didn't want to focus on any one holiday, so this concert will feature all the winter holidays." I went on to list them. "We'll have songs for Kwanzaa, Hanukkah, Christmas, and even the Hornbill Festival from India."

When his frown lines deepened, I added, "Believe me, I don't want to leave anyone out, either. In addition, the children have learned basic secular winter favorites like Winter Wonderland."

I was proud of my perfect song line-up. The children loved the tunes, and I was confident their parents would enjoy the concert. I smiled, happy that I could appease Dr. Love. But by the looks of his furrowed eyebrows, the man was not at all appeased.

He stomped his foot, causing me to flinch, and growled, "When I said no Christmas program, I meant no program at all!" He picked up the school newsletter. "But somehow, this was printed without my approval." He cocked his head. "Are you responsible?"

I leaned in to see the beautiful artwork my art teacher buddy, Jules, had designed for the program cover. The cartoon was adorable with children holding hands in a circle around the world. The concert date, December 20th, was posted clearly in the ad with the time of 7:00 p.m. The whole article was exactly as I had planned.

I stammered, "Well yes, I put it together, but I don't know how it was printed without your approval." I defended myself. "The date was marked on the office calendar. We've always had a Christmas—I mean winter program at Arrowstar Ele…" I trailed off when I remembered there hadn't been a Christmas program last year. Why was that? Oh yeah. Dr. Love was new, and he said it was too much in his first year.

The principal's face was beet red, but he remained silent. How could I fix this? And why didn't he want a concert this year? It was excellent PR for the school and the parents loved it. I pleaded. "Dr. Love, the concert is this Thursday. The children are prepared, and the parents have invited family from out of town to attend."

Dr. Love gave an audible gulp when I mentioned parents. Was that his aversion to special programs? Thinking back, he did stay hidden in his office during conferences and PTA meetings. No parents were allowed to attend our weekly assemblies. And just before last year's fifth-grade musical, Dr. Love suddenly called in sick. I wasn't sure I'd ever seen him talk to a parent in person.

The whole idea of a principal being scared of parents was so ludicrous I wanted to giggle, but this wasn't the time nor place.

He straightened his stance. "If it cannot be canceled, you'll have to do the introductions as I have a commitment Thursday night."

I gave a quick silent thanks that the show could go on and said, "That's fine, Dr. Love. I will be happy to do that. And just to remind you, it is customary to have a dress rehearsal in the cafegymatorium on the morning of the concert. Will you attend that so you can hear the children perform? I'm sure they would love for you to be there."

I only made that last statement to butter him up. Who knew if the kids wanted the grumpy man to hear them?

He sneered. "A rehearsal is not necessary. It would just disrupt the class schedule."

I started to panic. No rehearsal? I said, "Uh, but it's an all-school performance. 450 children need to practice moving to the risers and learning where to stand. I only need an hour to show them."

He gave a smarmy grin. "I'm sure you'll find a way to direct children during your class without losing learning time."

I contemplated how to convince him that a school-wide program without a rehearsal could be a catastrophe. But his smirk told me he didn't care if the program flopped. He lifted his hand and shooed me away. "That is all. Leave your lesson plans on Mrs. Finer's desk."

Not knowing what to say, I gathered my stuff and stepped towards his door, but I couldn't escape before he made yet another ridiculous declaration. "And you'll need to change the program so that no song mentions Christmas or any other specific holiday."

I froze and turned to him in disbelief. "What?"

He gave an evil grin. "Nobody should be forced to listen to something in which they don't believe."

I gulped. "But the kids have already learned the songs. Surely nobody would be upset to hear a wide variety of holiday songs. Besides, it is in our curricula to teach how holidays are celebrated in different cultures. Through the songs, the children not only learn music, but language, math, history, and social studies."

Dr. Love turned his back to me. "That is my decision."

I stormed out of his office, laid my lesson plans on Melanie's desk and fled before he could squash any more of my plans.

As I charged over to the art room to inform my buddies, I wondered again how we got stuck with such a horrible principal. When I slammed the door open, all three of my friends stared at me.

Becca, the PE teacher, said, "What happened to you? Your face is as white as Santa's beard."

I nearly cried at the thought of having no Santa for Christmas. The kids couldn't even mention his name with Dr. L's new rules.

Jules looked up from mixing red tempera paint and lifted her eyebrows. "What's got your goat?"

The gifted teacher, Jana, shook her head. "Does it have something to do with our fearful leader?"

I said, "Bingo!" and then let go, "First of all, he won't let me have a dress rehearsal—not even on the day of the concert."

Jana said, "That might be a problem with 400-plus kids to corral."

I let out my breath. "I know, but get this, he won't allow any songs that mention holidays. No Santa songs, Hannukah, or any Christmas classics, after I took so much effort to include every winter holiday."

I shrugged. "That leaves only three out of the twenty songs we have prepared that don't mention a holiday. We can only sing, Winter Wonderland, Frosty the Snowman, and Jingle Bells."

Jules wrinkled her brow. "Jingle Bells isn't a Christmas song?"

I shook my head. "Nope. It never mentions Christmas."

Jana said, "We've always had holiday programs. Nobody ever gets offended with your choice of songs."

I nodded. "I know. I kind of understood his aversion to Halloween parties, but this makes no sense."

Jules continued to paint a Santa hat on paper. "He's just doing this to make you crazy. I still say he's jealous because you are so tall and cute when he's, well, you know. He hasn't told me to stop painting Santas."

"Oh really?" That made my skin crawl. I had been on his hit list ever since he started last year. "Oh, and he won't come to the concert because he has previous plans the night of the program."

Becca shuffled a stack of scorecards and looked up. "Well, that's good! If Dr. Dreadful doesn't go, he'll never know what songs they sing. Just do your program like you planned."

I scowled at her. "He'd find out. He probably has spies."

Jules scoffed, "Ha! He has no cronies anymore."

I plopped down on one of the little blue stools attached to the white resin table and sighed. "Maybe I'll just cancel."

In unison, the trio said, "You can't do that."

Jules said, "Dr. Lucifer already canceled the fall carnival because he said someone could get hurt playing the games."

Becca grumbled. "I still don't know how anyone could get injured at the cakewalk or by picking up rubber duckies?"

Jana said, "And he canceled the book fair because he said our library has plenty of books already."

They were right. This program and the fifth-grade musical were the only other big Arrowstar events that brought in all the parents. There would be a riot if I canceled, and I would be blamed.

Becca said, "I'll bet he wants you to cancel."

I looked at the clock. "Probably. I'd better get ready for the assembly, but I don't know what to teach today, since the whole program is in limbo."

"Hang in there, Pity." Becca followed me to the door. "You'll think of something."

# Travel tip # 2

*Plan your own itinerary whenever possible.*

Reluctantly, I led the music for the weekly Monday assembly but refused to look at Dr. Love as he scolded students for tracking mud inside the building.

Afterwards, while leading Mrs. Ball's third graders to my music room, I said to the first boy in line, "Jason, I hope you are feeling creative today."

No. I wasn't planning to have him help write my car jingle for me, but on second thought, it wasn't a terrible idea. He was very clever.

Once the class of 25 kids was assembled on the risers in my music room, I wheeled up to them on my rolling stool and explained the concert situation to my captive audience of nine and ten-year-olds. "So, I'll need your help in making changes today."

Their faces went blank, but I went on, "For each song, we'll take out any holiday words and replace them with neutral winter words."

Still, they stared at me silently. I tried an example. "For instance, we'll change *Have a Holly Jolly Christmas*, to *Have a Holly Jolly Holiday*.

Nothing. No reaction. Perhaps the kids weren't fully awake yet.

Finally, Jessica, one of Jana's gifted students asked, "But, Mrs. Kole, why doesn't he want us to mention Christmas or Kwanza?"

When the others nodded, I realized the kids did understand me, but they were just dumbfounded as to why.

I shrugged. "I'm not exactly sure, but we need to comply."

So, we omitted all holiday names, an absurd idea, but I couldn't think of another way to save the program.

After a full day of confused children singing new lyrics, I went home exhausted. So much for spending my free time creating an outstanding jingle. I didn't even have the mojo to think about it.

While getting ready for bed, my policeman called. I hadn't talked to Mike for a few days, so I filled him in on everything, including the jingle contest and my issues over the school concert.

"How strange for your principal to be such a stickler. But then again, he is a strange man."

My eyes scrunched, then I said, "Oh, that's right. You met Dr. Love when he was writing trespassing tickets to neighbors on the playground last year."

"Yes ma'am, and it was a very special experience."

"Too bad you didn't lock him up. Well, at least you have someone to picture when I gripe about him." I twirled my hair around my finger. "He's not attending my winter concert Thursday night, so you won't have to see him if you come. You don't work Thursdays, right?"

"I'm sorry. I took an extra shift since a few officers are off."

I frowned. "Oh well. You had better come to the fifth-grade musical next Spring. It's a much bigger deal and such fun!"

"As soon as you know the date, I'll take that day off. Even crazy principals can't keep me away."

"Oh, you're invited to Mom and Dad's house for Christmas Eve dinner. The whole family will be there. You can even meet my oldest sister, Kay, who will be here from Los Angeles."

"Sure. I'd love to."

"Great, but I do have to mention one caveat."

"Oh yeah?"

"You have to eat at least one bite of oyster stew."

"Ha. I think I can handle that."

I gave him directions to my parents' house and said I would see him at 5:30 Monday, if not before then.

...

The next morning as I walked past the school office where Dr. L shook his head frantically while a frazzled Melanie tried to hand him a phone. What was going on? I snuck around the corner to the lounge where all the questions of the world were answered. When I entered, the staff members buzzed, but grew silent when they saw me.

Joe, a fifth-grade teacher raised his eyebrows. "Pity, you sure created quite a stir around here."

"What?"

He took his coffee mug out of the microwave. "Parents have been calling all morning complaining about your class. Apparently, the kids told them they had to change the lyrics to Christmas songs."

Oh no. Of course, they would be mad at me. I grimaced. "Do you think the parents are going to tar and feather me?"

He laughed. "No, but Dr. Love might want to hide. They are furious with him."

Rather than being happy, I slapped my forehead and said, "Now he'll think I did it to get back at him.'

The other teachers ate this up. Sue, one of the aides, said, "After today, maybe you'll get to sing the songs the way they were written."

"Or maybe I'll be fired."

When I entered the art room, Becca stood by a table, wearing her hot pink velour tracksuit. She said, "I knew you'd come up with something, girl! Dr. Dumbass is fit to be tied with your stunt."

I threw my head back. "It wasn't a stunt. I just followed his orders. Who knew it would cause such a kerfuffle?"

Jules ran her fingers through her curly hair. "Well, I love it!"

I wasn't loving any of it and sat down with a plunk.

Becca said, "Hey, on another topic, what are you getting your policeman for Christmas?"

I shrugged. I hadn't thought of a gift idea for Mike. Our relationship was still in the early stages, and I wasn't sure what to get him. I finally answered, "I don't know. Any ideas?"

Jules said, "Didn't you say he likes movies? Get him a gift card to the theater and maybe he'll take you with him!"

I said, "That's a great idea, Jules." It wasn't very personal, but I could buy one at the last minute if I didn't find something better.

As if she could hear my thoughts Becca said, "Well…if you want something more personal, I have a few ideas." She winked.

Jana, the more practical one said, "You could have a pen engraved for him or maybe get him a wallet."

Just thinking of all these gift ideas distracted me from my previous hysteria, but then it added to my list of things to do the next few days.

There was a crackle over the intercom, and we all stared at the speaker on the wall. Dr. Love's whiny voice came on loud and clear. "Ms. Kole please report to the office at once."

I gulped. My crew stayed silent as I stood and trudged slowly towards what I could only assume were the gallows. I could almost hear the slow cadence of drums as I neared the office. Both big and little sympathetic faces stared out of classrooms as I passed.

Dr. Love stood at his door with a face closely resembling a beet with glasses. It was round, bumpy, and deep red.

I entered his office, and the door slammed behind me so hard that I fell into the horrible chair. He turned to me with an evil stare, and I shrank back. He whined, "Well, well…I can't believe you stooped so low as to tell the parents to gang up on me."

My upper lip started sweating, which startled me since that had never happened before. I wiped it off and stammered, "Dr. Love, I was following your directions and changed the words you said might 'offend' someone. I didn't think the kids would tell their parents."

He nodded with sarcasm. "Right. Well, you got your way this time, but you can kiss your fifth-grade musical goodbye."

I almost choked. The fifth-grade musical was my baby. I lived for the excitement of producing a quality, full, off-off-off-off Broadway show. I had already drafted a new script tailored to fit this group of fifth graders. And what about those kids who have waited since kindergarten to be the stars of their own big production?

I said weakly, "But why would you do that?" I knew good and well, why. It was to punish me. But I wanted to hear him say it, and he did.

"It is my prerogative since I run Arrowstar. One program is plenty for a school year and this year, you chose the winter concert."

The bell rang, putting a bizarre end to his remark. Tears filled my eyes, but I could do nothing now about the future of the musical, now.

I stood and even with my thick throat, managed to say, "I need to go to my room unless you have anything else to tell me?"

I waited for him to add another ridiculous change for the winter concert. Maybe he wanted the children to wear all-black clothes or that singing was not allowed at all and only sign language could be used. Instead, he just nodded at the door. But he did it with such vigor his glasses fell off his nose and onto the floor.

. . .

The rest of the week went as previously planned with the holiday lyrics added back. Sadly, Dr. Love stuck to his no-rehearsal policy. What should have taken thirty minutes to explain to the whole school, took me three days to repeat to every class.

To make matters more frustrating, I was so busy I hadn't even started my jingle. If I wasn't careful, I'd run out of time.

On the night of the program, R.A. helped erect a giant, cardboard Christmas tree behind the risers. When the custodian opened the doors, families swarmed the building to watch their darlings perform. I crossed my fingers hoping the kids would remember where to stand.

With Dr. Love absent, I welcomed our guests from the microphone. Then I motioned for the "ornaments" to get in place while I found my seat at the piano. Brittany beamed from top in her star costume. Two bells stood on the step beneath her, with three shiny bulbs next. I almost squealed at the cuteness of the four first and second-grade candy canes standing on the bottom row.

Showtime! Facing the children, I played the introduction, and the ten "ornaments" began singing the silly song I had written.

*We are the Christmas tree ornaments.*
*We just hang around - on the Christmas tree.*
*We love to make people happy.*
*You know where we're found - on the Christmas tree.*
*Though we're used only part of the year,*
*Family love gives us plenty of cheer.*
*The Christmas tree is where we long to be.*

The candy canes sang their verse,
*"We are the candy canes. We are sugar sweet.*
*Our stripes go round and round us. Look, but please don't eat."*
They were so adorable this elicited an enthusiastic response.

After verses from the bulbs and bells, Brittany sang her solo,
*"I am the star of the Christmas tree. I sit way up high.*
*I shine above all the others, twinkling oh so bright.*

When the song ended with the chorus, the crowd erupted with a round of applause. The "ornaments" glowed and a fourth grader "dreidel" and a fifth grader "Kwanza drum" joined them.

All twelve animated characters described what it was like to watch a blended family celebrate the holidays from their vantage points. Then they introduced the holiday songs sung by each grade level.

The concert was a big success and very few problems arose. Thankfully, the classroom teachers were there to help with transitions.

I gave thanks to the audience for coming, Jules for her artwork, and the teachers for their help. I even gave a shout-out to Ree for helping with the costumes, but she ducked down in humiliation. Oops.

As people dispersed, Brittany's mom handed her a huge bouquet of flowers, which was fitting, as she was the "star." Her mother gave me a bouquet, too. Sweet.

My own family congratulated me, and I said, "I'm glad you came. I'll clean up, then meet you at our after-concert spot in a few minutes."

Kim and R.A. both said, "We can help you."

I handed Kim the flowers and said, "No, you go on. The custodian and I will get the risers and tree down tomorrow morning. I'll pick up some things and talk to a few parents. I shouldn't be long."

They made their way out the door along with droves of kids and their families. I was stopped by several parents who wanted photos of me with their children. All were complimentary.

I picked up a stray candy cane costume on the way to my piano to get my music. When I turned back around, I ran smack into Kenny. Yep, the one and only boring, and somewhat creepy Kenny Dicks. I stuttered in surprise, "Oh, hi."

I hadn't seen my friendly stalker in two months and hoped he had moved on to some other poor gal. The auditorium was now empty, and even though I figured Kenny was harmless, I made sure my phone was handy in case I needed to call R.A. "What are you doing here, Kenny?"

He gave me that adoring smile that made me cringe and said, "I'm so happy I saw the piece in the Broken Arrow Ledger about your program tonight, or I would have missed the most delightful performance. I mean, watching you play piano and speak into the microphone made my heart swell. You are so amazing."

How odd not to mention the actual performers tonight—the kids. But then again, Kenny was odd. I started toward the door and tried to act interested, "So, how have you been?"

"Oh. I've tried to stay busy, since you said you needed space."

Uhh. Those were not my words. I clearly said I wasn't interested in him. He's the one who said I just needed time away to miss him.

Kenny smiled as he walked and told me what he had been doing lately. "I took a delightful trip with my sister to find our family's gravestones. We toured cemeteries all across the country."

Oh, my…that did not sound delightful to me, but I nodded.

He continued. "On a whim, we took our metal detectors along and made a few stops along beaches to see what we could find."

Whew. At least they didn't use metal detectors at the gravesites. The mention of a beach surprised me though, and I looked at the pale man with his shirt buttoned up to his chin. He was the least outdoorsy person I knew. "I didn't know you liked the beach. Did you swim?"

He shook his head in disgust. "Oh, heavens no. I don't like the water. Due to my skin condition, I must be well-covered, so I always wear waders, long sleeves, and a hat. Otherwise, the sun and salt would irritate my skin. We only went there to find artifacts."

I pictured him in his odd get-up, holding the device. It was not a pretty picture. I didn't ask they had found anything, but just nodded. "Well, I need to go. It was good to see you again." I started to turn around, but like a magician, he pulled a huge bouquet of flowers from behind his back and held them out to me. He bowed and said, "I do hope we can start anew since you've had time to miss me."

I gave a big sigh and said, "Thank you for the flowers, but I can't accept them. You see, I'm dating the guy you met a few months ago. The tall policeman? He wouldn't be happy if I accepted flowers from another man."

Kenny's face lit up as if I'd said something wonderful. He shook his head dreamily. "I just love how you call me 'another man.'"

This guy was a wacko. "Look, Kenny, I have to go." I turned and left him standing alone, holding the flowers with his goofy smile.


When I got to *Braum's Ice Cream and Dairy Store*, my family gushed about the concert and how cute the kids were.

Mom said, "I just loved those adorable candy canes."

Ree bragged, "I painted them, Grandma."

I was pretty sure Mom was talking about the kids wearing the costumes, but I was glad Ree was proud of her work.

I told the gang about the encounter with my number one fan.

Mom said, "You have to be firm, or he won't leave you alone."

I rolled my eyes. "I thought I was firm."

Kim said, "Apparently, not firm enough."

R.A. shook his head. "I knew I should have stayed behind. No telling what that fruit loop could have done. He could be dangerous."

"No. Kenny's not dangerous. He's just crazy about me."

Dad said, "I sensed he was an odd guy when we met him. You really should be careful."

"I know," I sighed.

Ree said, "I'll get you a hot cocoa to forget all about him."

Chocolate with my family was the perfect ending to a busy night.

...

Once home, Ren hung her coat on the rack and said, "Now that your program is over, it's time to write your jingle."

I nodded. "Yes! You're right. Only one more day of school and I'll get on it, but tonight–I'm beat."

I had mostly good feelings after every show. I was relieved it was over, happy it went well, proud of the children, and content that I had such support from the staff. Unfortunately, this year I had to add two unpleasant emotions. I was fearful Dr. L would get back at me somehow and I was frustrated that Kenny may never leave me alone.

Despite the different feelings whirling around my head, exhaustion and a belly full of hot chocolate won over, and I fell into a deep sleep.

...

Relief flooded me the next morning when I wasn't accosted by Dr. Love. My entrance to the school was smooth. Teachers complimented me about the children's performances.

I spent the morning playing 'holiday name-that-tune' with me playing melodies on my flute and the kids guessing song titles. I ate lunch in the art room and finally told my buddies about the jingle contest.

"Aren't you scared to go to Europe?"

I looked at Jana, who wore a snowflake shirt. "Why would I be?"

"I don't know. Seems scary to be so far away from your girls. Something could happen."

Becca said, "If you take your policeman, he will keep you safe." Her head waggled and her Santa earrings swung side to side.

I smirked. "I thought about it, but I'm not ready for him to see me with bedhead. If I happen to win, I'll take Kim."

Jules frowned. "Lucky sister. I'd sure go with you."

I nodded. Any of my friends would be a blast to take along. I said, "Well, I've known about the contest for almost a week and haven't written a note or word yet and there are only four days before it's due! It's unlikely I'll come up with anything, and a miracle if I win."

Becca said, "I'll help you write it. It's a Greco, right?" She stood.

I braced myself for whatever the crazy gal might conjure up.

She picked up a stray paintbrush and held it like a microphone up to her Barbie pink lips. She swayed back and forth and sang a tuneless ditty, "This Greco car is so fast it will knock you right on your ass."

I laughed. "Not sure that's the direction I'm going, but thanks anyway, Bec."

We gave holiday wishes and hugs and finished the day. The halls had a festive feel as I left–that was until Dr. Love stopped me.

I closed my eyes, waiting for him to tell me what I had done wrong this time. He motioned me to move to the side of the hall and spoke in his squeaky voice without looking at me. "I hear the concert was well attended and the children did a nice job."

I nearly fainted at the apparent compliment. I squinted when I spoke. "Yes. They were very well-behaved and sang nicely."

He gave a smug grin. "See. You didn't need a rehearsal after all."

As much as I wanted to tell the man to bug off, I kept it to myself and said, "It wasn't easy, but we did manage to pull it off."

He cleared his throat. "I'll be making changes to your class size to give classroom teachers a special plan period. It will…"

I stopped listening at the words, 'changes to class size.' Dr Love would never give me fewer students, which meant he had another ludicrous plan to cause me pain. As he continued his lecture, I wondered if I could get a job at Quik Trip. I heard that the convenience store chain was a great company to work for, even if I couldn't use my music education degree while cleaning coffee machines. Or maybe I could become a street juggler? That wouldn't be stressful. I would just need to learn how to juggle.

Of course, a more realistic way out of my Dr. Love-induced nightmare would be to transfer to another school, except he would probably love that. But Arrowstar was in my neighborhood, my friends work here, my kids went here, and I loved it.

I stopped daydreaming of career options and focused on the man who droned on, "…it is imperative for you to incorporate all learning styles. With the new schedule, you'll be required to…."

I interrupted. "Um. Dr. Love, I'm getting hot in this big coat and these bags are heavy. I need to prepare for Christmas with guests coming from California, and…" I started to say, 'and write a jingle', but sidestepped with, "…and a hundred Christmas cards to send." I gave a fake smile. "Have a lovely holiday. I'll see you next year."

Without waiting for a reply, I did a 180 and went home.

I refused to let the man ruin my Christmas break. If he did indeed give me a horrible schedule, I'd just have to ask Jeff at Broken Arrow Teachers' Union if he could do something about it. Poor Jeff had already thwarted two of Dr. Love's crazy plans in the past year.

# Travel Tip #3
*Make sure your passport is valid for six months beyond your
return date in case of unexpected delays.*

Saturday, we spent a relaxing day addressing envelopes, baking cookies, and wrapping presents while watching Christmas movies.

On Sunday I announced, "I'm going upstairs to write the jingle!"

Ree said, "It's about time. It is due on Christmas Day."

Ren chimed in "Yeah, the day after tomorrow!"

I said, "I know. I won't come downstairs until I have a good start."

Ree said, "Good. We'll fix dinner for you so you can just write."

Ren added, "But don't forget we have to pick up Aunt Kay and the kids from the airport tonight!"

That was right. Mom and Dad didn't like driving after dark and Kim and R.A. were in Texas at my nephew's first band concert as a director. I had four hours until the holiday hubbub would start.

I entered my computer/music/craft room and shut the door. I said hi to Iggy, who lounged in her heated aquarium. I turned on my keyboard, the computer, and the printer, then straightened a crooked trumpet hanging on the wall. Hmm. Should I call Mike to see what he was doing? Stop procrastinating, Pity! I stared at the computer, but my treble clef clock ticked louder than usual. I turned to it and said, "Stop reminding me!"

Two hours later, I had written a few lines, but none were any good. Was it writer's block? I paced the room and cursed myself for telling everyone I was entering the stupid contest.

There was a light tap on the door. "Come in."

Ree entered, carrying a plate with a grilled cheese sandwich. Ren held a bowl of tomato soup and a drink. Yum. One of my favorite meals. Maybe that was all I needed to perk me up.

"Thank you! It looks and smells delicious." I motioned for them to place the dishes on my bass drum coffee table.

Ree grinned. "We even sweetened your tea the way you like."

"Aw. Aren't you nice?"

Ren licked soup from her finger and asked, "So, how's it going?"

I sighed and shook my head. "I may not have it in me, girls. I am at a complete loss. I think my creative juices are all dried up."

The girls chuckled and shook their heads.

"What?"

Ren opened the door. "You'll do it. We have faith in you."

"But if I don't, will you still love me?"

Ren nodded, but Ree shrugged. "We'll see." Then she threw her arms around my neck before leaving me alone again.

The next two hours went by with no more luck than the first two. I reluctantly turned off my electronics and joined the girls downstairs. "Don't even ask. Let's go get some cousins?"


We waited at baggage claim for the Californians. Cara bounded toward us full of energy, as usual. The petite blonde 12-year-old hugged me and made the rounds, talking the entire time. Such a cutie.

Next came my handsome nephew, Jon. At 19, he was much more laid back than his little sister. He gave us each a quick side hug and then searched the baggage conveyor belt for his skateboard.

Finally, Kay came into view. I hugged my big sister. The word "big" is not literal, since I'm eight inches taller than the eldest Kole sister. I grabbed her bag, emblazoned with a world map, and said, "How was the flight?"

"It was fine except for a baby screaming most of the time." She stopped short. "What are you feeding your girls? They are so tall."

I chuckled. Compared to her, I guess they were.

Once baggage was claimed, we drove to Mom and Dad's house on the other side of Tulsa, where we were greeted by our parents and homemade chocolate cake with fudge icing—oh, and Dad's cute stories.

...

The day before Christmas, I was in a good mood. It was my year to have the girls with me for Christmas Eve and Christmas morning. They didn't have to be at their dad's house until three Christmas day.

Ree entered the kitchen. "Mom, I forgot to get Smelly Shelly a present. Can you take me to get her something blingy?"

I snickered at the nickname for their dad's girlfriend, who apparently wore too much perfume. I had a different set of nicknames for the obnoxious woman but kept them to myself.

"Sure. I need to find something else for Kay anyway." I turned to Ren, who was painting her fingernails red and green. "Did you get Shelly something?"

"Yeah. She always talks about the new perfume, 'Nightshade.' I smelled it and figured it's better than what she usually wears."

How odd to name a fragrance after a poisonous plant.

Ree said, "Let's go to Goodwill. Maybe I'll find something there."

"Okay, but if you do, Shelly can't know where you got it. Miss Priss would be horrified to get anything second-hand."

I, on the other hand, have always loved scouring thrift stores and garage sales. Treasure hunting is my favorite sport.

At Goodwill, I found an old copper pitcher I liked so much I wanted it for myself. But Kay really loved copper, and since we only bought each other previously owned items, it was the perfect gift.

Ree rushed up. "Do you think Shelly will like this?"

I studied the leather purse in her hands. It was bedazzled with beads, and fake jewels in the shape of a horse. "Yes. It just screams Shelly." I looked inside and was surprised to find it was a brand name that even I had heard of. The price was high for a thrift store, but I had a coupon, so I said, "Good eye, Ree! She should love it."

Back at home, I wrapped last-minute gifts before heading to Mom and Dad's house for Christmas Eve dinner.

…

The whole family was there when we arrived. I sidled up to my band director-nephew. "How was your band concert, Mr. Ross?"

Eli smiled. "It was great. I have work to do with the jazz band, but all in all, I was proud." I was so happy he followed in my footsteps and majored in music. But he directed high school students instead of elementary school, so that was really cool.

"Well, I'm proud of *you*!" I frowned, "I wanted to attend your very first concert, but there was too much going on here to go."

"I understand. Mom said your winter program went well."

I nodded. "With no help from my principal. I pray you never have to work with anyone like him."

The doorbell rang and I rushed to greet Mike. "Hey there, Officer Potter." There he stood, wearing a blue dress shirt, khaki pants, and holding a bottle of wine. I gulped at the sight of my handsome guy.

With his infectious smile, he said, "Hey you."

I started to stand on my toes to kiss him, but a gaggle of family members appeared like magic behind me.

I stepped aside. "Mike, meet the rest of the Kole gang."

He handed the wine to Mom while I introduced the others to him. Soon after, Kay took me aside and said, "He's a cutie!"

While the guys visited in the living room, we gals drank wine and prepared dinner.

At dinner, all eyes were on Mike as he took his first bite of oyster stew. I expected his face to turn in disgust, but he announced his verdict with a smile. "Yum. It's great."

I, however, had to choke down my one obligatory oyster. Then I filled up with yummy shrimp and chicken. The one thing I saved room for was the rice cream. When it was time, I offered to spoon it up.

I explained to Mike, "It's a Norwegian tradition learned from our foreign exchange student years ago. It's just cold cooked rice, sugar, and whipped cream, but a peeled almond is hidden in one bowl."

Ree said, "Whoever gets the almond gets a prize."

Once small bowls were served, Mom reminded us, "No fair stirring to find the almond. Just take one bite at a time."

It wasn't long before Jon yelled, "I got it!" He pulled a white almond from his mouth to prove his luck.

Dad said, "Wait a minute. Are you sure that's an almond and you didn't pull a tooth out just to get the prize?"

We laughed as Mom handed a small package wrapped in tissue paper to Jon. He opened his prize and found a toy train. He wound it up and the red train chugged around the table.

Mike whispered to me, "So can I stop eating this now?" His face made it clear he wasn't a fan of rice cream.

"Good. Then I can finish what's left in your bowl." I grabbed his bowl and ate the remainder. "I love it."

Kim licked her spoon and turned to me with her eyebrows raised. "Have you finished your jingle, Pity?"

Since everyone knew about the contest, I didn't have to explain again. I frowned. "Um. I'm having a very slow start."

R.A. said, "I thought it was due tomorrow at midnight."

I nodded sadly. "I think I waited too long and now I have writer's block. I doubt I'll have anything ready to enter."

Kim's eighteen-year-old son, Alex, said, "You have 24 hours. How long does it have to be?"

I sighed. "A minimum of five seconds and a maximum of forty."

He scoffed. "Seconds? That's all? Aunt Pity, you could write a word an hour and be done with it."

I smiled at his naivety. "It sounds easy, but at this point, it would be a Christmas miracle for me to write the winning jingle in time."

After singing Christmas carols in the living room, I led Mike to the family room. "Have a seat on the couch and witness yet another tradition."

Once the whole group had seats, R.A. began. "Well…here goes." He lifted a small package in the shape of a CD. "This is for Jim."

Dad smiled. "It must be a baseball bat. I've been needing one."

We chuckled at Dad's age-old joke as R.A. put the small package under the tree. We continued to ooh, aah and make purposeful wrong guesses on the gifts' contents when our names were mentioned.

I leaned into Mike. "I'm sorry but you may be left out of this event…so if you want to leave, feel free."

"Oh, I don't expect anything. I'll just enjoy watching." He squeezed my hand, and I snuggled in closer to him.

When Mom and Dad presented their gifts, I was surprised that Mom held up a tiny package and said, "This one is for Mike."

He made his own silly guess. "Oooh, a golf club? I've always wanted to learn how to play." Everyone smiled to see the new guy get in the spirit by making a ridiculous guess.

We drank eggnog and ate cookies, then I wrangled the girls and walked Mike to his car.

He said, "I have a gift for you. Can I stop by tomorrow?"

I held my hands to my cheeks. "A gift for little old me? Sure. Can you come over after three. I may have something for you, too."

He gave me a sweet kiss then I joined Ren and Ree and drove home where we hung our stockings over the fireplace, of course.

After watching another Christmas movie, I said "Do you want to open one present tonight?"

"Sure!"

I watched as they opened matching packages and found new pajamas. "Are you surprised?"

Ree said, "Um. No, since we get new pj's every Christmas Eve, but I like them." She held up the pink set with dogs all over them.

Ren smiled at her blue pajamas with tiny polka dots. "Thank you, Mom. And thanks for not making us match this year."

"Now you had better get to bed or…"

They finished the sentence together, "Santa won't come."

I nodded. "That's right." I kissed them and watched them head to their rooms to put on their new pajamas.

Once they left, I filled the stockings, in case Santa didn't show up to do it. Harriet, dressed in her red Christmas sweater, acted like she wanted to help me, but I distracted her with a new chew bone I took from her stocking. The dog had an affinity for candy so once the stockings were filled, I hung them too high for her to reach.

I sat on the couch and enjoyed the glow of the Christmas tree illuminating the room. What if our little ornaments came to life when we left the room like in my silly program? What would they say about our family? Hopefully, nice things, since we tried to be good people.

I needed to go to bed since tomorrow would be a big day, but I was wide awake. I hummed a little tune and an idea hit me. Just like Santa going up the chimney, I flew up the stairs to work on the jingle.

My mojo was back! My jingle was written within an hour, and it wasn't half bad. I breathed a huge sigh of relief and shut down my computer. I could finally sleep.

…

Christmas morning was delightful. I took photos of the girls opening presents in their new pajamas. Harriet photobombed quite a few pics since she likes to be in the middle of everything. I was in an especially cheerful mood, having finally created a silly jingle. My girls liked their gifts. Thankfully, Ree had given up on getting tickets for the

Francesca concert. They gave me sweet presents too, but the funniest gift was a pair of readers from Ren.

I put the glasses on and said, "Hey, I can even read the fine print on the glasses package. Maybe I did need these. Thanks. I guess."

Of course, we gave gifts to all our animals. Harriet got a T-shirt, which looked funny with her long hair sticking out the sleeves. Edgar, our African Grey, ate a peanut while riding on his new rope swing. Ree gave giant iguana the special fruit mix Santa had chopped for him.

We were back at Mom's house by eleven, just in time for another tradition. Our whole family lined up in the hallway from youngest to oldest: Cara, Ree, Ren, Alex, Jon, Eli, Me, Kim, R.A., Kay, and Mom. As usual, Dad brought up the rear. We walked in a straight line from the bedroom, through the dining room, and out to the family room. In the beautiful light of the Christmas tree, the scene was magical.

We found seats and took turns opening presents. Kim looked at me and squealed, "Pity! You're wearing readers?"

Everyone stared. I cupped my hand beside my mouth as if my girls couldn't hear, and spoke in a stage whisper, "Well, when your kids get you a gift, you have to pretend to like it." I winked at the girls.

Kay said, "It's about time you caught up with your old sisters." She pointed to her own glasses and handed me a beautifully wrapped box. I opened it and gasped when I saw what was inside.

She said, "What?"

I suppressed a giggle and nodded. "Open that one from me."

She opened my box and sat stunned while looking at the identical copper pitcher. She shook her head and said, "How in the world?"

"I don't know! Fate? I love it."

Kim took a picture of us holding our matching antique pitchers.

I sat a little taller. "Speaking of Italy." With a finger drumroll on the table, I announced, "I wrote my jingle last night!"

Dad leaned forward. "Let's hear it."

I shook my head. "Nope. Nobody can hear it until I find out if I win or not. And even if I win, you can't hear it after the big reveal."

Ree whined, "Your darling children deserve to hear it now."

Kim said, "And your sweet sisters who have had to put up with you your entire life."

Alex said, "I encouraged you to write it, so let me hear it."

"Sorry - it's locked up safe and sound in my head. Nobody gets to hear it but little old me."

# Travel Tip #4
*Be open to new customs.*

After Christmas dinner, we took our haul of gifts home, and the girls prepared to go to their dad's house.

At 2:45, the doorbell rang. When Ree opened the door, Shelly waltzed past her, wearing a gaudy Christmas sweater and matching mini skirt. Todd followed her inside. Their sudden visit surprised us since Ren had planned to drive over to his house. The mystery of their visit was quickly solved when Shelly stuck her hand right in front of my face and squawked, "We're engaged!"

I sure didn't need my new reading glasses to see the rock on that ring. Of course, Shelly wouldn't settle for anything less showy.

When she whipped around to show it off to the girls, her red sequined Christmas purse flung into me and scratched my arm.

She put her hands up to her face and gushed, "Oh, Hot Toddy was so romantic. Last night he arranged a private carriage ride through Rhema's Christmas Lights. Then, in front of God and everyone, he knelt on the lighted bridge and proposed. He even had a friend there to take photos." She batted her thick false eyelashes at Todd.

I looked at my ex, who was preoccupied watching our parrot, Edgar, who stood on his swing doing nothing. Todd had to know Shelly would react this way, but he still looked embarrassed.

Shelly pulled up a gazillion photos from her phone. As the girls were forced to watch her scroll through the pictures from last night, their faces turned a sickly green. Poor things would be forever tied to the woman whom most of Tulsa made fun of for starring in the amateurish commercials for her father's *Big Jack's Cadillacs* dealership.

The photos were nice. Since when was Todd romantic? 20 years ago, while driving home from the fair, he blurted, "Hey wanna get hitched?" and for some reason I had agreed. The first years were great. That was before he started changing jobs monthly. He became a moocher, gambler, philanderer, and all-around jerk. But alas, if I hadn't married him, I wouldn't have my amazing daughters, so I don't regret it. Now, he was Shelly's problem, and she was his.

Mustering some enthusiasm, I asked, "Wow. Have you set a date?"

Oh boy, did I open a can of worms! Shelly practically screamed with excitement. "Not yet, but it will definitely be in May. Or June or maybe July. It will be an outdoor wedding with tons of daffodils. She paused and said, "I'll probably order artificial flowers since they won't be blooming then." She continued, "Daddy said we can have it at his ranch and he's footing the bill. I've already looked at dresses for you girls to wear. Orange will look great on you both."

My gaze flew to Ren and Ree, who looked nauseous–probably because they envisioned standing up at a wedding in a cow pasture and worse yet, being dressed like *Creamsicles*. They silently pleaded to their dad, but Todd looked at the ground as if he didn't notice. Coward.

When they turned to me, I shrugged my apology. As much as I wanted to help, it was not my call nor my business. I would never intervene unless they were in danger. Hm. Could forcing teenagers to wear orange in a wedding be considered child abuse? Probably not.

Shelly looked at me. "I'm sure our wedding will be the talk of the town. We'll invite everyone we know." Then she lifted her head in a haughty manner. "Well, most everyone. The children can tell you about the wedding afterward, Pity."

If she thought her dig would hurt my feelings, she was wrong. Sure, it was rude to rub it in my face, but I had no interest in attending my ex's wedding, except maybe to support my daughters.

Todd finally spoke. "Girls, we had better go. There are presents at my house that Shelly hand-picked for you."

Oh, my. As nice as it seemed, Shelly's taste was a far cry from that of my girls, so I could already feel their pain.

I scooted into the hallway and motioned them to follow me to get their bags. They joined me, happy to be away from the budding bridezilla, and we went into Ren's room.

Ree leaned on me. "Mom, can you stop this?"

I shook my head. "I'm sorry, honey. There is nothing I can do. You will just have to make the best of it."

Ren sighed, "They fight so much, I never dreamed he'd propose!"

I had to agree, "Maybe she won't be so bad when she settles down. Now be strong and get your stuff."

"I'm not so sure she can calm down," Ren said.

The girls slowly gathered their bags and left.


The doorbell rang at four and I checked my face and hair before opening the door for Mike. But there was no Mike or anyone for that matter. Instead, a large package, over 3 feet tall, stood alone on the porch. Ooh, that Mike was a tricky one. I looked around to see if he was hiding around the corner. When I didn't see anyone, I finagled the awkward box inside the house and shut the door.

There was no card, so I opened the box and found a handle connected to a long shaft with an electronic panel attached. Without taking it out, I stared at the contraption and picked up the manual. It read "13-inch professional waterproof metal detector."

What? Perhaps it was accidentally delivered here instead of to a neighbor. I started to shut the flaps when I saw an envelope taped to the handle. I pulled it out and opened it. Inside was a rusted key. The accompanying Christmas card read, "To my darling Kitty. I couldn't think of a better Christmas gift than one that keeps on giving. I hope you will go on many treasure hunts with me in the future." I threw my head back. It was a lost cause. Kenny never would give up!

The note continued, "I found this key to your heart with my metal detector, so when you are ready, you can unlock your love for me. Yours always, Kenny." I shook my head at the somewhat creepy note and odd present, then moved the whole lot to my bedroom closet to deal with later.

The doorbell rang again at five o'clock. This time, I was happy to see my visitor. Mike came in and set a gift bag on the stairs. Then he lifted me, twirled me around, and kissed me.

"What's gotten into you?" I said with wide eyes.

"Oh, it's a new Christmas tradition, don't you know?"

I giggled, "I like it."

The weather had warmed up, so we sat on my vintage glider overlooking my unusual backyard decorations. Harriet bounded over to us wearing her new green elf T-shirt. I patted her head while I told Mike about Christmas morning. I said, "And guess what? Todd and Shelly are getting married."

He nodded. "I figured she would get her claws into him sooner or later. How do you feel about it?"

"Mostly, I feel sorry for my girls. Now that she'll be a permanent fixture, I'm afraid she'll take over his house and the girls won't be welcome there anymore." I held his arm and laid my head on his shoulder as we glided back and forth. "How was your morning?"

"I had a great time at Sally's. I ate way too much and played with Jesse's new toys. Oh and, Sally and Scott are anxious to meet you."

"Same here. I mean, you've met almost every last Kole. Did little Jesse like the cars and racetrack you got him?"

He nodded. "Loved them."

"Well, speaking of cars and racetracks, I finished my jingle!"

He sat up straight. "You did? Let me hear it!"

"Sorry, Charlie. I'm not singing it for anyone yet. Not even you."

"Well, I hope you win the contest anyway."

"I'm not holding my breath. But I do have something else for you." I stood and led him inside where I retrieved the last two gifts from under our tree. "This is the one from my parents."

He took the small package. "Oh, goodie. The golf clubs."

I laughed. "You only have to do that on Christmas Eve."

Mike shook his head. "So many rules." He unwrapped the small box and found a gift card to the local movie theater. "How nice. Did someone tell them I like movies?"

I shrugged. "It wasn't me." I was glad I hadn't gotten him movie tickets after all. I handed him a heavy flat box. "This one is from me."

We sat on the couch and Mike opened the package. His face lit up when he discovered an old round film canister. "Cool!"

I said, "For your movie room!"

He lifted the round silver lid and revealed the movie reel. "What's the film?"

"Probably an educational film on the Oklahoma oil industry. Dad has had this in his garage for years and said I could have it."

"It's perfect, Let's see if we can figure out what movie it is." He held the movie reel up to the light and we could see an oil pump moving up and down as we followed the frames. "I love it." He gave me a kiss then went to the stairs and grabbed his red and green bag.

I dug through the green tissue paper and found a vintage Polaroid camera with two packs of instant film. "No way! I've always wanted one of these! Thank you so much. Let's try it out now!" I scanned the directions, ripped off the silver packaging, and inserted the film cartridge into the camera. Holding the camera away, selfie-style, I clicked. Only time would tell if we were even in the frame.

The photograph slid out of the slot, and we stared at it for what seemed like forever until slowly, a cute shot of us appeared.

I squealed, "I love it, Mike. Thank you so much." I gave him a long kiss and we lay on the couch, snuggling and giggling like teens.

After a while, he whispered, "Are you ready?"

I lifted an eyebrow. "Ready for what?"

"To go to my place. I made dinner for you."

"I finally get to see your house? And you are cooking? Let's go."

He drove a few miles farther east in Broken Arrow and we parked in the driveway of his newer model brick home. When we entered, a spicy aroma came from the kitchen. "Something smells really good."

Mike took me on a tour of the house. The walls were a pretty, tan color which gave the space a warm feel. The camel-colored leather sofa matched the recliner and a cozy off-white knitted throw was slung across it. "Did your sister make that?"

"No. I did."

I looked up to see if he was joking, but he just shrugged. "I have to do something while I watch TV, and I like learning something new. I tried whittling but ended up with sawdust everywhere. Don't tell my buddies at the department or I'll never hear the end of it."

A policeman who knits. How cool. I leaned over to stroke the soft throw and nudged him. "Hint hint…I really like reds and pinks."

Mike chuckled. "Duly noted."

As we went through the rest of his tastefully decorated house, I said, "I love your place. Did you do the decorating too?"

"No. I've bought original artwork over the years and chose the furniture, but Sally and her friend did the rest."

"Well, it's a far cry from my crowded and eclectic house. So, where is this movie room I've heard so much about?"

He opened a door and flipped on the light. I gasped. "This is an actual theater! It's amazing!" The space was bigger than I expected with its giant screen and reclining seats. I walked in. "Check out that popcorn machine. I could live in here."

He pointed to a spot to the right of the screen. "That is where the movie reel will go."

We had a lovely dinner of chili, cornbread, and beer. He even served brownies for dessert.

He apologized again. "I'm sorry it's not very fancy."

"Are you kidding? After all the rich holiday foods, this is a welcome change. It all hit the spot."

After cleaning up, we sat in his theater and watched one of my favorite old Christmas movies, *It Happened on Fifth Avenue*. The sound system was awesome and when the film ended, I didn't want to leave.

As Mike lowered his reclining seat, he said, "So when do you find out if you won the contest?"

I bolted upright and panicked. "Oh no! What time is it?"

He looked at his watch. "Ten o'clock."

I gasped. "Oh no! It's due by Eleven our time and I haven't sent it in yet!"

He jumped up and helped me out of the reclining chair. "Let's go. You have one hour to get home and e-mail that sucker."

He drove me to my house as fast as an off-duty policeman dared to go. With my heart pounding, I raced upstairs, wrote a quick e-mail, attached all the files required, and pressed send. Whew. I made it with only sixteen minutes to spare. Honestly, what was my problem?

I made my way downstairs to meet Mike and shook my head. "That was close. I'm so glad you asked me about it, or I would have missed the deadline. And I would never hear the end of it from Ren and Ree, since they already say I'm the worst procrastinator."

"Well, glad I could help. So now do I deserve a goodnight kiss?"

"I believe you deserve multiple kisses."

After he left, I went to bed, happy. The new year was going to be great, and I was relieved to know the jingle was on its way to Italy.

...

Before Kay flew back to California, all three Kole girls, R.A., and the kids walked through Rhema Park to see the incredible lights.

While strolling along, I showed my sisters where Todd had put a ring on Shelly's finger.

Making sure the kids couldn't hear, Kim said, "It serves him right to be stuck with her for all eternity."

Kay asked, "Is she still making those awful commercials where she dresses up for holiday car sales?"

R.A. nodded, "And they get louder and cornier every time."

Cara appeared by us and said, "Grandma and I saw her on TV last night. She popped out of a skylight dressed like Santa and yelled, 'Ho, Ho, Ho! You'll get the max from Big Jack's Cadillacs!'"

Kay cringed. "She was kinda cute when she was six, but probably not so much as a 45-year-old." We all nodded at the understatement.

…

The week between Christmas and New Year's was relaxing. On New Year's Eve, the girls and I went to Kim and R.A.'s annual party. Poor Mike had to work, but the usual crowd was there. I was glad to catch up with my best friend, Lin. Her eyes opened wide when I told her about the contest. "When do you find out if you won?"

"Tomorrow! I'm sure I didn't win, but who knows? I guess it depends on how many others entered."

Lin was also interested to hear about Todd and Shelly. "That's karma. Do you think he'll end up in a Big Jack's commercial?"

The thought of Mr. 'I'm such a cool cowboy-kind of guy', Todd, wearing a costume on TV was so funny, I snorted.

The evening was great with food, drinks and friends. At midnight, we all grabbed pots and wooden spoons and went to the front porch to bang them while yelling, "Happy New Year!"

R.A. poured champagne and we threw streamers across their Christmas tree, turning it into their New Year's tree. Then, after our annual egg casserole, the girls and I drove home at two a.m.

That night, I dreamed Santa had landed on my roof and the reindeer were stomping around. I awoke, but the reindeer continued to thump. Just how much did I have to drink at the party? There it was again. Clump, clump, skitter-scatter. I rolled over to go back to sleep, but the noise kept going. When Harriet looked up at the ceiling, I knew I hadn't imagined it. Were squirrels running on my roof?

I had to get to the bottom of it, so I stepped outside and shone my phone flashlight up to see who was partying up there. I saw no reindeer or squirrels. All was quiet. Maybe whoever it was finally left.

I went back to bed and the thumping started again. It wasn't a good sign that the new year was already wearing on me, but after a while the noise stopped, and I went back to sleep.

Despite little sleep, by ten o'clock on New Year's Day, I was sitting in the living room eating orange rolls and watching the Rose Parade.

I sighed. "You know, years ago I marched in that with my high school band, right?"

Ren replied flatly. "Yes, Mom. We know."

Ree imitated me in a bright voice, "And the fragrance of the flowers was intoxicating!"

I defended my excitement. "Well, it was. Someday, I'll take you both there and you can smell it for yourself."

During a commercial, I went into the kitchen to get coffee. Ren yelled, "Mom, they are talking about Greco Motors on the news."

Surely, they wouldn't announce the winner of a silly jingle contest on TV. I ran into the living room just as the local announcer said, "The Greco family had a huge loss today when the youngest successor, 43-year-old Matteo Greco, was killed in a car accident."

How tragic. I felt awful, having just read about the bright, heir to the Greco dynasty. My heart broke for Isabella losing her only son. The reporter said, "An investigation is taking place to determine the cause of the accident."

Ren asked, "Do you think they will cancel the contest now?"

"Could be. I'm sure the family will have a tough time with this. It's just terrible and he was so young."

I was still thinking of the Greco family and how tragic it would be to lose a child when Shelly appeared on the screen dressed as Baby New Year. She was holding a giant pacifier. I escaped into the kitchen, so I didn't have to hear her obnoxious voice. From the living room, I heard Ree say to her big sister, "And to think that big baby in a diaper is going to be our stepmother."

I wanted to laugh, but also felt like crying for the Greco family.

Moments later, Ree yelled, "Mom, we just heard a cat."

I stuck my head around the corner, "What?"

Ren chimed in, perplexed. "We did. A cat just meowed."

Just then, a loud meow came from the return air vent above us. I nodded. "Oh. So that's the rascal who kept me up all night."

Ree said, "How did it get there?"

"Beats me." I found my phone and called my trusty brother-in-law. "Um, R.A., we seem to have a cat in our attic. What do we do?"

"Give me an hour, and I'll be over to check it out."

45 minutes later, R.A. appeared wearing leather gloves and a headlamp. He was also carrying a trap.

I said, "You look like a miner with your birdcage."

He chuckled and started up the stairs.

"Wait. Don't you need to climb the ladder in the garage?"

He shook his head. "Nope. You have an access panel upstairs."

"I do?" I followed him up and sure enough behind my sewing table was a small opening with a sheet rock door. He and Todd must have put it in years ago. R.A. pulled it free and climbed in.

After a bit, he yelled in a muffled voice, "I saw it! It's gray."

A few minutes later he said, "It won't come anywhere near me though." When he came back out, he asked, "Got any tuna fish?"

"Jeez, R.A., are you really that hungry?"

He chuckled, "I'm not going to eat it. The cat is, I hope."

Of course. Embarrassed, I shook my stupid head and ran downstairs to open and drain a can of tuna.

Ree and I watched R.A. set up the trap. He carefully balanced the can on the flat section he called the trip pan. According to my smart brother-in-law, if we left the access door open, the kitty might be hungry and go for the fish. Then, when it stepped inside and touched the can, it would trip the trap and we could catch it.

Ree asked, "Will it hurt the cat to be in there?"

"No. This is a live trap. It might get a little scared, but it will be fine. I'm just glad I had the right size trap."

I said, "When can we check to see if we caught it?"

"Maybe in a few hours. If there's nothing, check before bed, then again tomorrow morning."

We shut the upstairs door quietly so as not to trip the trap and went downstairs. R.A. said, "Now I want to figure out how it got up there." It wasn't long before he came back from the garage and said, "I think the cat got trapped in your garage, was cold and warmed up by the water heater. Then when you came home, it must have climbed up the hoses into the attic."

"Well, thank you, R.A. But what do we do with it if we catch it?"

He scratched his big white beard. "Well, maybe it belongs to someone nearby. You can print some Found Cat posters."

"Good idea. Thanks so much, R.A."

As he left, he said, "If nobody claims it, you can keep it."

"Um. No. I already have a dog, a parrot, an iguana, and two backyard fish. I don't need any more pets."

# Travel Tip #5
*Never let your luggage out of your sight.*

New Year's Day became increasingly stressful. I had no responses about the cat and checked my e-mail every few minutes to see if a jingle winner had been announced.

After a few hours, the girls and I sneaked upstairs. Lo and behold, there in the cage lay a big, beautiful cat. I fumbled around with my phone and Face Timed my sister. "Kim, you have to see what we caught." I pointed the camera at the cage.

She said, "Oh, it's a Tortie."

"No, Kim. It's not a tortoise. It is definitely a cat. It just meowed." I scoffed. "Now who needs glasses?"

"Pity, you are so goofy. It's called a Tortoise shell cat. See, it is bi-colored; gray with golden spots and nicknamed a Tortie."

I looked at the cat and nodded, "OK. Now I get it. I need to make some Found posters. What do I do with it for the time being? I don't know anything about cats and sure don't have cat food."

"Well, when you come to Mom's for lunch, bring it along and I'll take care of it until someone claims it. Oh, and Torties are usually female, so it probably is."

That made no sense to me, but I didn't push it since she was willing to take care of the cat. "Oh, thank you so much!"

Ren printed Found Cat signs with my phone number, then hung them in the neighborhood while I posted it on Facebook.

We made our way to Tulsa for New Year's dinner with the trap on the back seat next to Ree. Shortly after we arrived, Kim and R.A.

arrived with a cat carrier, a bag of food, and a blanket. Kim wrapped up the cat and sat cooing to it on Mom's couch. I instantly hoped nobody would claim it because Kim looked like she was ready for another kitty after losing K.C. a few months earlier.

She put the Tortie in the carrier with the blanket, and we all sat around the table for a New Year's Day ham dinner.

Mom passed the bowl of black-eyed peas to me and asked, "Did you hear about the poor Greco boy dying in that car accident?"

I nodded. "So sad. I may not have paid much attention to the story if I hadn't just researched the family. Matteo was one of the siblings who recently took over the business when his mother retired."

Alex stopped chewing and said, "Wait. Who died in an accident?"

I said, "Matteo Greco."

He picked up his phone and googled the story about the crash.

Kim asked, "Do you think they will go ahead with the unveiling of the new car next month?"

I shrugged. "I don't know."

Alex, who was fascinated with race cars, said, "This seems kinda weird. He wasn't in a race, so what could have caused an expert driver like him to just lose control and crash?"

R.A. told his son, "Maybe he was being reckless like I've warned you about. And you better not try any of your video game stunts in real life either." He turned to me. "You still haven't heard who won, have you?"

I shook my head and changed the topic to the Rose Parade while the guys talked football. I missed most of it because I was checking my phone for a response on the cat or news about the contest.

After our late lunch, we played board games. My energy level was at zero–probably the anxiety of waiting to hear something. I stretched my arms out and said, "We should get out of your hair."

Dad said, "Stay as long as you want."

Mom chimed in. "We can have ham sandwiches for supper."

Kim said, "Actually we should get this cat home, so she can get out of the carrier. Poor thing."

Mom piled us up with baggies of ham and we said our goodbyes.

Back in my kitchen, I put the food away and glanced at the clock. It was 4:45 and there was still no contest news. I sighed. Maybe they put everything on hold due to the death in the family or, more likely, someone else had won. It was OK. Life was good and I still had a few more days before going back to school. I plopped down on the couch.

Ren cocked her head. "Why are you smiling? Did you win?"

"No. I'm just thinking about the ecstatic winner who is probably already packing for their big trip in February."

She frowned. "I'm sure you made up a good jingle, Mom."

Ree said, "Well, if you didn't win, can we at least hear it now?"

I sighed. "Why not? I sat up and ran through the short ditty in my head before sharing it." My phone rang just as I opened my mouth. I looked at the unknown number and answered, "Hello?"

"A woman's heavily accented voice said, "Allo. May I please speak with Pity Kol-a?"

My stomach gave a little flip, and I said in an unsteady voice, "Um, yes, this is Pity." I stared at the girls with wide eyes.

After a brief lag, the caller returned. "Allo. This is Zophia from the Greco Motor Company in-a Rome, Eetaly. I am calling you to tell you dat your jingle… eet has won de contest."

I could hardly breathe as I tried to absorb her words.

She continued, "You are 'appy to take a trip to Eetaly, no?"

I cleared my throat, "Yes. Oh, yes I am! Thank you so much." I started panting like Harriet, but managed, "What do I need to do?"

"Well, eef your passport ees good-a, you will be ready to go. Look at your e-mail for information and to tell of your companion choice. For questions, you must reply to dat e-mail."

The girls, sensing my excitement, hovered beside me. Ren whispered, "Who is it?"

Ree jumped up and down clasping her hands. "Did you win?"

Without answering, I squeezed my eyes shut in disbelief. Did I really win? Am I going on a free trip to Italy?

Sophia said, "Ms. Kol-a, are you steel on the line-a"

Sophia's accent was so cute. Every sentence ended with a question mark. "Yes. I am here. I just can't believe it. And I want to say I'm so very sorry for the loss of Mr. Greco."

"Yes, we are all so sad about thees. Matteo was very nice-a man."

Alex had put some questions in my mind, and I said, "Have they discovered the reason for his accident?"

"Jes. He had a healthy problem with hees heart and hees Mamma is so so sad." She paused, "But she cannot stop-a thees event." Then in a brighter voice she said, "And everyone here thinks your leettle song ees very cute-a and we are excited to met you next-a month-a."

Excited, I said, "Me-a too. When-a will I geta de email-a?"

When my girls gave me an odd look, I realized I had imitated Sophia's accent aloud and cringed.

Luckily, Sophia didn't seem phased and said, "I'll send it tomorrow. Ehh…eet is very late for us 'ere now."

I took a deep breath and said, "Thank you so much for the fantastic news, Sophia. I appreciate the late call. Please have a nice night's sleep." Since it was New Year's Day all over the world I said, "And Happy New Year!"

She chuckled and said, "And Buon Anno to you-a, Pitico."

I put my phone down and stared at the girls, then screamed, "I won. I won the contest!"

We all three jumped up and down and danced around the living room like crazies. Harriet got in on the fun and jumped up. Ree held Harriet's shaggy front paws and danced around with her. Even Edgar, our African Gray parrot, joined in by whistling.

When I tired out, I sat down and recounted the details of the phone call to my girls.

They pelted me with questions: "How will you get the plane tickets? What do you have to do while you're there? Are you going to learn some Italian before you leave?"

I shook my head. "I know absolutely nothing yet. She'll send me an email with the information tomorrow. And as for the language, I guess I'll use a translation app."

Ree said, "Now can we hear the winning jingle?"

I shook my head. "Nope. It is in the rules that the winner can't let anyone hear it until the presentation."

She pouted. "Darn, if they had just called you five minutes later."

I laughed. "Yep. Missed it by that-a much-a. I wonder what the time difference is there." I pulled up the World Clock app on my phone and typed Rome, Italy. "Wow. They are seven hours ahead of us, so when Sophia called me at 5:15, it was after midnight in Italy."

Ree pouted. "It will be tricky to talk to you while you're there."

"We'll manage. I promise." I wasn't going to like being so far away from my girls, which reminded me I should let Todd know, so he could arrange for them to stay with him and Shelly. I looked at my happy girls and decided I'd wait to remind them of where they would stay when I was gone.

When my stomach started to growl, I remembered I had only picked at Mom's ham dinner. But now that the tension was gone, I was famished. I stood and said, "I need a ham sandwich before I call everyone with my news."

As I got everything out, I said, "I'm really sorry I can't take you two along, but I promise someday I'll take you to Europe."

Ren raised her eyebrows at her little sister. "You heard that, right?" Ree nodded with a smirk.

After eating, I called Kim. "So…is your passport up to date?" My hearing would probably be gone for days after all her squeals. Once she calmed down, she peppered me with tons of questions which I couldn't answer. Before hanging up, I asked, "How is that cat?"

"Oh, she's so soft and sweet. Has anyone called about her?"

"Not yet." Kim sounded so hopeful that I hoped nobody would claim the cat and she could keep her.

Then I called Mom, Kay, Lin, and finally Mike with the news.

. . .

The next morning, I checked my e-mail before getting out of bed. Amid a bunch of ads and spam messages, there was one from Sophia@Grecomotors.it. As I read the sweet e-mail, I just could hear the Italian gal's cute accent. I grabbed my new reading glasses and opened the attachment with the itinerary. As I scanned the pages, my stomach fluttered. I was going to Europe in five weeks!

We would fly from Tulsa to Atlanta and then on to Rome where an employee would meet us and take us to our villa just outside of town. Mamma Mia, a real Italian villa!

I skipped ahead to read about the next day when we would take a tour of the Greco factory and meet the owners. Wow! I would get to meet Isabella Greco and her husband, Mario Conti! Apparently, their twin daughters, Rosa and Anna, run the business now and we would get to meet them too. This was too exciting, but my stomach turned when I remembered Matteo was now out of the picture. Apparently, Kim and I would get to go to a fancy gala.

The following morning there will be the rehearsal for the big unveiling event. I almost choked when I read who would be singing my jingle. I shouted, "Ren, Ree, come here!"

When nobody came, I looked at the time and remembered the girls were still asleep in their rooms. I would just have to wait a few hours to tell them the unbelievable news.

With my heart even pounding harder, I read on. After the morning rehearsal, we would have free time to tour Rome. Then at 6:00 p.m. it would be showtime for the big shindig.

According to the information I had read so far, I wouldn't have any duties. We would just be honorary guests. How sweet!

Overwhelmed by all the information, I forwarded the e-mail to Kim and printed off the attachment.

Her reply a few minutes later was, "Eek!"

I brewed a pot of coffee and smiled when Ren entered the kitchen.

She yawned and asked, "Why are you singing a Francesca song?"

I hadn't realized I was singing, but turned to my eldest with a head waggle, "Well because *she* is slated to sing my jingle."

That woke her up. Ren's jaw dropped and she yelled, "What?"

I shook my head having trouble believing it myself. Francesca, the world famous Italian pop singer and actress known for her smoky voice and her dark beauty, was going to sing my jingle!

I said, "I know! It's ridiculous, but I'm not holding my breath. When she looks at my silly jingle, she'll probably back out."

"Well, don't tell Ree about it, or she'll try to squeeze into your suitcase."

"Probably, but I'd better tell her anyway."

I took my coffee and settled into my recliner. When Ree emerged from her room Ren said, "Guess who is singing Mom's jingle."

She shrugged, "Maybe Mom?"

Ren was bouncing up and down as she said, "Nope. Francesca!"

She slapped her hand over her opened mouth and her eyes bugged so much, I was afraid she might hyperventilate. "What? Wow! How big is your suitcase?"

Lauren and I smirked at each other. I said, "Not nearly big enough for an almost 14-year-old.

Marie carried on. "Mom, you have to get a picture of her, or with her…and an autograph."

"I will see what I can do about a picture, but no promises."

Ren said, "She probably won't even give Mom the time of day."

I thought back to last spring when I had gotten to know two very famous people. They were so kind to me and said, "Well if Francesca is a tenth as nice as my Hollywood friends, she might."

Ree warned. "Please don't name-drop, or she'll think you're a snob. I just can't believe you get to meet Francesca and I don't."

. . .

The next three weeks went by so slowly I could hardly stand it, so I worked extra hours at my second job. At school, there were no changes in my schedule yet. Instead, Dr. Love was focused on having our hallway murals painted over with giant school rules. I felt awful for Jules, since she had designed and painted the colorful images with her art students years ago. Our principal was something else and not a good something else.

I tried not to obsess too much about the trip but just happened to find Italian songs to teach my classes. Who knew the children would enjoy singing, 'Funiculi Funicula'? And what better time to introduce them to my favorite Italian composer, Giacomo Puccini?

Kim and I spent most of our free time discussing the schedule and planning what to pack. One night we met at Mom and Dad's house to borrow their big suitcases and travel adapter plugs.

While standing in the hallway looking at bags, I said, "So, how's the cat fitting in now that you decided to keep her."

She smiled. "I love her, and R.A. must too, because he said he gets to name her since he's taking care of her while we're gone."

Dad joined us by the coat closet and said, "Pity, I'm so proud of you for winning the contest. It is quite an accomplishment."

"Thanks—I guess. It seems silly to get a whole trip from writing a 25-second jingle but get nothing for teaching and writing original musicals. Or what about Kim who manages a whole library? And Dad, you write books, for heaven's sake!"

Mom walked up and I turned to her. "And what did you get for starting the Oklahoma Native Plant Society? Nothing!" I shook my head. "I was just really lucky on this."

Dad smiled. "Well, just enjoy every minute of your adventure. You both work so hard and deserve a special trip."

Mom pulled the suitcases from the closet and said, "Don't forget to leave space for souvenirs, Pity. We know you like to shop."

That was true. I wanted to buy things for my family and get something for Mike, Lin, Becca, Jules, and Jana. Then, there was E.J. who would be watching Harriet, plus Melanie, our secretary, and friends from my second job. Just thinking about how much it would cost stressed me out. And would there even be time to shop?

Dad cleared his throat and said, "Pity, are you okay?"

I snapped out of it and noticed that not only had we all moved to the living room while I was making my internal list, but Dad was trying to hand me an envelope. I looked inside and found $100. Problem solved. Kim had an envelope too. We both squealed our thanks.

He put his hand on my shoulder. "Now please stay out of trouble."

Mom added, "Kim, we're expecting you to keep an eye on Pity."

She nodded. "Don't worry. I'm on it."

I scoffed and said, "Maybe I should be watching her."

Kim and my parents snickered. Dang that responsible sister.

…

I had already collected a pile of things to pack, and it was time to get organized. I sorted everything on my bed in groups.

For the airplane: a small pillow, snacks, a blow-up footrest, headphones, a laptop, ear plugs, gum, eye mask, slippers, jacket, books, reading glasses, water bottle, hand sanitizer, disinfecting wipes, chargers, travel adapter, flashlight, pens, and a notepad.

Clothes: undies, socks, pajamas, robe, five shirts, five pants, four dresses, two nice dresses, a swimsuit, towel, two pairs of dress shoes, walking shoes, raincoat, hat, gloves, and flip flops.

Personal items: a make-up bag with toiletries, brushes, shampoo, conditioner, laundry bag, extra plastic bags, safety pins, and Bandaids.

Unfortunately, I had a lot of heavy stuff too.

Yikes, the entire bed was covered. Would this all even fit?

"Are you cleaning out your closet?" I turned around to find both girls staring at my bed.

"No. This is what I'm taking on the trip." I smiled.

Ree said, "I thought you would only be gone five days."

"That's right."

Ren walked around the bed and shook her head. "Looks like you are packing for five months. This will not fit in your suitcase."

"Well, I have to be prepared for any kind of weather."

Ree picked up my coffee pot. "Mom, you are going to Italy. Isn't that where Cappuccino was invented? You can probably get it there."

"Hmm. Maybe you're right." I put the little pot and mug aside.

Ren said, "Do you really need to take your big camera? I mean, you won't be there very long, and your iPhone takes great pics."

She was right. I had worried about lugging my big camera and its lenses around, so I put it back. The girls helped me take out a few more things and I felt better about my packing situation.

Ren said, "Can you take two bags?"

"No, just one suitcase. I can carry on my backpack and a purse."

"Well, then put all the stuff you need with you on the plane in your backpack, and maybe the rest will go in the big suitcase. Maybe."

# Travel Tip #6
*Try to get good seats on the plane.*

On the last school day before my big trip, I left extensive substitute plans on my desk and rushed into the art room. Jules rinsed out paint jars while Becca and Jana wrote lesson plans.

I announced, "Arrivederci, my friends!"

Jana clapped her hands together. "I can't believe you actually get to go to ancient Rome! You know how I love history!"

I nodded and Jules said, "Take lots of photos of the Sistine Chapel for me. I'm doing a study on Michelangelo in March."

The last of my buddies, Becca, said, "And send photos of your villa and maybe bring back a tall, dark, handsome Italian for us."

"Forget the guy, I want a Greco sports car." Jules joked.

Jana said, "Just try to stay out of trouble, Pity."

"I will definitely try." Why did everyone tell me that?

"Well, a *little* trouble never hurt anyone." Becca smiled.

Jules cocked her head, "True, but we're talking about Pity."

I shook my head at her. "Jules, I'm sorry I won't be here to fight the mural war with you. Good luck!"

She rolled her eyes. "Thanks. I'll need it."

After hugs, I made sure my lesson plans were perfect and left the school without a peep from Dr. Love. For weeks, I had anticipated getting flak from him about my upcoming absence and was shocked that he never brought it up to me. I was also skeptical about his big "schedule change", but I wasn't going to worry about it or think of the man at all for the next five days. Ahh.

Even though I was confident my daughters would be in good, albeit annoying, hands with Todd and Shelly, I called my ex to make sure all was set. I said, "Just a reminder, we leave on the 12th and return on the 16th. Mom and Dad are available anytime. Make sure Ree does her homework and Ren doesn't miss swim practice."

I could sense him rolling his eyes. "I know how to take care of my own kids. Shelly has already made up the guest room for them."

I heard a commotion through the phone and suddenly Shelly's brash voice blasted into my ear. "So, I was thinking… when you go over to that I-talian country, maybe you could put in a good word for me to do commercials for those Greco cars."

I slapped my hand over my forehead. No way an elite sports car company would be interested in having Shelly wear a kitschy costume and say some corny line with her thick Okie twang.

I tried to be tactful. "Um. Shelly, I'm sorry but I think they use an Italian advertising agency for their commercials."

"Well, why did you get to write a jingle? You are not I-talian!"

Just the way she said I-talian proved she would be horrible at the job. I said, "Right. But I won't be singing it." I stopped myself before telling her Francesca would do the honors, or Shelly would go nuts.

I finally got off the phone but didn't feel any better about the girls staying with them. Why was I worried? It was only a few days.


The night before our flight, Mike took me to a Chinese restaurant. He grinned as we were given our chopsticks. "I thought you might enjoy something completely different from spaghetti."

"Good idea. I probably won't see many eggrolls in Rome, but I sure plan to eat some good pasta and red wine."

"So, are you all packed and ready to go?"

"As ready as I'm going to get. My suitcase will barely close. So, Mike, what would you like me to bring you from Italy?"

"Sounds like you won't have room. Your gift to me is to be safe and try to stay out of trouble."

He was the third person to tell me that. Sure, I had managed to find myself in some dangerous situations in the past year, but seriously… Maybe all those warnings just meant people cared about me. I said, "I plan to be a very professional jingle-writer/tourist."

He took my hand and said, "Well, since you'll be gone on the actual holiday this weekend, I have this for my Valentine."

He handed me a small box and I cringed. I had forgotten all about Valentine's Day. "Uh, I didn't get anything for you."

"This is just so you don't forget me while you're gone. I don't want you hopping on the back of a Vespa with some handsome Italian dude and riding off to Tuscany to live."

I pictured myself on the back of a Vespa and scoffed. "I really don't think that will happen. I don't even like motorcycles." He raised an eyebrow, and I quickly added, "And there is no chance I'd forget my own handsome man back home." I winked.

Inside the box, there was a gold chain made of tiny gold hearts.

"Oh, it's gorgeous. I love it. Help me put it on, please."

I took off my special silver necklace I had worn since getting it as a gift last March and placed it in my coin purse. Then I scooted across to his side of the booth, lifted my hair, and turned around so he could fasten the clasp. I faced him and planted a big kiss on his lips. "Thank you, Mike. I promise I won't run off with anyone."

. . .

Finally, the big morning arrived. It was time to fly to Italy! I kissed my girls. "Here's a little something for you." I handed them each a little bag of Valentine's treats I had grabbed at our Walgreens the night before. I also put spending money in a card and gave it to them.

Ree read the card and gave me a hug. "Thanks, Mom. I'm going to miss you, too."

Ren handed me a package. "We have something for you."

I opened the box and found a beautiful leather passport cover with flowers tooled on the front. "I love it! Did you make this?"

Ren beamed. "I stamped it in my leatherworking class."

Ree said, "The note inside is from me."

I read the sweet note covered in airplanes, wine bottles and hearts. I hugged the cover to my chest and said, "It's amazing. I will be the envy of all the other travelers." I ran to slip my passport inside and put back it in my purse before I had the chance to lose either one.

"I'll call you girls every chance I get and will bring you something special from the trip."

When R.A. and Kim arrived to take me to the airport, I reminded the girls, "Feed the animals and go visit Harriet at E.J.'s house. Do your homework, and say thank you to anyone who helps you, even Shelly. And text me all the time so I won't miss you so much."

Ren said, "OK. Bring me back a young Italian in a sports car!"

I laughed and Ree said, "Tell Francesca I love her new album and I really wanted to go to her concert in Dallas. And don't forget to get a picture with her!"

I waved to my girls as we pulled away and tears started to form. Stop it, Pity. You'll be back in a few days.

Tulsa has a great airport; not too big or small. I looked at the cool mural depicting the city's history and growled at the thought of Dr. Love. He would probably paint it over with giant TSA rules if he could.

At the airline's counter, Kim and I got our tickets for the flights to Atlanta and then on to Rome.

Kim said, "I've got a window seat on the long flight, but I'll switch with you whenever you want."

"Thanks, sis. Can you believe we're doing this?"

"No!"

R.A. schlepped Kim's big bag onto the scale and the ticket agent tossed it on the belt. Wow, she's strong.

When R.A. lifted mine, he said, "What's in this? It weighs a ton."

Before I could answer the woman looked at the scale. "Ms. Kole, your luggage is well over fifty pounds. You'll need to pay the heavy bag fee or remove items. But to do that, move away from the counter."

Kim said, "What did you bring that is so heavy, Pity?"

I shrugged as R.A. pulled my bag off the scale. I opened the suitcase and tried to hide my underwear from nearby strangers.

Kim leaned over. "How many pairs of shoes did you bring?" Before I could answer, she blurted, "You brought Mountain Dew?"

"It's just a six-pack. I read they don't have it over there."

She rolled her eyes. "I think you can live without it, dork." She took the heavy cans out and put them on the ground.

R.A. took out my pillow. "You'll get a pillow and blanket on your flight, and why a big hairdryer? Won't they have them there?"

"I don't know. Better safe than sorry." I stuffed it down deep.

Kim said, "Don't you have a smaller umbrella?"

"Yes, but I couldn't find it."

"There's no rain in the forecast, and you have a raincoat."

"And what is this?" R.A. lifted a bulky notebook.

I smiled. "My photo album! People there might want to see pictures of life in America. There are old pics of the Golden Driller, my girls, of me with a Fiat Spider, which proves I like Italian cars."

R.A. shook his head, and I handed him the huge binder.

Kim said, "Honestly, Pity, I'm not sure how your brain works. Give me your phone." She took a photo from its pocket, snapped a picture with my phone, and then repeated the process a few more times. "There. Now you have those photos to show them from your phone. I'll admit, the one of you and the girls beside Lin's Fiat is great."

I frowned and said, "Thanks for hijacking my belongings."

R.A.'s eyes widened. "Shhh. Don't use that word in an airport! You can be arrested." He put my bag back on the scale. It weighed 46 pounds. That was a relief, but I could only get feathers for souvenirs.

I hugged R.A. goodbye, then Kim gave him a kiss. She said, "I wish you could come, too. Take care of that cat while we're gone."

He nodded. "Just have a blast After we watched him haul my excess items away, we took our smaller bags through security. I sat on a bench beside Kim to put my shoes on again. "Well, we have over an hour. Whatcha want to do? I can't get souvenirs here."

She zipped her boot. "Yeah. Who wants something from Oklahoma?"

I brightened. "Wait. Why didn't I think of that? I should take gifts to the people who hosted the contest, or the owners of the car company, or at least to Francesca for singing my jingle. Come on!"

Kim followed me into a souvenir shop filled with expensive Oklahoma items. I said, "Too bad I didn't get affordable stuff at Walmart. How about a shot glass with a buffalo on it."

She made a face. "I don't know," then picked up a liquid tornado. "This is cute, but they probably don't know Oklahoma has tornadoes."

I picked up a Tulsa shirt. "I could get shirts but don't know sizes." I walked past coffee mugs since they were heavy and breakable.

Kim said, "What about this?" She picked up a small canvas bag with a cowboy riding a horse. It said, 'You're doing fine, Oklahoma!'"

"Perfect. Let's get six. And look at these cute Tulsa magnets with my boyfriend on them." I picked up six of the black magnets with the Golden Driller oil man statue printed on them.

She pulled out her card. "I'll pay half, since I'm on the trip too."

Once the goodies were paid for and stuffed into carry-ons bags, we found our way to the gate and people-watched until we boarded.

We had three hours to kill in the Atlanta airport. In a souvenir shop, we bought six decks of United States playing cards to put in the tote bags. I googled what kind of candy they only have in America and found a big bag of Tootsie Rolls with plans to add to each tote bag.

I laughed. "Who would dream I'd shop before we left the States?"

She cocked her head. "Um. Everyone who knows you."

When our boarding section was called, we lined up. I was proud of my new leather passport cover and couldn't help but show it off. The gate agent wore a red and green 'Stivale Airways' uniform. She smiled, scanned our tickets, and said a cute, "Sank you."

When we found our row, we saw that R.A. was right. A pillow and blanket were on every seat. I sat down but worried my long legs would be cramped up in the tight space, especially on a 10-hour flight.

Kim pointed to the back of the seatback in front of her. "I forgot we would each get our own movie screen."

"Sweet! Glad we brought headphones."

An enormous guy who smelled like cigarettes and alcohol took the aisle seat beside me. Shoot. I had hoped it would remain empty so we could spread out. I smiled at my new neighbor, but he just looked away as he sat down. His gigantic arm took up the whole arm rest, so I was forced to shift close to Kim. I couldn't arm wrestle a 300-pound bear.

We scrolled through the movie icons and giggled as Kim pointed. "Ooh, I want to see that, and that, and that."

Once all passengers had boarded and the cabin door was closed, the flight attendants started the safety demonstration. I watched intently, but who in the world wasn't familiar with buckling a seatbelt? I did pay close attention to the lifejacket info since most of the flight would be over water.

Moments later, a male flight attendant with a red and green tie handed us earbuds in tiny packages. "Thank you!" I exclaimed.

As the plane hit the sky. I squeezed Kim's hand. "Next stop…Italy!"

I turned to say the same thing to the man beside me, but he was sound asleep already. Maybe he flew all the time.

Kim pulled some snacks from her bag and said, "I figure I should eat something when I take my motion sickness pill. Shall we?"

"We shall!" I took a pack of Ritz Bits and started chomping. "I'll get my snacks later. For now, I just want to watch *Roman Holiday*." Since my headphones were in my backpack up above, I opened the little pouch and put on my free earbuds. The sound was horrible, especially with all the background noise from the airplane. I could barely hear the dialogue. Why was my backpack in the overhead bin? Oh well, I couldn't exactly crawl over the guy while he slept. I'd just have to wait until he woke up. I finally figured out how to get the captions on, so I could at least tell what Audrey Hepburn said.

About 20 minutes into the film, I smelled food. I nudged Kim. "I think they are serving us a meal!"

We paused our movies, unplugged our cheap earbuds, and pulled down the tray tables. The same attendant leaned over the sleeping giant and asked us in an alluring accent, "Sheeken or bif?"

I said, "Beef please."

Kim said, "Same for me."

He spoke to another attendant and turned back to us. "Oh, I'm so sorry, we are out of bif. You can have sheeken or vegetarian."

I nodded. "Chicken is fine."

He handed us each a plastic tray with dividers. There was salad, a roll, chicken and rice dish plus a brownie in a little cup.

"What would you like to drink?" A tall woman with a red and green scarf stood by a cart full of bottles of wine, cans of beer, and other drinks.

I asked, "Can you tell me how much a glass of wine is?" I hoped the price wasn't outrageous.

She smiled. "They are all included with your flight."

"Really? Well, then I'll have a glass of red wine, please."

Kim overheard the conversation and said, "Same here please?"

She handed our drinks across the top of the snoozing man. I asked, "Do you think we should tell him the food is here?"

She said, "No. Just let him sleep." The look on her face warned me that waking him might be a bad idea.

Kim and I toasted our plastic cups. I enjoyed my wine and hoped it would help me sleep. But after the attendant picked up our trays and refilled our wine glasses, I could only think about getting my headphones down to finish my movie with proper sound.

I asked Kim, "Do you think I can sneak across him? I need my headphones, so I can hear the movie."

"I don't see how you can do it without waking him."

"I do have long legs."

She shrugged. "Give it a try then."

I pushed myself up from the seatback and lifted one foot as high as I could over the guy's wide legs. Just as I straddled him, he woke up and growled something in a foreign language.

I froze. It was like I was face-to-face with a grizzly bear just coming out of hibernation. I pointed up and said apologetically, "Um. I need to get something from the overhead compartment."

He grumbled in a heavy accent, "You should have done that before you sat down."

I lifted my other foot over him. "I didn't mean to bother you."

He growled and settled back to sleep. Since I was up, I should go to the bathroom. I mouthed my plans to Kim, who said, "What?"

After doing a sort of sign language to explain where I was going, I went to the bathroom. When I returned and got my backpack, I lifted my foot even higher and crossed him without a problem.

Kim said, "Hey, I'm going to need to go pretty soon. How can I get out? I'm not as adept at high stepping as you are."

"Well, maybe he'll wake up and need to go himself. Then we can jump up when he's gone."

She nodded. "I'm going to sleep now but tell me if he gets up."

# Travel Tip #7

*Sleep on the flight and power through the time change when you land.*

I watched the rest of *Roman Holiday* with my noise-canceling headphones and the difference was unreal. The experience was so good that I also watched *Under the Tuscan Sun.* How cool that they added Italian movies to the in-flight entertainment. When the movie ended, I was totally pumped to get to Italy.

Kim slept just as soundly as the dude next to me. I needed to get some shut-eye, myself. Unfortunately, I wasn't sleepy. I blew up my footrest but couldn't find a place for it in the small space. There was nowhere to lean my head, my back was cramped from avoiding touching the guy's arm, and my stupid seat only reclined an inch. No point trying to sleep. I pulled my small laptop from my backpack and looked over my list of fifth graders. I was determined to write the new fifth-grade musical even if Dr. Love wouldn't allow it to be performed.

I had already developed the storyline–a light mystery set at an elementary school. In the story, the school children had free reign to solve the mystery because the substitute was clueless. Maybe I could make the principal be the bad guy. That would be easy to imagine.

I started a new document for the script and began writing. At one point my arm slipped over and hit the armrest, so I jerked my head to see if I had touched the grumpy guy, but he wasn't there. I had been so engrossed in writing the dialog that I hadn't noticed he got up.

"Kim! Wake up!"

"What?" Her eyelids looked like they were glued shut as she tried to open them.

I urged, "It's time to go to the bathroom!"

"You're not my mommy." She put her head back against the window and settled back in.

"Kim. It's now or maybe never. Get up."

She slurred her words, "But I'm groogly."

She made no sense. "Why are you so sleepy?" I demanded.

"I took two."

"You took two what? Motion-sickness pills? Why?" I remembered she also had two glasses of wine. Yikes. She would be out for the rest of the flight, but I knew she needed to go to the bathroom. I shook her. "Come on. You can come back and sleep. Get up." I pulled her arm and she collapsed towards me. I finally lifted her to a standing position. With my arm around her waist, we wobbled to the bathroom. Despite the dark cabin, I sensed other passengers staring at us.

I propped her up against the wall and opened the accordion door leading to the small area. "Here, I'll help you in."

Once inside, she woke up enough to realize where she was. When she started pulling down her pants, I stood guard outside the door.

I smiled as another lady came up to wait for a turn. It felt good to stand up. I bent my legs and marched in place. After all, I heard you could develop blood clots from sitting too long.

The woman behind me tapped her foot and I didn't think it was her form of exercise. What was taking Kim so long? I put my mouth to the door. "Kim, are you OK?"

There was no answer and so I told the woman, "It's my sister. I'll just check on her."

I opened the door and found Kim sitting on the toilet, slumped against the wall, sound asleep with her mouth open.

I squeezed inside the tiny space and my first thought was how in the world did people join the mile-high club in one of these cramped cubicles? I shook my sister. "Kim, wake up. You can't stay here."

"Hmm?"

"Get off the pot."

She looked around, confused, and said, "Oh. Ok, I'll be right out."

I slipped back outside and told the impatient woman, "Sorry. She took two motion sickness pills and had wine. She fell asleep on the toilet. Haha. But she should be right out."

"This is ridiculous." The woman huffed and walked to the back of the plane to a different restroom.

Kim finally emerged and was able to weave her way down the aisle without much assistance. In a very loud voice everyone could hear, she said, "I feel so mush better after going potty."

She sounded drunk. Maybe I should have just let her sleep. As funny as it was, she would be horrified if she knew about this so I vowed not to tell her.

When we got to our row, my seatmate was back, sound asleep again. I tapped his shoulder. "Excuse me?" He didn't budge so I said, a little louder, "Excuse me, sir. May we get to our seats?"

There was still no movement and without warning, Kim tried to step over him but ended up sitting right on his legs. She leaned in and patted his face. "Your chin is so shiny. Not like R.A."

He snapped awake and pushed her towards her seat. "Che cosa?"

I cringed. "I'm so sorry. We tried to wake you so we could get back to our seats."

He shook his head but finally stood so I could pass him. Then he said something under his breath, also in his native tongue. I only understood one word–Americans, and it wasn't said with joy.

Kim slept soundly while I worked on my musical. I was proud of myself for being productive, but by the time we landed, I was finally sleepy. I looked at my watch. No wonder. It was 1:30 a.m. our time, but the pilot announced it was 8:30 in the morning in Rome.

I nudged Kim and said, "Wake up sleepyhead. We're in Italy!"

She stretched her arms and smiled as if she had just had a good night's sleep - which she had. She said, "Let's get this party started."

I wanted to tell her she had a party earlier but kept it to myself.

The grumpy man woke up and I turned to him. "I'm sorry for bothering you earlier."

He rolled his dark brown eyes and said with a thick accent, "Next time, get an aisle seat."

"Good idea."

We gathered our belongings and checked the floor and seatback pockets as directed. Then, we followed Mr. Grumpy Pants out.

As we passed our flight attendant, she asked Kim, "Did you get enough sleep?"

My sister nodded. "I did, thanks."

A little girl pulled Kim's sleeve and said, "You were so funny."

Kim's eyebrows knitted. She asked me, "What was that about?"

I shrugged but hoped I could get by without telling her. Since there was no jetway, we had to walk down a stairway from the plane onto the tarmac and then catch a bus to the terminal. I smiled on this beautiful, crisp, clear morning. How strange to think it was the middle of the night for me, but who cared? I was in Rome! Woohoo!

While waiting at the bottom of the stairs, the woman who couldn't wait for the bathroom walked by and shook her head in disapproval. When Kim scrunched her eyes, I said, "I'll tell ya later."

We boarded the bus, but we had to stand up because of the crowd. I held onto a rubber loop hanging from the ceiling and swayed back and forth, praying my backpack wouldn't hit anyone in the face.

A man winked at Kim and then in an undeniably Italian accent he said, "So, too much-a wine last night, no?"

She slowly turned her head to me. "What in the world?"

The bus let us out at the terminal, and we followed the signs to baggage claim. While we waited for our bags, Kim grabbed my arm. "I feel like I'm in *The Twilight Zone*. Everyone is acting weird."

I sighed. "Actually, you were in a twilight zone last night."

"What?"

"You took two pills and drank wine."

She shrugged. "So. You know how I am. I have trouble sleeping and was worried about turbulence."

"Do you even remember going to the bathroom?"

"No!" She sucked in a breath and looked down at her crotch.

"Not in your pants–in the restroom." She shook her head. I added with a smirk, "Perhaps you remember snuggling up to my seatmate?"

Kim's shocked face was priceless. "What? I did not."

I giggled. "Yes, you did. You were so out of it I had to practically carry you to the bathroom. It was like you were drunk. I wasn't going to tell you about it, but now I wish I had recorded the whole thing."

Her face turned a deep shade of red as I explained it all to her. She covered her eyes with her hand. "Well, that explains all the odd comments." Then she hid behind me. "I'm so embarrassed."

"It's okay. We'll never see those people again."


Once we picked up our luggage off the belt, we started toward the exit, but a uniformed man ushered us down a hallway. A huge sign in English read, 'Welcome to Roma. Please proceed to immigration and customs.' We opted for the long line with an American flag.

Finally, we approached a turnstile. A laminated photo directed us to scan our passports. Once on the other side, we were called up to a booth where we handed our passports to a young man with dark curly hair. He asked where we lived and how long we would be in Italy. When he gave them back, I frowned at my blank passport and asked, "Will we get our passports stamped somewhere else?"

The man grinned, took my passport back, and stamped it. The date was now stamped in red with Rome, Italy. I showed it to Kim, and she handed hers back to the man too.

Whew, that was easy! We followed the other travelers and found ourselves in yet another line. This time, it was more like TSA with some people walking through and random people being stopped.

A stocky woman in a blue uniform came up to me and said curtly, "Customs declaration form?"

"Uh. I don't know?"

She nodded for us to go into the line where bags were being searched. An adorable beagle walked toward my suitcase, and I leaned over to pet him, but a man yelled something at me in Italian. I jumped back and stared at the dog. Maybe the pup was a biter?

Then the beagle got to work sniffing my bags, probably for drugs. The dog seemed very interested in my backpack and the uniformed man motioned for me to open it. My heart pounded. Had I inadvertently brought drugs with me? Or had someone slipped them in my bag, like they do in the movies?

I nervously unzipped the big pocket, worrying I would find a bag of white powder and be carted off to an Italian jail. Wearing gloves, the man dug through my belongings. He pulled out a banana and the beagle went wild, which was not surprising. Harriet loved bananas too.

The agent said, "Not allowed!" He threw my banana into a trash can. Then he nodded his head as if the rest of my stuff was fine. Whew.

I shook my head as I caught up with Kim. "I thought for a minute I would be arrested for smuggling a banana into the country."

Kim pointed. "Look, she's holding a sign with our names on it!"

Sure enough, a petite woman dressed in a smart red blazer was looking for us. I felt like such a celebrity - except they probably don't wave wildly and run to their greeter squealing, "Hi, I'm Pity Kole!"

"Allo, Pitico. It's me, Zophia. I'm 'appy to meet-a you." The small, peppy gal oozed kindness with her bright smile and twinkly black eyes. Her dark ponytail swung back and forth as she spoke.

I said, "Hi Sophia! Wow, you are so beautiful, just like your voice. This is my sister, Kim Ross."

"Allo Kim-a. Deed you have a nice flight?"

We nodded.

"You are tired, no?"

I nodded again. "I'm very sleepy, but I heard we should power through and stay awake the whole day."

"Dat will be good, for der is much to zee. You can take a rest in your rooms if you like."

She led us to a parking lot and right up to a silver Greco SUV, of all things. A large man stepped out of it and put our bags in the back. "Thees is your driver, Aldo. You vill know him so much this weekend." She hopped in the front passenger seat.

I looked at the burly man with his heavy dark beard and wondered if he was as mean as he looked. Not knowing if he spoke English, I just waved meekly and said, "Ciao, Aldo."

He broke out with a huge smile revealing a gap in his front teeth. He belted, "Buongiorno, Belle!"

We brightened. Kim said, "Hi Aldo, I'm Kim and this is Pity."

"Kim e Pity." He bowed down and I half expected him to kiss our hands. "Welcome to Roma!"

He opened the back door, and we climbed into a spacious backseat that resembled the interior of a limousine–I only knew that because of my odd date a year ago with Kenny. Aldo drove us north from the airport to an area Sophia called Trastevere. Along the way, she pointed out places of interest. We passed through a gate and followed a winding road lined with unusual trees until we reached a gorgeous villa.

I couldn't help but gasp at its beauty. I whispered to Kim, "It's just like the villa in season two of *White Lotus.*"

Kim shook her head. "I know! And we're staying here!"

Aldo pulled up to a set of wide marble steps leading to the entrance. The steps were surrounded by perfectly sculpted bushes, manicured hedges, and stone fountains on each side. When I climbed out of the Greco and turned around to get my suitcase, my mouth dropped open. Kim must have seen the same thing because she too was speechless. The view overlooking Rome was incredible.

Sophia stood next to us and said, "Lovely, no? Many people want to come to thees hill to take-a the photos."

Stunned, I could only nod. The city was painted in reds and pinks with domed roofs pointing skyward – just gorgeous.

Kim pointed. "Look. I think that's St. Peter's Basilica!"

Sophia smiled. "Jes eet is. Come, and we'll find your rooms."

I looked for my luggage, but Aldo was already hauling our big, heavy suitcases up the steps as if they were briefcases.

The entryway was adorned with so many pieces of art that I wondered if we even needed to visit a museum. As we followed Sophia, I marveled at the way her heels clicked and echoed throughout the massive place. Our rubber-soled shoes made no sound, but we made up for it with our loud oohing and ahhing.

We followed the two Italians through a courtyard to a separate side entrance. After climbing a few flights of stairs we walked down another tile hallway where Sophia and Aldo stopped in front of an ornate wooden door. Sophia pointed, "A room for one and the other is across. Please pick-a up the phone if there is a need. A light meal for you is downstairs at Mezzogiorno, uh…" She counted on her fingers in English and corrected herself, "at-a twelve."

We both said, "Oh, thank you!"

Once alone, we opened the first door and stepped inside. The room could easily have been the setting for the two Italian movies I just watched. It was small but beautiful with an intricately carved headboard, and gold frames around the oil paintings that may have been painted by DaVinci himself. I rubbed my hand along the rich textures of the bed covering and curtains. The tiny bathroom had a toilet, a pedestal sink, and a clawfoot tub with a handheld shower head. The small mirror frame was as ornate as the rest of the room.

Kim glanced out the window and said, "Pity, there's a pool."

I rushed to join her, and my jaw dropped to find an ivy-covered courtyard featuring a small oval swimming pool right below us. There were even fish statues spouting water into it.

We both said, "I want this room," then, "jinks!"

I twisted my mouth. "Maybe we should at least look at the other room."

We crossed the hall to a room that was equally elegant with similar neutral colors and a terracotta tile floor. I checked out the view. "No way. It's an actual vineyard!" I was in disbelief. "I don't care which room I get. They're both amazing. You can choose, Kim."

She went to the hall and rolled her suitcase into the vineyard room, so I pulled mine into the pool room and unpacked. Once I put my clothes away in drawers, I lay on the bed - Ahh this was the life.

. . .

I awoke to a pounding on the door and opened my eyes to find a naked boy standing beside my bed. No wait. It was just a statue of a cherub on a nightstand. Where was I? I lifted myself up on my elbows and saw my suitcase standing in the corner. Oh, right. I was in Italy! Had I been drugged? Why was I so sleepy? I looked at my watch, which was still set on Tulsa time—5 a.m. That was why.

When the pounding continued, I yelled, "Come in!"

Kim marched in and sat on my bed. "I've been knocking for five minutes. It's time for lunch, sis. Why were you asleep? It's noon."

I scoffed. "Unlike the slumber queen, I didn't get a six-hour nap on the flight, so I really didn't want to wake up."

"Well, you're gonna have to because there is a meal waiting for us downstairs. Come on. You can sleep tonight."

I was so groggy, I cursed myself for sleeping at all, but dragged myself off the bed. As the two of us made our way down the stairs, I said, "Should we should leave breadcrumbs to find our way back?"

"Maybe, but right now let's follow the delicious garlic aroma."

We entered a room through a brick archway. I stared at the décor and whispered to Kim, "This is just like *Olive Garden*. It even has greenery around the windows and Chianti bottles on the table."

"Except…this is the original style that *Olive Garden* copied."

I nodded. The scene was so iconically Italian, I snapped a photo.

A tall, willowy 20-something girl wearing an apron, motioned for us to sit at a long, empty table. Once we were seated, she placed a plate in front of each of us. The array of meats, hard cheeses, and bread with bruschetta made my mouth water. Before I could take a bite, the girl said something to us in Italian and then poured red wine into our glasses. I was so sleepy that wine seemed like a bad idea, but heck, when in Rome…I took a sip. It tasted incredible.

After we finished the delicious charcuterie, I patted my tummy, which I hoped was the universal sign to show the food was delicious. The gal nodded and left us alone.

I said, "I'm stuffed. Kim, let's go check out the rest of the villa."

Before we could stand, the girl came to us with new plates. My eyes grew wide at the sight and smell of a beautiful pesto pasta. I looked at Kim and we shrugged. All we could do was settle back in.

After one bite, I leaned my head back in ecstasy. As much as I like *Olive Garden* and *Zios*, their food could not compare to this.

Kim licked her fork as though she was trying to get every last drop of olive oil from each bite. It really was that good.

When the girl came back to fill our empty wine glasses, I held my hand over my glass to stop her. I pointed to my empty plate. "Who made this pasta? It is incredible!"

She dipped her head down shyly. "Mi cuoco de villa."

If the word cuoco meant cook, I was shocked someone so young was that talented. I pointed to myself. "I am Pity. What is your name?"

"Mi chiamo Martina."

I attempted one of my new Italian words., "Grazi, Martina."

Kim nodded. "Ciao, Martina. Mi chiamo Kim."

Martina pushed her long chocolate brown hair behind her ears and said, "Mi inglese is no buono."

I nodded. "Well, my Italian is terrible."

When we stood, Martina's face crumpled. I turned to Kim. "You don't think there is *more* food, do you?"

I lifted my hands. "More food?"

When Martina nodded and took our plates, we sat back down. I turned to Kim. "We'll gain 20 pounds if every light meal is like this."

"How do these people stay so slim?"

In a minute, Martina returned with small plates. We thanked her. I wasn't sure what the dessert was but took a bite. It had hints of coffee, chocolate, and something else I couldn't identify.

Kim said, "This is the best tiramisu I've ever had."

"So that's what it is. It's great, but I can't pinpoint one taste."

"It's probably the rum."

Well, that made sense. We managed to break away from the feast and thanked Martina again. Kim asked me, "Should we leave a tip?"

"I think everything is included, but we can ask Sophia."

# Travel Tip #8
*Respect local culture.*

With no apparent plans for the day, we took a walk around the estate. Every time we turned, there was a photo-worthy shot. At this rate, my phone memory would be full on day one.

We managed to find the courtyard with the pool, and I dipped my fingers in the water. As expected in February, it was very cold.

I nearly fell into the pool when a person with a deep voice belted, "Do you wish to go for a swim?"

I whipped my head around to find a tall, handsome man with dark stubble leaning against a wall. He looked like he was a model posing for Armani suits. Mamma Mia!

Kim stuttered, "Um, no. We're just wandering around looking at this beautiful place." I was glad she spoke because I was speechless.

He used his hands while speaking perfect English. "That is fine. Enjoy. I'm Luca. If you need anything, let me know. No place is off-limits for you. When the others arrive, I'll call you down for drinks, so you can get acquainted." He turned and left.

Still dumbfounded by his good looks, we made our way back to our floor. We found our rooms and sat on my bed.

Kim said, "What others do you think he's talking about?"

"I don't know, but that Luca is gorgeous! I only wish I'd been quicker on the draw, so I could have snapped a photo for Becca."

"Well, if you take a picture, you might not show it to Mike in case he's a jealous type." She nudged me. "Hey Pity, don't close your eyes. You'll fall asleep again. We're supposed to power through."

I nodded. "Easy for you to say. What time is it?"

"It's three o'clock."

"So, it's still just 8 a.m. at home. No wonder I'm groggy. I'm not sure I can make it until it's evening here."

She yawned and lay down by me. "I'm tired too, but we should try to stay awake until seven or eight. We can wait that long, right?"

. . .

Ha. Best laid plans. We both fell asleep again and within what seemed like minutes the phone rang.

We bolted upright. The room was dark, and I grumbled, "Where's the phone?"

Kim climbed from the bed and found the light switch. When I spotted the phone on a desk, I stumbled over and answered, "Hello?"

"Hallo. I hope I did not disturb you. It is Luca. Please come join us for a light dinner and drinks."

"OK, we'll be right down. Thank you." I rubbed my eyes. "I'm still full from lunch, but they want us to go for dinner and drinks? How do I look? Can I pass for a human? Should we change clothes?"

"Well, you might want to brush your hair and wipe the drool from your mouth. I'm too tired to change, myself. Let's just go in our travel clothes." Kim promptly left to freshen up in her room.

I ran to the bathroom, washed my face, and attempted to make myself presentable for whomever we were about to meet. Being so tall, I had to squat a little to see my eyes in the low-hung mirror. I expected to see red eyes with bags under them after so little sleep, but they looked better than I felt. With such dark eyes and eyelashes, I didn't need much mascara. I could almost pass for an Italian, but my dull brown hair was missing the luster of those we had met, and at this moment, it was in dire need of fixing. Since I didn't have time to heat up my straightener, I just ran a comb through my hair and called it good. I stood on tiptoes to see my outfit in the small mirror. Hmm. The leggings weren't so bad and at least my long top covered my bum.

We heard voices and approached a big room. When we entered, we were shocked to find a group of beautifully dressed men and women standing around as if at a cocktail party. I quickly realized it *was* a cocktail party and we were very underdressed. We did a 180, hoping nobody saw us, but Sophia rushed over and caught my arm. "Pityco and Kim. I hope you got to rest after the long flight."

I smiled and said, "Oh. Yes, thank you. This place is amazing." I leaned into her and whispered, "I wish we had known to dress up. Who are these people?"

"Oh, do not worry. Everyone knows you have traveled to here. You are fine. I will introduce you."

Before we could stop her, she clinked her wine glass with a fork and said, "Allo, everyone. This is Pitycol-a. She won zee contest for writing the leetle song for Macchina Forte. Thees is her sister, Kim. They travel from America. Please introduce yourself to them-a."

My face grew hot. How embarrassing to be presented while in this getup. Even I knew better than to wear tennis shoes to a cocktail party. Everyone else looked like they were from the *House of Gucci.*

Nobody seemed very interested in us, some even gave us looks of disdain, like we were lowly Americans who just won a contest. I leaned over to Kim. "I feel like a slob. Why didn't we dress up?"

"I'm sorry. I thought we would be fine. Who knew?"

We were interrupted by an older woman with a wrinkled, but kind face. She had short white hair and wore a beautiful blue dress which accented her hair. She said, "Allo. Welcome to Italy, my dears. We were enamored with your little jingle."

"Thank you. It's nice to meet you…"

In perfect English she said, "Oh, my name is Isabella Greco."

I almost stumbled to meet the namesake of the car company—the woman who ran Greco Motors for over sixty years. I recognized the same kind eyes that looked out from the image in ads and commercials, but they had softened over the years. Kim's eyes were wide.

I said, "It is so nice to meet you, Señora Greco. We were so sorry to hear about Mattteo. He seemed like a very nice man."

The woman said, "Thank you. It has been very difficult for us. He was our bambino." She wiped away a tear and then smiled. "We will see you much more this weekend, I hope."

When she walked away, I whispered, "Kim, that was the Isabella Greco, the face of Italian sports cars. Meeting her is like meeting the Pope or Chef Boyardee himself."

"I know what you mean. We grew up seeing her face on TV."

I frowned. "Do you think it was bad that I brought up Matteo?"

"No. It was a nice gesture. I wonder if her daughters are here?"

I looked around for Rosa and Anna but was distracted when Luca appeared in front of us carrying a tray of hors d'oeuvres. I looked at the appetizers and back at the gorgeous man, then picked up a toothpick with an olive, tomato, and cheese. "Grazi, Luca."

Kim took one too. As he moved on, she said, "I wasn't sure which looked more delicious—Luca or the food."

We giggled and sipped our wine until Sophia brought four impeccably dressed people over to us. One woman who looked to be about my age had short, cropped brown hair with bright red lipstick and a gorgeous green dress. The other gal was not as tall, had longer hair, and a classy Sophia Loren look about her. Both were gorgeous.

Sophia motioned to the first couple. "Thees is Rosa Greco and her husband Carlo Bruno." She turned to the others. "And this is Anna Greco with her husband, Giacomo Rossi. I leave you to visit." Sophia flitted away, leaving us with the people who now ran the company.

The faces of the twin girls were similar, but not identical. I held out my hand to the taller of the two. "Nice to meet you, Rosa…" I was going to name them all in greeting but had already forgotten the husbands' names. I turned to Kim. "I also have my sister with me. This is Kim." Rosa took my hand and smiled politely.

Rosa's husband, (what was his name?) was of medium height, clean-shaven, and looked in his fifties. When he gave me a curt nod, I blanched and focused on his serious face and his salt-and-pepper hair.

I turned to the other twin, Anna, who forced a smile. She hesitated before taking my hand as if she might catch something from me. Anna's husband, with another name I'd already forgotten, was tall with dark hair and a neatly trimmed beard. He kissed the back of my hand and said, "Welcome to Rome." He rolled his R beautifully and gave a dazzling smile – what a charmer.

I smiled and turned back to the sisters. "Thank you so much for including us in this amazing weekend."

Kim nodded. "Yes, and this villa is beautiful."

Rosa gave a slight nod, but apparently the four weren't much for small talk. Anna took her husband's arm and they all walked away.

Kim leaned over to me. "Maybe the girls don't speak English?"

"Or maybe they are just rude."

As if to punctuate my statement, Anna glared at a woman who wore a cropped, pink sequined top baring her skinny midriff. Then she yanked her husband aside as they passed her.

Was she jealous? I couldn't even imagine why someone so rich and beautiful would be. But, when the sparkly gal turned around, that thought disappeared and I almost fainted. It was Francesca. Her iconic, heavily made-up eyes familiar from album covers and concert posters, were unmistakable. I elbowed Kim and then waved at the superstar as if I was a crazed fan. Unfortunately, things got worse when I stepped forward and opened my mouth.

"Hello, I'm Pity and you're performing my ditty." My face heated instantly with my unintended rhyme, but I continued, "I hope it's not beneath you to sing the silly jingle. If you need any help, let me know."

Kim nudged me - a sign I was talking too much. I closed my eyes in embarrassment.

When I opened them, the superstar looked down her long nose at me and spoke with only a slight accent. "I have not yet seen the song sheet, but I believe I can do it without your help. It is not a concerto or anything, right?"

Had I just insulted "the" Francesca by insinuating she couldn't sing a jingle? I backpaddled. "Oh no. Of course not. It will be so easy for someone like you. Oh, and my daughter is obsessed with you."

For some bizarre reason, I bent low and bowed and then backed up as if she were a queen. When I turned to stand up straight, my head knocked a wine glass out of someone's hand and it shattered on the tile floor, spattering the burgundy liquid everywhere.

I apologized, "I'm so sorry," then looked up, staring directly into the dark eyes of…no! It was the big guy who sat next to me on the plane!

I wrinkled my nose. "What are you doing here?" When he didn't respond with anything except a frown, I gulped. "I'm really sorry I broke your wine glass. It was an accident."

He rolled his eyes and, in a smarmy manner, said, "Unbelievable." Then he walked away. Within seconds, a girl dressed in black rushed over with a bucket and rag to clean up the spill.

I leaned down and picked up the biggest piece of the broken wine glass. "I'm so sorry I made such a mess. Let me help you."

"No, no. I do eet." With her head still down, she took the shard from my hand and put it in the bucket.

When the girl carried the bucket away, I was shocked to recognize her as our chef/waitress, Martina. Did she do everything at the villa?

Kim leaned in and said, "Please tell me that wasn't the guy who sat by you on the plane."

I nodded and watched the big man as he inspected his pant legs for damage. "Yes. He's still just as rude." I turned to her. "I'm surprised you even remember him from the state you were in."

"How could I forget him? I just hope he forgot about me. But why is he here? Do you think he followed us here?"

I gave her a side eye. "Why would he? I doubt they would let him in without an invitation, anyway. Maybe he's a friend of the family or a sports car driver. But aren't the drivers usually really small?"

She chuckled. "You're thinking of a jockey for horse racing."

"Oh, right. Still, how could a man that huge squeeze into a little sports car?" The burly man stood to the side with an eyebrow raised as if the whole event was beneath him. Another server rushed to him with a fresh glass of wine. He took it without thanking him. Why was he here? He looked bored and certainly didn't interact with anyone.

Sophia popped up, and in her adorable, accented voice, said, "Come-a, you must meet-a the rest of the guests."

I wanted to ask her who the man was, but she whisked us off and introduced us to a few other Italian-looking and sounding men and women, whose names I knew I would never remember.

At one point, Francesca strode by us and rolled her eyes at me. I sure wasn't making any friends here.

When our hostess finally took a breath, I asked, "Sophia, who is the man standing over there?"

She followed my line of sight, but the grumpy airplane guy wasn't there. I searched the room, but he must have gone. I explained, "The guy I spilled wine on?"

She still looked confused, so I continued, "Big man, brown hair with a European accent."

That probably sounded dumb since everyone here had some sort of European accent. When her face scrunched up again, I figured she didn't know the guy, so I said, "Never mind."

The gathering thinned out as most people left in cars and a few walked to their rooms in the villa.

I smiled at Sophia. "Thank you so much. This was lovely. We do have some ques…"

Before I could ask about our schedule for tomorrow and whether we should tip our amazing chef/server/cleaner, Martina, Sophia rushed away to talk to someone else.

Kim and I shrugged at each other, then went back to our rooms where we sat on Kim's bed looking out at the lights over the vineyard.

She sighed, "Can you believe we are in Italy? And we just had real Italian wine in a real Italian villa with Isabella Greco?"

"And I made a mess at our very first real Italian function?"

She cocked her head. "It was an accident. But why were you backing away from Francesca in such a weird bent position?"

"Don't ask me. Did you see the girl who cleaned the glass and wine from the floor? It was Martina, the sweet cook."

Kim's eyes narrowed. "Really? I guess I didn't get a good look at her. Does she take on all the duties at the villa?"

"I don't know, but there is no question now about tipping her. She deserves to be paid extra."

While Kim texted R.A., I went to get my laptop. I googled the Greco family and found a family photo with about a dozen family members. There, majestic as she was in person but a little younger, sat Isabella, the matriarch of the family. Next to her sat an older man, probably her husband, Mario Conti. He must not have been at the reception tonight or I would have remembered seeing his pure white hair. My finger moved to the people standing behind them. I recognized Rosa and Anna along with their brother, Matteo.

When I got to the back row of taller people, I blinked to clear my vision and grabbed my reading glasses to confirm who it was. Amid the other family members, stood Mr. Grumpy Pants! Was he a Greco? Oh, no! I hoped not or I made a terrible impression on a member of the family. Just thinking of the words "the family' made me think of Italian mobsters. What if the big, surly man was a henchman who killed people who crossed the family? I shook my head. What a ridiculous thought.

I took my laptop across the hall. "Kim, look at this! Our favorite airplane passenger might be a Greco. I'm trying to find out his name."

She sat beside me and said, "He sure didn't act like he knew anyone there tonight. Maybe he's their security guard and just lurks in the background…or maybe he's the black sheep of the family?"

"He sure acts like the odd one out." I scanned the screen for another image of the family that might include their names. I found one but didn't know how to make the screen bigger on my new laptop, so I grabbed my phone, snapped a photo, and zoomed in on that picture–voila! It was an old people trick, but it worked.

I pointed. "There he is again." The bulky man who looked nothing like the rest of the Greco clan, frowned as he towered above everyone. His name was Xander Greco. I turned to Kim. I said, "Exander? What a weird name to start with an X."

She took my phone from me and said, "You don't say the X. It's pronounced 'Zander,' like xylophone. It's a Greek name. And Greco literally means Greek. Since the two countries influenced each other in language and art, it makes sense for him to have a Greek name. You know–the whole Greco-Roman thing."

I stared at my librarian sister; having forgotten she was so smart.

She shrugged. "Sorry but I just love history! And don't get me started on Greek and Roman mythology."

I cleared my throat. "Well, back to the big burly guy who may hate us both. How is he a member of this family? Look at Matteo, Rosa, and Anna. They are half his size and have no similar features."

Kim said, "Maybe he's a cousin, or was adopted?"

I frowned. "Yeah, maybe. But why was he in America?"

She scoffed. "People travel, you know. Especially rich people."

I nodded. "Oh yeah. I just hope he doesn't bad-mouth us to his family and they decide not to use my jingle."

"They wouldn't do that. Besides, he doesn't seem the type to talk to anyone, much less gossip. And who cares if your song isn't played? We already got the free trip."

I stared at the names below the picture. "I wonder why none of the kids have Conti as a last name. I assume Mario is their dad."

"Well, you kept your maiden name when you got married."

"True. And maybe since Isabella started Greco Motors before she got married, they all used her famous name instead of taking Mario's." I was on a roll. "Neither of the twins took their husband's names either. Speaking of…what were their names? Seems as though one was Giacomo like my favorite Italian composer, Giacomo Puccini."

Kim tilted her head, thinking. "I think one had the last name Bruno."

I quipped, "We don't talk about Bruno, no, no, no!"

She rolled her eyes at my Disney reference. "That's actually a good use of mnemonics."

I hated telling her I wasn't sure what that word meant, and considered looking it up but couldn't if I wanted to because I had no idea how to spell it. Instead, I said, "The girls should be home from school now, so I'm going to call them."

"I'll go call R.A., then Mom."

"OK, tell Mom and Dad that I'll call them tomorrow."

I sat back on the bed and called Ren's cell phone. Before she even said hello, I could hear Shelly bickering in the background.

"Mom, is that you?"

"Yes! How are you, sweetie? I miss you so much."

"We miss you too." She whispered, "I'll go to the other room so I can hear you." There was a rustle and the sound of Shelly's grating voice diminished. Then Ren shouted, "Ree, Mom's on the phone."

"So, how is Italy?"

I smiled to hear Ree's voice. How strange to talk to my girls from another continent. It was like they were in the next room. I answered, "It's incredible so far. We're staying in a beautiful Italian villa on top of a hill overlooking Rome, and we each have our own room." I rushed as if we had limited time to talk, but remembered I paid for the international plan for four days, so I relaxed. "Kim's room has a view of a vineyard, and my window is above a courtyard with a fancy swimming pool surrounded by statues. I'll send you photos soon."

Ree said, "Are you going to swim?"

"No. The water is freezing." I described the plane ride and gave a brief description of the cocktail party but didn't mention any of our embarrassing moments. When they pelted me with questions, I tried to answer as best as I could; "Yes, the food is amazing. No, I haven't bought any souvenirs yet. We did meet a very handsome Italian guy named Luca who works in the villa, I think. No, I didn't meet the Pope. But Ree, I did meet Francesca. No photo yet, but maybe later?"

"You did? Oh my gosh! Was she nice?"

I hated to tell her how rude her idol was and said, "I didn't talk to her much, yet." I took a breath. "How is everything with you two?"

Ren said, "We're OK, but Shelly doesn't talk about anything except the wedding. She's driving us crazy."

Ree added, "I think she's driving Dad even crazier."

"Well, I have faith that you two can handle her. Got anything planned for Valentine's Day?"

Ren said, "Chris is taking me out to dinner."

"Ooh fun. Tell him hi and don't stay out too late. Ree, is everything set for your birthday party at Okie Karaoke?"

"Yep. Just as we planned, Caitlyn, Sydney, Jai and Emma will meet us there next Saturday after Ren's swim meet. I'm so excited."

"Great! I can't wait for it, and remember we'll have our family party on your real birthday Monday night at our house." I yawned. "Look, I'd better go to bed, but I'll call again soon. I miss you gals and wish you were here. Give Harriet a kiss for me. Oh, by the way, I found a new job for her–she can sniff for bananas at the airport."

After hanging up, I lay back down on my bed and a tear trickled from the corner of my eye. I wiped it away, sat up, and announced to myself, "You'll see them in just four days."

I crossed the hallway but could hear Kim still talking to R.A. and made a quick call to Mike.

Leaning against the wall, I smiled to hear his deep sexy voice. "How's your Roman holiday?"

I said, "Well, except for the very long uncomfortable flight, everything is great so far. Are you working?"

"I am. So, what are you doing tomorrow?"

"We're going to tour the Greco plant, then we'll be on our own to explore Rome. Then tomorrow night, we'll go to a big, fancy gala."

"Sounds exciting. I'm going to take my sister and Jesse to dinner since Scott has to work and my Valentine skipped the country."

"Yeah. Sorry about that. But I'm sure you'll have fun with them. I just wanted to check in with you and let you know we made it safely."

"Okay well, call or text when you can, but just make sure to stay out of trouble."

"I'll try. Miss you!"

Kim popped into my room and in an overly cheerful voice, said, "So what do we do now? It's only 10:00."

"Sleep."

# Travel Tip #9
*Don't draw attention to yourself.*

I awoke to a sunny morning and opened the window overlooking the pool and my private courtyard. The air was cold, but I felt like a million bucks after getting real sleep. Stretching my arms as if I were in a musical, I belted out 'O Sole Mio!' from my own little balcony."

I couldn't help but smile when my voice echoed throughout the courtyard. I shut the window so I wouldn't freeze while taking a much-needed bath/shower. It was rather awkward fitting my long legs in the small tub to wash, but I managed to clean off all the travel grime.

Feeling refreshed, I put on a thick robe that I found hanging in the bathroom and wrapped a towel around my wet hair to cross the hallway. I gently knocked on Kim's door. When she hollered something, I entered and found her still in bed.

She yawned and said, "You are already up and showered?"

"Yep. It's a glorious day to explore Rome!"

"OK. I'll be over in a bit."

Back in my room, I dried my hair, very thankful I had brought the hairdryer and adapter plugs. I dressed in what seemed an appropriate outfit for touring the car factory and sightseeing: a 3/4 length top and nice jeans with Sketchers.

Kim came over and said, "I'm in dire need of coffee."

A wonderful aroma of baked goods wafted through the hallway and my stomach growled. "And I'm starving."

Kim and I made our way downstairs and entered the dining room. I smiled at a group of people who were already eating. A few glanced our way, but nobody greeted us.

We sat at the other end of the long table, feeling a bit uncomfortable. I leaned into Kim. "They don't seem very friendly."

Martina popped in carrying a tray and walked to us. Her eyes sparkled as she set down a basket full of pastries. "Buongiorno. Cappuccino, yes?"

I nearly yelled my answer, "Yes, please."

Kim nodded. "Si."

The adorable girl smiled and turned to retrieve our drinks.

I said, "Look at all the types of bread. There are croissants, biscotti and that one looks like it might be filled with whipped cream." I grabbed one and took a bite. "Yep, Ree would love this. I wonder how I could take one back to her."

Kim chose another pastry with lemon pudding on the top. When she took a bite, she leaned her head back. "This is amazing."

A man from the other end of the table said something and everyone laughed. Of course, we didn't understand his joke since it was in Italian, so we continued eating.

When a lady sang "O Sole Mio", the group burst out in hearty laughter, and I saw them looking our way. Oh, no. Had they all heard me singing this morning? My face burned with embarrassment.

"Pity, what's wrong? Why is your face red?"

"Oh. I'll tell you later." When Martina arrived with our coffee, I quietly asked her, "Martina, did you hear me singing this morning?" I added singing gestures so she would understand.

She smiled. "Si. It was 'appy." She chuckled and walked over to the other group.

I covered my eyes with my hand and said, "I'm such a dope."

After hearing of my newest faux pas, Kim said, "That's funny, but I wouldn't worry much about it. They'll never see you after this weekend. But what in the world were you thinking?"

I shrugged. "I thought it was my own private balcony. I'll be good from now on, I promise."

"Right." She smirked as she licked lemon pudding from her finger.

The cappuccino was hot, strong, creamy and delicious. I sighed when the rowdy group finally left the table.

"Buongiorno, ladies!" Sophia popped into the room wearing a colorful flowered dress. I couldn't help but smile at the compact ray of sunshine. She raised an eyebrow. "You are ready to adventure, no?"

I said, "Yes! We just need to get our purses and jackets."

She nodded. "Perfetta. I'll wait with Aldo een the front."

"Oh, Sophia, do you know what this is called?" I pointed to the pastry filled with whipped cream.

She nodded. "Maritozzi."

"I may need to find some to take to my daughters."

"Have Martina wrap some for your last a day."

"Really?" I pulled a few Euros from my pocket and put them beside my plate and stood.

"What you are doing? There is no need. Keep-a your money. All is taken care of."

I stammered, "But Martina works so hard."

"Buy her a present if you must, but no tipping, please." She smiled sweetly, turned, and left.

I sheepishly put the coins back in my pocket. Kim said, "How weird. Maybe they don't tip much in Italy?"

"Then we will definitely give both of these gals Okie bags."

As we walked toward the stairs, Xander lumbered down. He made a low growl as he brushed past us in a hurry.

I whispered, "I hope he didn't hear me sing this morning, too!"

When I got to my room, I was startled to see Luca leaning over my bed holding my pillow. What was he doing? The gorgeous man looked up and, in his deep voice, said the sexiest thing a girl might want to hear; "I've cleaned and straightened your room for you. I hope it is to your satisfaction."

I looked around and saw that everything was perfect. "Um. Yes, it looks great." I hadn't expected anyone to clean my room and hoped I hadn't left any underwear lying about.

He bowed slightly and went to the door. "Just call if you need anything." He gave me a little wink and I nearly fainted. What a hunk.

Sophia waited for us beside yet another limo-looking Greco. I had no idea Greco Motors made anything but sports cars. As we climbed into the spacious back seat, I marveled at how different it was from my Volkswagen Beetle.

I said, "Ciao, Aldo."

"Ciao, Pity e Kim" His voice was big and jovial.

Sophia sat in front and proclaimed, "Down we go to Greco Motors! Not so many people can go there. You vill luf it."

I said, "We're very excited." Although, to be honest, the only car I was interested in seeing was the Macchina Forte.

We rode down the beautiful twisty road, and I snapped photos as we went. "Sophia, what is that tall umbrella-looking tree called?"

"It is a penis tree."

Kim and I stared at each other. My throat caught as I asked cautiously, "a penis tree?"

She nodded, "Jes - where we get pignoli for pesto."

Kim grabbed her phone and searched for something then handed it to me, giggling. There were photos of the crazy-shaped pines. I read '*Pinus Pinea* is a special Mediterranean Stone Pine tree also called Umbrella Pine. The pine nuts are used for pesto.'

We stifled more giggles about her pronunciation until Kim asked, "So do you have olive trees too?"

"Si. Everywhere. You may see many when we turn the corner." A few seconds later she pointed. "Look."

Perfect rows of small olive-green trees lined the hillside. I said, "Oh, is that an olive grove?"

"Si, the Grecos they make the oils from olives and even wine."

Kim said. "That's cool. I sure wish we were here longer so we could watch the production."

I leaned over to Kim and whispered, "Then we could stomp grapes like Lucy and Ethel did on their trip to Italy." I sat back up and asked, "Do they sell their olive oil and wine in shops?"

Sophia turned from the front seat with a chipper smile. "Yes, but I will-a send bottles home-a with you."

Kim and I stared at each other. Why was she being so nice to us?

As we entered the busy city, I was surprised to see ancient Roman architecture around every corner. "This place is amazing!"

Kim said, "Look, that's the National Gallery of Modern Art."

I nodded and, trying to act semi-knowledgeable, pointed, "Ooh, and that's the… what is the name of the beautiful building with the statue out front?" I knew it had to be something incredible.

Sophia followed my sightline and said, "Oh, it ees a money bank."

I had to stifle a giggle, but how was I to know? It looked nothing like the Bank of Oklahoma. I was afraid to point out any other ancient-looking monument for fear it would be a laundromat. I said, "Well, tell us if we pass something more important than a bank."

She pointed out a few places, but even I recognized the huge, Colosseum as we approached. I gasped to see the iconic landmark and wanted the car to stop so I could take photos but hated to ask.

As if she read my mind, Sophia said, "Not to worry. I have made you tickets to tour the Colosseum and Vatican for thees afternoon."

Kim and I grabbed each other's hands in excitement.

Aldo pulled up to a huge stone building with large glass windows and stopped. It didn't look much like an automotive plant or a Roman building with its clean lines and modern architecture.

"Come," Sophia urged as we exited the SUV. "This way, please."

We followed her past beautiful landscaping through large glass doors and stood dumbfounded in a showroom filled with shiny cars of all colors and styles. I expected to see price stickers displaying outrageous prices, but the windows were as pristine as the vehicles. Sophia stood by a small sports car, speaking in Italian with a man whose back was turned to us.

As we walked around marveling at the similarities between the styles, Kim said, "These are so beautiful, and they all have such a sleek design. I didn't know Greco had so many models."

"Me neither. I'm pretty sure James Bond drove this one." I stood next to a sporty black car and held up a pretend gun like a spy. I asked Kim to take my picture, but Sophia appeared beside me, and I took my finger-gun down.

"You like-a thees one, no?" We both nodded, and she explained, "Only five hundred made. Eef-a you find one now, it will cost you a pretty nickel."

I figured she meant pretty penny but didn't correct her. "Are all these cars for sale?"

"Oh, no. Thees is the collection of Signora Greco and Signor Conti. It is every vehicle the company made since the starting."

"So where is the Macchina Forte?" I tried to spot it.

She shook her finger at me. "Ohoho. Not yet, Pitico. It will be uncovered at the event tomorrow night."

I nodded. "Of course. That makes sense."

Sophia pointed to the man she had been speaking with. "I leave you to the expert for to tour, Carlo Bruno. You met heem last-a night. Carlo knows eet all. See you later, crocodile." She smiled, and I couldn't imagine anything cuter than this peppy Italian gal.

We smiled at Carlo, glad to know his name again. He looked much different wearing a Greco Motors shirt with work pants than he did last night all dressed up with his wife, Rosa Greco.

I said, "Your name will be easy to remember, Carlo, since you work in a car factory."

Kim smiled, but he did not. He waved for us to join a group of important-looking men—possibly bankers? I guessed they were touring too. We wove through even more immaculate cars to a hallway lined with portraits of the Greco family members and photos of cars being unveiled. There were framed photographs of the factory as it was being built. I stopped to study a black-and-white photo of Isabella as a young woman. It was a different image from the one everyone was familiar with. She was a gorgeous dark-haired beauty with none of the wrinkles and age spots she had today, but I couldn't miss those friendly eyes. It was hard to imagine a girl of only 26 starting a motor company on her own. What an incredible woman. I was anxious to see her again and meet her husband.

Kim whisper-shouted, "Pity, come on!"

I rushed to catch up with my sister. When Carlo opened a big door, the whir of machinery was deafening. I held hands to my ears to muffle the sound. Accordingly, a man ran up and handed us each a hard hat and a set of headphones. I fiddled with the hard hat and tried to take a selfie with the cars behind me, but it was awkward. As I put the headphones on, I expected to hear a narration explaining what we would be seeing on the tour, but there was nothing except complete silence. Wow, these noise-canceling headphones would sure come in handy in my classroom when the kids were learning to play recorders.

We followed Carlo, who pointed to various components of car manufacturing. A whole line of engines sat to our left and cars of varying stages of assembly hung from cables while machinists stood beneath them welding pieces together. Huge conveyor belts sent bumpers and parts along. The place was enormous and so busy that watching in complete silence was surreal. I was glad to only imagine the noise.

Carlo moved his hands and talked as he walked. Since we couldn't hear him, I wondered why Kim was nodding. I would have to tell her I was impressed with her acting skills. Surprisingly, I had questions about cars. For example, did the hanging cars ever fall? And who got to choose the colors?

I tapped Carlo on the shoulder and pantomimed spray painting. I mouthed the words, "Where do they paint the cars?"

He cocked his head as Kim stared at me. Then she grabbed my head and tipped it forward. What the heck was she doing? While I was forced to stare at the floor, I could suddenly hear Kim's voice loud and clear. "Goofus, you didn't turn your headphones on."

I shrugged. "Nobody told me to."

She sighed. "Yes, he did. You were busy focusing on your selfie."

One of the businessmen smirked, but Carlo gave me a slightly annoyed look and continued explaining everything about the building of cars, thankfully in English. I knew my face was red, but oh well.

As we walked along, I learned that Carlo had been the manager of the plant for 15 years.

One of the men asked, "Can you explain the conflict among the new successors about how the company should be run?"

Carlo waved him off. "Just growing pains. It will work out soon."

It made sense that he wouldn't say much derogative since his wife was one of the successors in question.

Another businessman said with a French accent, "Can you discuss the drop in sales since Isabella left the company?"

Carlo hesitated, then brightened. "The Macchina Forte will be a game changer. You will see."

As we continued, I heard way more facts about making a car than I ever cared about. I was not at all excited about the chassis, engines, or electrical systems. The parts of a car I recognized, like steering wheels and dashboards, were much more interesting to me. I especially enjoyed watching the workers as they attached the upholstery.

As we walked through, I saw a stray set of beautiful taupe bucket seats sitting off to the side and tried to figure out what kind of vehicle they belonged to. Just past them, I walked up to a black car that looked almost finished. It had the exact taupe interior as the stray set, and I couldn't help it. I just had to feel the fabric.

I was at the back of our tour group again and looked to make sure nobody watched me before carefully opening the car door. I quickly scooted inside the driver's seat of the brand-new Greco vehicle to experience the luxury on my own. Oh my. The upholstery was as soft as Mom's kid leather gloves. And the smell was heavenly.

I pulled the handle to jump out before anyone could notice I had snuck in, but the door was locked. I was trapped and the electric windows wouldn't open. What the heck? Suddenly, there was a jolt, and the car was being lifted into the air—with me in it! Up I went, high above the floor. My heart pounded harder as I rose. I had a sense of vertigo and grabbed the steering wheel to steady myself. My sister, oblivious to my plight, grew smaller as I distanced myself from her.

What if the cables couldn't hold my extra weight and it fell with me in it? I quickly put my seatbelt on, just in case that might help. I knocked on the window, but nobody heard me. Then I remembered I had a two-way microphone and yelled, "Help!"

I watched through the car window as Kim started looking around for me. I pounded on the window harder, but she didn't see me.

I yelled, "Help! I'm stuck in a car."

All the men started scanning the area for me too.

I yelled, "Look up!" The group finally saw my face plastered in the window my fists pounding on the glass. Carlo immediately took off his headphones, picked up his phone, and dialed a number.

"Pity, what are you doing up there?" Those words sounded familiar, and I remembered hanging high above my sister on another occasion last year, but that was another story. And here I was again. I would never hear the end of this.

The car and I turned a corner so I couldn't see Kim anymore.

I murmured my answer, "I just wanted to feel the seats." Why did all my explanations sound so lame when spoken aloud?

I heard a loud buzz despite the noise-canceling headphones. Within seconds, the car stopped moving forward but it began to sway back and forth like a gondola at the top of a Ferris wheel.

Workers halted production and rushed around pushing buttons and turning cranks in fast motion, all the while staring up at me. It only took a few minutes for a crew to find a safe place to land my car, and I found myself being lowered gradually. When it touched down, someone opened the driver's side door and I climbed out, thankful to be on safe ground again.

"Pity, you are exhausting! What if you ruined the car? Or fell?"

Carlo stormed up to me. "Didn't you hear me say not to touch anything?"

I gulped at the reprimand. "I guess I didn't have the sound on when you told us. I'm so, so sorry, Carlo. I'll be good, I promise."

"We have not had an accident in the plant for six years, and you almost caused one today." His face was as red as Dr. Love's, and I expected him to throw me out. But he closed his eyes, took a few deep breaths, and said, "Keep your hands to yourself, please."

"Yes, sir." Humiliated, I hung my head, but adrenaline continued to pump through my body.

Kim grabbed my hand, so I couldn't get into more trouble but dropped it right away. "Eew, your hand is sweaty."

"You'd be sweaty, too, if you were trapped in a flying car!"

I calmed down considerably as we followed along. I learned that all the painting was done in the paint shop. Go figure. When we entered the paint shop, we were given masks so as not to breathe in the fumes. I vowed not to spill paint on anyone or touch a single thing.

"Kim, look at that color of red. It looks like maraschino cherries. I want my next car to be that exact color."

"You don't deserve a car after today."

I forgot Carlo could hear everything we were saying but his rolling eyes reminded me he could. I really should act more like an adult.

When we finally finished the tour, we thanked Carlo and met Sophia outside. She walked us across the busy street for lunch. We sat at a table situated right beside a keg of beer. The servers ran back and forth filling drink orders. Since there was a nozzle right next to me, I ordered a beer to go with my pepperoni pizza. Kim got a Margherita pizza and Sophia ordered a salad. No wonder she was so tiny. I waited to be scolded about my flying car trick, but nobody brought it up. I guess Sophia hadn't heard about it…yet.

The pizza was nothing like what we were used to. It had a lighter crust with such fresh sauce as if they crushed real tomatoes instead of pouring sauce from a jar. The big blobs of cheese might have been buffalo mozzarella. I was a bit disappointed in the pepperoni because it was more like thick salami, but I guess that's what I get for expecting American pizza. Kim's Margherita pizza tasted amazing. We insisted on paying for Sophia's lunch.

As we got in the car, Sophia said, "I must now go back-a to work, but Aldo will drive to the Colosseum. Thank-a you for lunch." Then she skipped off down the sidewalk. So cute.

# Travel Tip #10
*When in Rome, do as the Romans do.*

Aldo dropped us off across the street from the enormous amphitheater. "I will pick you up here in 90 minutes."

I made note of the spot where we stood, but there were so many intersections and cars that I hoped we could find it again. We said, "Thanks, Aldo!"

I squealed, "Kim, we're on our own in a foreign country!"

"Just promise not to break this 2,000-year-old building."

I looked up at the ruins of the ancient arena, thinking that much of it was already broken. The tour of the world's largest amphitheater was amazing. It was hard to believe gladiators fought in this very spot so long ago and that the huge structure held 80,000 people who watched the bloodbath. We also learned all local Romans were admitted for free. They were given numbered shards of pottery to direct them where to sit. Fascinating.

Our guide told us that the filmmakers of the movie, *Gladiator*, had permission to film inside the ancient wonder of the world, but instead, they built a replica. Crazy if you ask me. I must rewatch the movie again when I get home just to see if I could tell it was a fake.

Kim and I finished early enough to walk around the exterior. It was so much fun people-watching the other tourists. We heard probably 20 different languages as we snapped oodles of selfies. The overcast sky was perfect for photo—well until it started pouring rain.

We hadn't brought our raincoats, so were both soaked within seconds and couldn't find any overhangs to protect us from the downpour. People rushed around bumping into each other in the chaos. A guy walked up to us and tried to sell us roses. We brushed him off, but when another man approached us with disposable ponchos for sale, we quickly paid him two Euros each.

After donning our flimsy ponchos, we walked through the puddles to venture around the monstrous building, hoping to find the meeting spot. The plastic covering stuck to my skin and chilled me to the bone. My shoes were soaked through and started rubbing on my heels.

The sky had grown dark, and we couldn't tell which corner was the pick-up spot? I had forgotten to get Sophia or Aldo's phone numbers, so we were in a pickle, and a soaking wet pickle at that.

Kim yelled through the din, "Where do we go? We're late."

I hoped Aldo would understand, considering the crazy storm. We trudged along, trying not to run into tourists heading the opposite way. It was complete mayhem until we heard a honk and a deep voice yell, "Pity e Kim!"

Even though we could barely see the black vehicle through the driving rain, we rushed toward the sound of Aldo's voice. We jumped inside the plush backseat and thanked him profusely for saving us and apologized for getting his car wet.

"Is okay Kim e Pity. You dry up and see museums tomorrow."

My teeth chattered as I said, "Good idea!"

. . .

Once back in my cozy, dry villa bedroom, I peeled off my clothes, filled the tub with hot water, and climbed in to warm up. Ahhh. It felt so good. Why didn't I take more baths at home?

While I soaked, I started humming a new melody for my school mystery. I splashed and sang while I made little whirlpools in the water. I was having a glorious time when there was a knock at my door. I called out, "Come back later, please!" I hoped they had heard me.

I leaned my head back and closed my eyes until a loud deep voice spoke so loud and clear it was as if someone was right next to me. "Miss Kole, I have extra towels for you." My eyes flew open and saw Luca standing beside my tub!

I gave a little squeak and quickly covered the few parts of my body I could with my small washcloth. I said with a shaky voice, "Um. Thank you? Just leave them there."

He set the additional towels on the cabinet beside the toilet but didn't seem to notice that I was embarrassed being naked. Nor was he phased to see me in my birthday suit. He just stood there, gorgeous as could be. Finally, he said in a bright voice, "The car will take you to the gala at eight. There will be food, but you may want a snack downstairs before you go. For now, I will take your wet clothes to be laundered." At this, he nodded and left.

My breathing started to slow down again. Whoa. How was I going to explain this to Mike? 'Oh, by the way, the world's most handsome man watched me take a bath in Rome. Hope you don't mind.'

I was unnerved that someone could just walk in whenever they wanted, but strangely I hadn't felt threatened by Luca. Dying to know if Kim had the same experience, I popped out of the water, toweled off, and dressed in the warm guest robe. I peeked out the door and tiptoed across the hall. Her door was shut, so I knocked. She opened it a crack, looked at me, then opened it fully and ushered me in while wearing a matching robe.

She blurted, "Oh my gosh, you won't believe this."

I said, "I think I just might."

After telling similarly odd tales, she said, "Do you think that's an Italian custom or maybe they just aren't self-conscious at all here?"

I chuckled. "I don't know, but for once I wish I had used bubbles in my bath."

With lots of giggles and discussion about our surprise "guest," we covered my bed with possible outfits to wear to the gala. After modeling a couple of dresses, we chose those we deemed classy enough for the evening. Mine was gold with black stripes and Kim chose one with pretty, muted flowers.

A few hours later we went downstairs to the little dining room to see if Martina had a snack for us. The place was empty, so we just stood around looking at the artwork.

When I heard sounds coming from the kitchen, I opened the door a crack. Inside, Martina was in a passionate embrace with Luca! My eyes grew wide, I stepped back and closed the door quietly.

Kim said, "What?"

"Shh." I motioned for her to follow me out to the hall. I told her what I had seen. "I mean, it was intense. I'm starting to believe in the whole Italian lover thing."

"Ooh, do you think they are a couple? Or maybe he kisses all the young girls?"

I shrugged. "Well, she's beautiful and I can also see how she couldn't resist him."

We were heading back to our building when a familiar man's voice said, "Miss Kole and Miss Ross, were you interested in a small meal?"

We turned to find Luca leaning in the doorway. How in the world did everything coming out of his mouth sound so sexy?

I stammered, "Um, sure but we don't want to bother anyone if it's the wrong time."

"No problem at all. Martina will have something set out for you shortly. Please have a seat."

We looked at each other, wondering what to do. I lifted a shoulder and followed him back into the dining area with Kim close behind.

Martina came in with a bright smile and a tray of assorted cheeses, crackers, and spreads. "Allo?"

I said, "Ciao, Martina."

Luca made a bow and said, "I will leave you, ladies. Enjoy." Before he turned, he blew a kiss to Martina.

When she blushed, I asked softly, "Do you like Luca?"

She nodded. "Jes. He is um…amore mio." Then she pointed to a ring on her left hand.

"Kim looked at it and exclaimed, "You are getting married?"

"Jes". She pulled up her phone to the calendar and held it out for us to see.

I squealed. "On Saturday? How exciting!"

She was beaming when she left, and we practically melted. I marveled, "What gorgeous kids those two would have."

Kim took a bite of cheese and said, "Do you think they run this place by themselves?"

"It kind of seems that way."

We finished our snack and went back to the rooms to call our families. I talked to Mom and Dad, both girls and Mike and wished them all a happy Valentine's Day. I finally sent them photos and posted some pics on Facebook.

A few minutes later, I fixed my hair and make-up and put on my above-the-knee dress that I thought was kind of sexy. I tried on shoes with heels, but my right foot hurt. Shoot. I knew I'd get a blister, and there it was on my heel. Stupid rain. I couldn't find my Band-Aids, so I tried on a gold backless shoe. Much better.

At seven o'clock Aldo was waiting for us out front. He looked us over, kissed his fingers, and yelled, "Magnifico!"

We giggled at the compliment and climbed into the back seat feeling confident that we were appropriately dressed this time.

When we arrived at the venue, I almost choked. I knew it would be a swanky affair but didn't know it would be in a place that could have come straight out of a *Mission Impossible* movie. The people getting out of their chauffeur-driven cars fit the profile too. So many backless, strapless evening gowns, gorgeous wraps, and tuxedos. Oh my.

I slowly said, "Toto, I don't think we're in Kansas anymore."

Kim made a face and looked down at her flowery dress. "I guess we're underdressed yet again."

Aldo opened our doors, and we had no choice but to get out. "Thank you, but we are nervous. Do we look like fish out of water?"

"Fishes? No. You are Bellissima!"

I didn't know what that meant, but it sounded nice. Maybe Aldo didn't attend this kind of affair often and wouldn't really know, or he was just being nice.

Kim walked behind me as we climbed the steps to the place, or maybe palace. As I made my way up the stairs, I felt lopsided, like one leg was longer than the other. I glanced down at my shoes and realized in horror that I was wearing two different shoes. One was my heeled shoe with an open toe. The other had a covered toe but was open in the back for blister relief. But even worse than that - they were different colors! I looked back frantically, but Aldo was gone.

I froze and Kim ran into me. "What? Come on. People are behind you. Keep walking."

I kept moving and once inside, we gave our names and got our table assignment. Meanwhile, I crossed my legs awkwardly so I could cover up one shoe at a time.

"What are you doing? Do you have to go to the bathroom?"

"I'm trying to hide my shoes. Look." I pointed to my feet.

She looked down. "Pity, why didn't you notice you had one gold shoe and one black one? You are unbelievable."

I tried to explain. "My blister..."

She cut me off with a sigh. "Oh well. I'll bet nobody will notice. Besides, you can hide your feet under the table when we sit down."

I nodded, feeling better about my situation.

When we finally looked up, we saw red and pink heart decorations and a banner reading, 'I Motori Greco Dicono Buon San Valentino!' I gasped. "I didn't know they celebrated Valentine's Day in Italy."

"Me neither. That's cool."

As we entered, we were offered champagne. I took a big swig and made a face, but drank it to get me through the shoe fiasco.

As we stood there, looking for our table, Sophia appeared in front of us wearing a stunning steel blue gown. "Allo, Pitico and Kim. You look-a lovely."

I shook my head. "But look at you. You're gorgeous!"

"Ah, you-a so nice. Is that a new style from America?" She pointed down at my shoes.

I blushed and Kim jumped in, "Sometimes people do that."

She nodded. "Hm. Deed you find your seats? I belief they are over with some of the family." She pointed to a table near the stage. "Have-a fun tonight."

I said, "Thank you so much, Sophia." Then I tiptoed on one foot to match the taller one. I whispered to Kim, "Nobody would purposefully wear different shoes in America unless they were deranged, but thanks for covering for me."

We sat down as soon as we saw our place cards. I started snapping pictures of people. I mean the gowns were just gorgeous.

To our surprise, Francesca and a handsome man I recognized from somewhere approached our table. She eyed us with suspicion and sat across from us. I gulped. In what world were we allowed to sit at the same table with a megastar?

We nodded at the two as they took seats across from us and I straightened my top. Kim whispered to me, "Isn't that Marco something from the new action series streaming on Max?"

Aha. That was where I had seen him. I nodded. "I think so. Cool."

I wanted to take her photo but instead snapped some photos of people in their designer clothes so I could take a closer look later. When I spotted Xander walking alone past the bar, I slapped Kim on the leg.

"Ouch. Why did you do that?"

"Look."

We stared at the large man we had encountered on the airplane who was now clean-shaven and wore a stylish tuxedo. He sure cleaned up nicely. For the first time, he didn't look like a beastly grump but seemed to fit in with this type of crowd. When he walked our way, we sunk into our chairs and I prayed he would go to another table, but nope, he headed straight to ours. As soon as he saw the two of us, he gritted his teeth and then sat beside Francesca. The two spoke cordially in Italian and she introduced him to the man next to her as Marco. Kim was right again for the big guy's name was pronounced "Zander."

I looked at Francesca and wondered how I could ask her to take a selfie with me to appease Marie. But she still didn't seem very receptive. I had to settle for the next best thing. I turned around with my back to the table and took a selfie of me, making sure the superstar was in the background. Unfortunately, when I faced the front again, I stared into the annoyed face of Francesca. She lifted her eyebrow and scoffed at the lowly fan. Guess I wasn't the first person to try that selfie trick. I put my phone down and cringed at my faux pas.

Of course, Kim noticed and whispered, "Way to go, paparazzi."

Luckily, the attention turned from me to another couple who sat at our table. They smiled and introduced themselves as Anthony and Gia. We nodded, and the woman waited for us to give our names. I cleared my throat and said, in what sounded to me like a super hick Okie accent, "Hi, I'm Pity, and this is my sister, Kim."

"So, you are from America?" the woman said.

We nodded and Kim said, "Yes, from Oklahoma."

Her husband started singing, "O-------kalahoma where the weend-a comes a-swipping down the pains-a."

We chuckled, and I said, "Yes! Good job." It was nice to sit with someone who wasn't so stuffy.

The woman shook her head as if embarrassed, but patted her overly friendly husband on the back. "We work for the Grecos in pubblicita—um…advertising. Did you write the leettle jingle?"

I nodded.

"Well, we loffed it."

Her husband opened his mouth, apparently ready to sing it, but she said. "Nono, Tony. That is for tomorrow, and Francesca will do a much better job performing it than you, my lof."

He belted out a big laugh. I liked this couple!

A server poured red wine into each of our glasses, then he left two sleek bottles with a red sports car racing across the gold label. The wine's name was Pino Greco. I snapped a photo of the bottle while the others inspected the wine in their glasses. I copied them by lifting my glass, breathing in the aroma, swirling it, holding it up to the light, and taking a tiny taste. Of course, I had no idea what I was doing, but I could tell it tasted wonderful.

I clinked glasses with Kim, and we sipped wine with confidence as if we belonged at this fancy gala.

A screech came over the microphone at the stage near us. I resisted holding my hands over my ears like my kindergarteners do at school assemblies. The Greco sisters, Rosa and Anna, stood at the podium and took turns speaking in Italian, of course. People intermittently clapped and laughed as they talked. I wished we had someone to translate for us.

When everyone got quiet and the mood turned solemn, I had to assume they were mentioning their brother, Matteo. The giant screen on the wall behind the stage lit up with photos of him as a child. The pictures flashed every few seconds and revealed pictures of all three children. In one picture, the kids sat around the same pool from below my window in the villa! In the next, they were joined by a much bigger boy I recognized as a young Xander.

Kim nudged me when she saw him. If he was also a sibling, why wasn't he running the company along with the others? I looked at the profile of the real Xander sitting across from me just as a tear slid down his cheek. So, he was human after all. My heart ached for him.

The photo display continued showing Matteo, both with and without the other children, as he grew up. There were shots of him standing by Greco cars, on horseback, and at the beach. Of course, some of the photos were with their parents.

When the Matteo montage ended, people clapped, and then Rosa and Anna stepped up to the mike again. As they spoke, I surveyed the nearby tables. The lovely Signora Greco was wiping her eyes. Sitting next to her was her husband, Mario, looking rather feeble. Beside them, sat both twins' husbands. I cringed at the sight of Carlo and hoped he wasn't going to hand me a huge bill for halting production at the factory.

Anna's charming husband, Giacomo nodded encouragingly to Anna as she spoke. What a supportive spouse. When I was married, Todd sure never did that when I spoke publicly. If he showed up at all, he was usually playing games on his phone the whole time.

I was surprised that Sophia sat at the family's table too. What was her role with Greco Motors? Why wasn't Xander sitting at their table if he was family? I took more pictures to capture memories of the incredible evening.

As soon as the twins left the stage to join their family, the food came. And oh, what a spread it was. I had been to a fancy sit-down dinner at Southern Hills Country Club for a wedding once, but even that was nothing like this.

After we were served individual plates of cheeses, olives, and meats, we were each served the oddest and ugliest-looking thing on a pretty plate. It was a brown, spiky thing that had been cooked to death. I wasn't sure if it was animal, vegetable, or even mineral.

I turned to Kim. "How the heck do we eat this?"

Kim turned to the nice woman beside her. "Excuse me, Gia. Can you tell me what this is?"

She smiled, took a shriveled-up leaf from the outside, held it up, and answered, "It is fried Jewish artichoke. Deliziosa!" She then popped the whole leaf into her mouth.

I studied the object and saw it indeed resembled half of an artichoke. I copied the woman and took a small bite of a leaf. Wow, it was crunchy like a potato chip, but with a rich olive oil flavor.

When I got to the bottom of the leaf, the soft meaty part was even better. We watched the others for hints on how to proceed. After pulling off the outer leaves with their fingers, they used utensils to eat the heart. The combination of textures and the nutty flavor was just divine! "Kim, this may be the best thing I've ever tasted. I'm going to make these for the family when we get home."

She savored her last bite and said, "I'm not sure that's a good idea, Pity. You with a pan of hot oil is a recipe for disaster."

But I wouldn't be dissuaded. I would make them.

Then came the pasta. I was already stuffed but kept eating. Why on earth had Luca told us to eat beforehand? Luckily, my dress had room for me to grow. How do Italians stay so thin eating like this?

Oh, and the wine…so good. The servers must have been hovering out of sight because every time I drank my last drop, my glass was full again. I started to feel tipsy and forced myself to stop. There was no choice of non-alcoholic drinks at our table. I considered asking for a glass of water, but it didn't seem to be a thing at this gala.

After dinner and sampling several delicious desserts, the dishes were cleared, and a band started playing. I hadn't even noticed the dance floor earlier. Couples rose and we watched them dance. I wanted to get up and join the fun, but I couldn't go out there alone.

I leaned over to Kim. "Look, even Isabella and Mario are dancing." I stared at the couple doing a slow dance to the fast music and sighed at how sweet it was. "Come on, Kim, let's go. Other ladies are dancing alone."

She shook her head vehemently. "No way. I'm not embarrassing myself here."

I sighed and drank more wine. What else was there to do? Everyone at our table was off dancing except grumpy Xander. I watched Francesca and her date move perfectly on the floor as if they had taken lessons together. The other couple from our table, especially Anthony, had a much more creative style.

"Come-a dance with me, Pityco and Kim-a!" I looked up from my glass and saw our perky friend, Sophia, looking at us with an expectant smile. When she glanced at Xander he turned away quickly. Interesting.

"I'd love to." When I popped up, the room tilted a little. I steadied myself with a hand on the table and then followed her to the dance floor, leaving Kim alone at the table with Xander.

I'm not exactly sure what happened, but after moving around for a while, the alcohol seemed to hit me even harder. It was quite the challenge trying to dance while slightly intoxicated, but it was even more difficult with uneven shoes. I had a blast anyway.

After a while, I went to our table to drop off my shoes figuring it would be safer. I said a little too loudly, "Come on, Kim!" She shook her head. I frowned at her, and then maybe out of pity for the man who had just lost a family member, I walked over to Xander. With no inhibitions, I took his hand and urged, "Come dance, Mr. Grumpy Pants! It'll be fun."

He wrinkled his nose as if I smelled disgusting and pushed my hand away. Kim stared at me with huge eyes, so I stuck my tongue out at her. Determined to find out what the big man's problem was, I made my way back to the dance floor and found Sophia. While moving my bare feet, I asked, "So, what is the story with Xander? Is he related to Isabella and Mario?"

She held her hand behind her ear, so I shouted, "What's the story with Xander?"

She looked over at our table with an odd expression and said something I couldn't hear. In retrospect, a dance floor was probably not the best place for a serious conversation, but I yelled, "What?" Unfortunately, the music had just stopped, so people stared at me after my outburst. Sophia was distracted by an older man who spoke to her, and I decided it was time to go back and sit down.

I gave Kim a light shove. "You should have joined us. It was fun!" I turned on Live Photos and snapped a few more random shots to immortalize the evening.

Kim said, "I can't believe you grabbed Xander's hand and called him a name! You need water. I'll go to the bar and get you a glass."

I defended myself. "I was just being friendly."

"And obnoxious." Kim stood up but sat back down when Rosa and Anna walked to the microphone again and the music stopped. This time, the twins were joined by Anna's handsome husband, Giacomo. The other guests returned to their seats. Once they had everyone's attention, the trio spoke in Italian, so again we had no idea what was being said. But even without understanding the language, I could tell Giacomo wowed the crowd when he spoke. Everyone smiled and looked enthralled except for Francesca who was uninterested in what any of them had to say.

I opened my mouth to yawn, but it was interrupted when someone from the crowd shouted, "Attento!"

I heard a crack and looked up to see a huge glass chandelier break free from the ceiling. It fell amid screams toward the stage, aimed directly at the three people standing by the microphone!

# Travel Tip #11
*Don't forget to buy souvenirs.*

Just before the chandelier hit, Giacomo pulled Anna away and Rosa jumped to the side. The crash was deafening, but the worst sound was the agonizing scream of Rosa. Apparently, one of her legs was trapped beneath the enormous and heavy fixture. I sat stunned as she shrieked in pain.

In an instant, the place turned chaotic as people rushed to lift the chandelier from Rosa. Carlo leaped onto the stage to tend to his wife. Sophia had her phone in her hand, dialing for help. I had no idea how to help, but I worried about the elderly Isabella and Mario, who sat only feet away from the stage. Although they looked physically fine, their table was littered with broken crystals. I could only imagine how shaken they were to witness their children come so close to death. Anna left the stage to hug her parents.

Kim said in a flat voice, "I wonder if there is anything we can do?"

Neither of us had medical training, so that was out. We didn't know the family well enough to comfort them, but one thought occurred to me; I remembered a similar scene last year when a recording came in handy. I pulled my phone from my purse and said, "I'm going to take videos to document everything in case this wasn't an accident."

"Oh Pity. Don't turn this into another mystery." She looked up. "It was just a faulty cable." As soon as Kim said it, she must have remembered the same incident from the Tulsa Fairgrounds, because she twisted her mouth, looking less confident.

I ignored her statement and recorded the scene, hoping to catch anyone acting suspiciously. I was too shaken to pay much attention to what I was getting on the video but tried to capture everything.

It wasn't long before a team of medical professionals rushed in wearing Tecnico Emergenza Medica uniforms. The people whom I assumed to be like our EMTs, soon freed the young Greco from her trap, loaded her onto a gurney and took her away. She was moaning, so I considered it a good sign that she was still conscious.

I continued to scan the ballroom with my phone and then focused on the ceiling where the chandelier had been. When I zoomed in on the shattered light fixture below, I saw Xander standing near the family's table. I trained the camera on him and gawked as he hugged Sophia. What? I nudged Kim and pointed to the couple, which caused the camera to wobble off course. I managed to focus my camera back on them just in time to see Xander look directly into my lens. Even from the distance, I could see his evil stare.

I pulled my phone down and groaned. "Maybe it's time to go."

"Are you already finished sleuthing? Don't you want to see what Xander is up to?"

"Nope. Let's go." I was sober enough not to poke the bear further.

We gathered our things, and I hobbled down the stairs to the lobby where a crowd stood around. Why weren't they leaving? We wove through the people, all the time saying, "Mi scusi." When we reached the exit, an officer with 'Polizia' on his uniform held up his hands and said, "No." He pointed to a table with a sign marked, Investigatore.

So, I wasn't the only one who doubted the so-called "accident."

I said, "Looks like they're going to question everyone."

"Well, I hope they speak English, or we won't do very well."

After an hour of watching couples speak to the two plain-clothed detectives, we got our turn. We walked up to the table where a young lady sat with a computer and an older man held a notebook.

The woman rattled off something and Kim said, "We don't speak Italian. Do you know English?"

The notebook guy said, "Names? And connection?"

I said, "I'm Pity Kole, and she's Kim Ross. Our connection is that we are sisters."

When they rolled their eyes, Kim said, "I think he means why are we at the party?"

I went into a long explanation on how I had won the contest but the woman interrupted and said, "Passports please?"

We dug around in our purses and handed her our passports. I got a whiff of the new leather cover and smiled as I handed it to her.

The officer looked up at me with a heavy eyebrow raised. "This says your name is Kitty, not Pity."

I nodded. "Yes. That's my nickname. You see, when I was born, my sister…" I nodded toward Kim, "called me Pity. I think it's because I was a very pretty baby."

Kim interrupted with a scoff. "Nope. You really weren't. I just couldn't say Kitty."

Glaring at her, I said, "Anyway, the name stuck and I'm Pity."

By this time, the detective's faces had gone blank. The man finally spoke. "Just describe the accident."

Our stories were identical and finally they said we could go, but the man handed us each a business card in case we remembered something else. I turned to them and asked, "Are you considering this suspicious because the Grecos had a recent death in their family and now this accident happened?"

The two looked at each other, and the male officer shifted in his seat before they shook their heads. Aha, I guessed right. All the more reason to have gotten a video.

We walked outside in the chilly air and spotted Aldo standing along with some other drivers beside a huge statue of a horse. When he saw us, he put his cigarette out on a hoof and motioned to us that he would be right back.

Kim sighed. "What a night. I can't get the picture of Rosa's smashed leg out of my mind."

"Or her screams." I cringed. "I don't think it was an accident."

She cocked her head. "OK, I'll bite. Why not?"

I started to answer but Aldo jumped out of his car and opened the back door for us. Once we were belted inside, Aldo turned back with a frown on his big face. "Bad luck this night, no?"

We both nodded and said, "Yes."

I leaned forward. "Do you know Rosa?"

"Of course. I drive her many years." He pulled the car forward.

"Do you know anyone who would want to hurt the Grecos?"

He waited before answering. "All families have crunches."

Not sure what crunches meant, I said, "I sure hope she'll be okay."

Since we had a captive audience, I asked him, "You knew Matteo too, right? Were you aware of any health problems?"

"No. He was very active and healthy and was an excellent driver."

I nodded as we rode the rest of the way in silence, but my mind whirred. Was the chandelier tampered with? Who did it? Who was the target? And why?


Back at the villa, we sat on Kim's bed. She said, "It's late and I want to go to bed but tell me why it might not have been an accident.

"Well," I took a deep breath, "Matteo died only six weeks ago and now a second heir to the dynasty was injured in a freak accident. Doesn't it seem a little odd?"

"But he died of a medical issue."

I raised an eyebrow. "Or did he? You saw how the detectives acted when I brought it up. Aldo is close to the family and didn't know of any issues? And why did they question everyone if they thought it was a true accident? I rubbed my chin and pondered aloud, "I wonder who else I can ask about Matteo's death?"

She shrugged. "Maybe Sophia?"

"Maybe. Speaking of Sophia, did you see Xander hugging her?" I raised an eyebrow again. "Or maybe it was the other way around?"

"Yeah. I didn't even know they knew each other. There are a lot of unanswered questions."

I pushed my hair behind my ear. "Right! That's what I'm saying."

Kim sat up and looked at the clock. "Well, we're only here one more day and it's late. We should get to bed and leave this investigation to the experts. Tomorrow you will focus on…" She counted on her fingers, "1. Your jingle performance, 2. The car's unveiling, and most importantly, 3. Making sure you wear matching shoes."

I punched her lightly on the shoulder about the shoes, but we both knew I couldn't leave a mystery alone.

...

I awoke to my cell phone ringing. It was still dark, but I found where it was plugged in and managed a hello.

"Hi Mom! Whatcha doin'?"

I croaked, "Hi Ree. I was actually sleeping." I looked at the time. It was 5:30, which meant I had only had five hours of sleep.

"Oh, I'm sorry. Want me to call you back?"

"No. It's okay. What day is it there anyway? I'm so confused."

"It's still Valentine's Day. I'm at Caitlyn's house and we just watched two rom coms. She's already asleep and I wanted to call you."

"How much candy and pop did you have?"

"Uh. Probably too much. Grandma and Grandpa gave us little heart boxes full of chocolate, then since Trish and the Judge are at an event, Andy let us have whatever we wanted."

That explained it all. The girls wouldn't have had much fun if Caitlyn's parents had been there, but Andy always came through. I wondered why the handsome young man didn't have a date on Valentine's Day. "Well, aren't you lucky he was in charge this time?"

"Yep. Did you buy me something Italian yet?"

I sat back on the bed and started to wake up a little. "No, we haven't had time, but hopefully today." I rubbed my eyes open. "Oh, yesterday, we toured a car factory, got stuck in a rainstorm, and went to a big fancy party where I wore two different colored shoes."

She giggled. "Ha. You're a dork. I'll have to tell Ren about that."

I didn't want to mention the flying car or the tragic chandelier incident just yet.

She said, "Well, I'm finally getting sleepy so guess I'll go to bed."

"Okay. Nighty night, sweetie."

I texted Ren and asked about her dinner, then thought about all that had happened the night before. I pulled up the videos and played the first one. When I saw and heard Rosa screaming in agony, I shuddered and turned off the sound, so I didn't have to relive the whole thing. My camera had brightened up the scene so much that everything was easier to see than when we were there in person with the dim, romantic lights. By zooming in on the video, I could see Rosa's blood on the floor. Ick. I winced when I noticed crystals sticking out of her crooked leg.

As I continued to watch, I looked for people I recognized to see their reactions. Off to the side was Francesca with her hand covering her mouth. Her famous date looked equally horrified. The camera suddenly turned and did a slow 360-degree pan of the ballroom.

There were probably two hundred people, some gawking at the gruesome scene and others turning away to avoid seeing it. Funny how people reacted differently.

The next video zoomed in on the ceiling. I was now able to see a walkway high above the stage. That would have been the perfect place to reach the cable and make a cut.

When the camera focused on the stage after Rosa had been hauled off with Carlo at her side, I saw Giacomo help Anna walk away. How awful to witness her sister being injured.

Oh, there was Xander. He approached the elderly Grecos and hugged them. When he turned to Sophia, she clearly embraced him. The camera then jiggled and focused on a shot of the stage floor where there was a big tool with handles. When the video straightened again and Xander came back into view, he glared straight at me and that's when the video ended.

Was that tool used to cut the cable? It sure wasn't there to cut artichoke or pasta. I replayed it and paused the video to get a better look. I took a screenshot and texted it to R.A., the expert on all tools.

I wrote, "R.A., can you identify this tool? And could it be used to cut a cable holding a huge chandelier?"

He wrote back right away. "Yep. It's a high-leverage cable cutter. It could snap a cable easily. Why? Please don't tell me you aren't trying to solve a murder in Italy!"

I replied, 'Not sure yet, but maybe?'

He let out a sigh and said, "Just promise you'll stay safe and please don't drag my wife into your shenanigans."

"I'll try. Thanks, R.A."


I couldn't fall back to sleep with the new information zipping through my mind. I didn't want to wake Kim yet, so I threw on jeans and went downstairs looking for coffee.

I found Martina sitting at one of her tables crying and hurried over to her. "Are you okay? What's wrong?"

She buried her head in my shoulder and whimpered, "Wedding no buono."

Oh, my. Had Luca broken up with her? That jerk! I wish there wasn't such a language barrier so I could hear what happened. Just then, Luca walked in and before I could give him a piece of my mind, she released me and ran to him and sobbed into his arms. He took her over to sit on the sofa where she rattled off a string of emotional sentences. I watched the scene unfold as if I was watching an Italian soap opera with no subtitles. When Luca gave her a passionate kiss, I turned my face away to give them privacy.

It seemed I had jumped to the wrong conclusion about him and regretted calling him a jerk in my head.

He finally said in English, "Thank you, Miss Kole, for comforting my sweet Martina. I'm sorry. You must have come down here for a reason. Do you need food?"

I shook my head. "Oh, it's no problem. I just came for coffee. Is everything okay?"

"The Grecos had said we could have the small wedding here next Saturday, but now Carlo says it must be moved so a group of investors can come to the villa for the weekend. My love does not want to wait any longer. The flowers and everything have been ordered already and she is very upset. I also don't want to wait any longer either."

Oh, the poor kids. Were the investors the same men who toured the factory with us? I didn't know what was going on, but it sure didn't seem nice to make Luca and Martina move their wedding date just so some rich guys could have a meeting. I wasn't so sure I liked Carlo very much anymore. And why was that a priority instead of his injured wife?

I asked Luca, "Could you have it earlier? Would a weekday evening work for you? Maybe the Grecos could allow that."

He leaned down to Martina and translated. She sniffed a few times as the idea sank in. She nodded and spoke rapidly. I understood the word, "famiglia."

Luca smiled and said, "She said that might work after everyone who is here for this weekend leaves. Our families are all nearby and why not have a weekday wedding?"

She kissed him, jumped up, and got me a cup of coffee. When she set it down on the table, she hugged me. I sure hoped my suggestion would work. At least she was her sweet self again.

While I had Luca alone, I asked him, "This is a strange question, but do you happen to know what kind of medical problem Matteo had? I mean can you tell me how he died?"

He shook his head. "I do not know of any conditions he had. It shocked the family for him to have a heart attack so young."

I nodded slowly but wondered if something else had caused his heart attack. "It's so sad. Oh, have you heard how Rosa is?"

He tilted his beautiful head and said, "Why? What happened?"

So, Luca hadn't heard about the incident. I recounted the evening in much more detail than I had with the investigators.

He shook his head and said something curt in Italian. Perhaps he could give me clues as to who might have beef with the family. I said, "Do you think someone may have wanted to harm the Grecos?"

"There is always some fighting about money in big families, but I don't know."

I shook my head. Money, money, money-the root of all evil. At least our family wasn't rich, so we never had to worry about that.

I drank my coffee and took a cup to my sister who was awake and dressing when I arrived. She smiled, took the coffee cup, and gulped it down. "Ahhh." As she put on socks, she said, "So I hear you already told R.A. about our evening?"

"Not really. I just asked him one question." I filled her in on everything I'd learned.

"Gee, such drama in the morning. I want to talk about it, but you have to get ready. Sophia called and said Aldo will pick us up at 7:30. That's twenty minutes."

I rushed to my room and dressed in basic tourist clothes; jeans and a nice T-shirt—nothing fancy since the morning event was only a rehearsal. I checked the weather app to make sure rain was not in the forecast this time, put on a jacket and met Kim in the hallway.

She said, "This is the big day! Are you excited?"

"Kind of. Hopefully there won't be any 'surprises' like last night."

Aldo met us in his usual place and greeted us with his enormous smile. "We will go to Roma Superstrada for rehearsal."

As we rode along side streets, I wondered if I would have to do anything at the rehearsal, but I forgot about it when I heard church bells ringing. I rolled down my window and savored the sights and sounds of Rome on a Saturday morning. A few children played with a ball on the sidewalk, women watered flowers on their balconies and a street merchant sang a ditty while selling pastries from his cart. How charming! Kim and I both snapped photos from our windows.

Aldo pulled up to a gated entrance. Looming in the background was a large stadium. He drove up and let us out by the steps to the raceway. "I will be just there." He pointed to a spot by a tree. "Wave and I will get you."

I leaned inside the car and said, "You are so great, Aldo. I wish you could drive me around Oklahoma."

"If I visit, I will drive you."

I laughed and followed Kim towards the shindig. I stifled a yawn. It was still early, especially after such a crazy and late night. As a matter of fact, it was so early, that we seemed to be among the first to arrive.

The racetrack was huge, but not old and amazing like the Colosseum. The stage was set up by the finish line and men were hooking up the sound system. I felt nervous when it hit me; Francesca would soon be singing my little ditty. I turned to Kim. "What if people hate my jingle? It is pretty dumb."

"It can't be that bad if they chose it out of all the entries."

"What if I was the only entry?"

She scoffed. "No way."

We sat in the bleachers and shaded our eyes from the bright morning sun. I was glad I had worn a jacket because it was chilly in the unprotected area. I snapped photos of the stage and watched as men set up giant ramps leading to it. I asked Kim, "Do you think they will park the Macchina Forte right on the stage behind the microphone?"

"Maybe. The car *should* be front and center for the unveiling."

"I hope we get good seats to watch." I looked around. "Where is everyone else? And why do you think they even invited us to the rehearsal if we aren't doing anything?"

"So, you can make sure Francesca doesn't butcher your jingle?"

"Ha! As if I'd dare tell her if she messed up."

"Pitico and Kim! You made it!"

We turned to see sweet Sophia coming from another entrance. She was lugging a large box.

I stood up. "Can we help you carry something?"

"Oh, that would-a be nice. Can you get others from Greco?"

"Sure." I wondered which Greco would give us the box, but once we made it down from the bleachers and to the parking lot, I realized she meant the Greco car. I lifted a long, heavy box from the open trunk and grunted. "What's in this? Bricks?"

Kim grabbed one and said, "Looks like I got the light one."

We lugged the boxes back and found Sophia forming stacks and stacks of programs on the stage. There must have been thousands of programs. How many people were they expecting tonight? Yikes!

I glanced in my box and saw what looked like a rolled-up banner.

Kim's was filled with bundles of small red, green, and white Italian flags. I whispered to Kim. "I hope I get one of those to take home. And remember today is our only day to buy souvenirs."

Kim whispered back, "More importantly, it's our last day to see the Vatican Museum and the Sistine Chapel."

Oops. I had forgotten that important detail.

Sophia, with her supersonic ears, said, "After thees, Aldo will take you to Holy See to take-a your tour. He will then show you a shopping area for to take things to America."

I nodded and walked over to her. "Thank you so much for organizing our entire stay." Her uncanny hearing reminded me of our partial conversation on the dance floor and said, "Oh, Sophia, remember last night when I asked you about Xander Greco? With the loud music, I couldn't hear your answer."

She put a stack of papers down on the edge of the stage and said quietly, "We were once man and wife."

# Travel Tip #12
*Take lots of photos.*

I blinked, taking in the incredible news. "You were married to Xander?"

She nodded. "Jes, but it did not go so right for us." She looked at the ground. "It ees hard to explain."

It was hard to believe sweet little Sophia had been married to big grumpy Xander. But I was sad to have upset her. I nodded. "I understand. I was married once, too. Sometimes people just change." I thought Xander must have changed an awful lot because I couldn't imagine her with him as he was now.

She continued, "It mostly was because of the Greco Motors. He didn't believe…"

"Sophia, vieni qui!!"

We turned at the sound to see a group of people enter, all speaking excitedly in Italian. Sophia said, "Mi scusi" to us and ran to meet them. Among the people, I recognized three: Anna, Giacomo, and Carlo. I imagined Rosa was probably lying in a hospital somewhere.

Kim said, "I'll bet Rosa was supposed to be here too."

I said, "That's what I was just thinking. So, what do you think about Sophia being married to Xander?"

We sat down on the cold bleachers and Kim said, "It's really hard to imagine them together, but…if Sophia was part of the family, it explains why she is so involved in Greco Motors."

I nodded. "Yeah. And I kind of get why she didn't sit with him at the gala.  I wouldn't want to sit by Todd, either." I shook my head at the thought of my aggravating ex-husband. "So, what do you think she was going to say about Xander and the company?"

Kim sat beside me and said quietly, "Maybe he didn't believe in the way it was being run or who should be in charge?"

I gulped. "Do you think Xander cut the cable? Maybe he wants to run the company."

Kim rolled her eyes. "Pity, nobody has confirmed the cable was cut. But still, we might want to stay clear of him."

The group of well-dressed people climbed the steps to the stage, pointed at the equipment, and tried out the microphone. I picked up one of the programs and, even though it wasn't in English, I could decipher the order. Francesca's name was listed twice; once at the top beside the words, "Fratelli D'Italia. Maybe it was the Italian national anthem. The other time was toward the bottom – maybe with my jingle. Eeek. I looked around. Where was Francesca anyway?

I studied the program more closely and frowned when I didn't see my name listed. Oh, for goodness' sake, get over it, Pity. They never include the name of Francis Scott Key, they only acknowledge the singer of the *Star-Spangled Banner*. Oh, so now I was comparing my jingle to our national anthem. Good grief. I shook my head and focused on my surroundings.

The place was bustling with workers cleaning the stadium and setting up chairs on the stage. Carlo barked orders to a couple of men dressed in black while he pointed to the spot where the car might go.

Another man smiled and nodded to us as he pulled a huge banner from my box. He took it to the back and along with another guy, strung it up onto two tall metal poles. As the banner straightened, I recognized the famous Greco logo with the iconic photo of Signora Greco to the side. Giant words read, 'Presentando il Macchina Forte!'

My stomach flipped a little. This was getting real. And so exciting! I took several more photos and sent them to my family and Mike.

Anna stood behind the podium and hollered something to her husband, who had climbed to the top row of the bleachers. She tapped the microphone, producing a loud thump. In a silky voice for all to hear, she counted, "Prova. Uno. Due. Tre."

Giacomo yelled back to her, "Buono," and gave her two thumbs up. We watched as he bounded down the steps. He was so quick and agile. I now understood how he was able to jump aside so fast to miss the falling chandelier.

I got up my nerve and said to the woman at the microphone, "Anna, how is Rosa today?"

Anna jerked as if a ghost had spoken. Maybe she hadn't seen us sitting just feet away. She focused on our faces, probably trying to place u, then said, "Not good, but she will get better soon we think." She noticed the stack of programs in front of us and picked one up.

Kim said, "We really hope she recovers quickly."

Anna was distracted by the program, but said quietly, "Grazie."

She met Giacomo at the edge of the stage, where they looked over the program together. They got into a heated discussion and suddenly she ripped up the folder and stomped off toward Carlo. She spoke in rapid-fire Italian with her hands flailing.

Kim looked at me with eyebrows raised. "What is that all about?"

I shook my head. "Well, something sure upset her. So where did Sophia go? Where is Francesca? And why are we even here?"

As if summoned by my question, Sophia entered the stadium with Francesca. Her hair was a mess and she wobbled as she walked. The superstar diva looked hungover at best.

I leaned into Kim and sighed, "In that state, I'm pretty sure she won't be able to sing or even stand by herself."

Kim nodded. "I hope she'll be fine by tonight."

I was in the process of nodding my agreement when all hell broke loose. Anna pointed to Francesca and said something in Italian. Francesca straightened and walked right over to Anna spouting her response. The two shouted at each other and looked as though they would get into a fistfight any second. Sophia managed to turn Francesca around while Carlo held Anna back.

I whispered, "We really should have learned Italian before coming here. I'm dying to know what they said."

"Well, whatever it was, I don't think it was very nice."

"Yeah. I doubt some of those words are even taught on Babbel."

As the gals cooled off in their separate corners, Giacomo advanced toward Anna slowly as if approaching a lioness. Who could blame him? He said something to his wife, but she shoved him away.

Whoa. I picked up the program again but couldn't see what all the fuss was about. Maybe it had to do with Francesca singing two songs? Then I remembered Anna's sour expression when she saw the singer at the cocktail party. Something was going on there.

Finally, Sophia came to us and said, "I'm-a so sorry, but we must cancel the practice. Do not-a be worried. Everyone knows where to go. You may leef and enjoy the city."

I said, "So that's it until tonight?"

"Yes. Sorry for the long-a wait. We are back here before seven."

Kim said, "Okay. Oh, Sophia, where should we sit tonight?"

Sophia pursed her lips, then brightened. "How about right-a here? By the stage?"

My eyes widened. "Great. Thank you. And what should we wear?"

"No need to dress up. Just wear happy clothes."

We snickered as we exited the raceway. I asked Kim. "So, what happy clothes will you wear tonight?"

"Well, I doubt she means my pajamas, so I guess I'll wear jeans?"

Aldo pulled up to long wide steps leading to Vatican City and announced, "Benvenuto to the smallest country in the world."

My jaw dropped. I had forgotten that fact. I had read it was only about the size of Central Park in NYC.

Before we exited the car, Aldo asked, "Pity e Kim, do-a you have my phone number, thees time?"

I checked my phone and smiled at him. "Si, Aldo."

We climbed the stairway. When a church with a beautiful dome appeared. Kim gasped. "I can't believe we are standing in front of St. Peter's Basilica. This is so cool."

We showed our skip-the-line tickets to a uniformed woman, and she directed us to a security checkpoint. There was no beagle this time but I asked the guard who looked through my bag, "Where can I get my passport stamped?"

He said, "No passports needed."

"But can I have it stamped anyway?"

"We have-a no stamps."

I pouted and then caught up with Kim who was showing her ticket to another guard. This man pointed to a group forming to the side. Our tour guide, who introduced herself as Bianca, gave us each a lanyard with a listening device so we could hear her spiel. I quickly turned mine on, so I didn't miss anything this time.

We followed our guide to an open atrium with an enormous spiral walkway and escalators spanning several floors. The modern look was not at all what I expected in the centuries-old city. As we rode the escalator up, I was mesmerized by the shapes and shades of blue glass in the transparent ceiling.

At the top, Bianca asked us to stand to the side. With a heavy Italian accent, she told us our tour would be ninety minutes long.

Kim made a face and whispered, "I read it would take three to four hours to tour the Vatican Museum and Sistine Chapel. I sure hope we get to see most of it."

Bianca proceeded to pull out a picture book and show us photographs of what we were going to see and what we would not see. The fifteen people on our tour tried to look at the pictures, but it was nearly impossible to see the details from the small pictures. I listened to her describe the artwork in the book for a while, but quickly grew impatient. I wanted to get the party started.

Kim was even more annoyed. We were both anxious to see the artwork in person rather than looking at a book. She leaned over to me. "Why are we looking at a book? You don't have to go to Rome to do that. I want to see it all in person. This is ridiculous."

Some of the other tourists were getting antsy too and I was fed up. It was one thing for me to be bored, but this museum and the Sistine Chapel were what Kim was most excited to see in Rome.

I walked right up to Bianca and said, "If we only have an hour left, can we go inside soon please?"

She looked surprised at the request, but when everyone else nodded in agreement, she shrugged, put her book into her bag, and led us in. We walked past incredible Roman sculptures and beautiful Renaissance art from around the world. It was a magical collection amassed by the Catholic church throughout the centuries.

I enjoyed seeing the paintings, statues, mosaics, and tapestries, but Kim looked like she was in heaven. Sadly, we didn't have time to stop and read anything or even take many photos because Bianca practically raced through the museum. We had to hurry to keep up.

Kim and I both got way behind the group when we stopped to take photos of the unbelievable paintings on the ceilings. How did someone paint so high up, on a curved roof, no less? Almost every room and hallway had murals or frescos on the ceiling and my neck began to hurt. How could everything be so ornate and beautiful?

After we caught up with the group, we saw our first sign that read, "Cappella Sistina" with an arrow pointing downstairs. We picked up our pace since we were dying to see the Sistine Chapel. I had told Jules I'd take lots of photos of Michelangelo's most famous and massive work. I was primed and ready for duty.

We reached the bottom step and followed yet another arrow, then another, then another. Where was this 600-year-old chapel? Finally, we got to the entrance just to find posted signs with a line through a camera. Guess I couldn't take pictures in the Sistine Chapel. Dang.

As we entered the massive chapel, Bianca put her finger to her lips. We joined what seemed like thousands of tourists facing upward. It was eerily quiet since nobody was allowed to speak above a whisper.

But before I looked up, I stared at the beauty of the frescoes that lined the interior walls. When I finally tipped my head back to see the massive, famous ceiling, I found the artwork even more majestic than expected. It was awe-inspiring to think the 33-year-old Michelangelo painted this entire masterpiece and did it in only four years! He even designed a special type of scaffolding to reach it. I contemplated breaking the rules for just one photograph, but there were so many guards around, that I dared not risk being put in Italian jail.

It was a good thing I didn't yield to temptation because a guard snatched a camera from the woman right in front of us. Yikes. I would just have to use my eyes and hope I would remember the beauty of the immense painted ceiling.

Bianca ushered us forward and out of the chapel. In a stage whisper, said, "You must hurry. St. Peter's Basilica is closing in a few minutes."

Even though Kim wanted to see the Basilica, she refused to rush anymore. Once we left the incredible Sistine Chapel, we took our time walking along St. Peter's Square. It was a huge area with thousands of chairs set up, probably for tomorrow's Mass. We walked slowly, taking in the beauty and history of the place. I could just imagine the Pope standing at his apartment balcony greeting people with prayers and blessings. I snapped lots of photos outside since it was allowed.

I held my phone up to record a video of the square. I did a whole 360-degree turn, then walked backward, giving what I was sure was a fascinating narration. As I walked, I recorded Kim smiling with the Basilica behind her. Then she pointed beyond me and yelled, "Pity!"

Just as I turned, there was a loud rip. I saw in horror that my shoe was planted on the hem of a priest's robe. I jumped away, horrified to discover I had torn the holy man's garment—all the way from the hem up to his knee.

My hand flew to my mouth. "I'm so very sorry, Sir. I didn't mean to rip your robe!"

The priest, who was flanked by a few other clergy, said something in Italian and nodded to me. He didn't seem angry at all. I was surprised when he took my hand and kissed the back of it. Then he turned and walked away with the other priests, hands folded as if in prayer. I couldn't help but glance at the rip in the robe. Whew. He wore long pants underneath.

Kim shook her head. "Pity, what were you thinking?"

"I don't know. I didn't mean to do it. But why was he so nice?

"Well, that's what priests do. They forgive. But, whatever happens, face the front from now on."

I nodded. "I will." I took a few steps and said, "Why did I call him Sir? Maybe I should have called him Father. I'll bet he was embarrassed to have that happen in front of that whole flock of priests."

She looked at me strangely and said, "I don't think a group of priests is called a flock? You're so weird."

Once I got over my newest humiliation, we ate a quick slice of pizza and called Aldo to meet us. He took us to a street with lots of shopping. Yes! I could finally shop for souvenirs.

Most stores had similar versions of kitschy things: magnets, shirts, key chains, and little replicas of the Colosseum. But I was surprised there were adorable wooden Pinocchios in every size. I guess that made sense, since the wooden boy and his father, Gepetto, were Italian. I picked up some Pinocchio figures, ornaments, and wine stoppers and hoped the delicate wooden noses wouldn't break off in my suitcase.

While I chose a pretty letter opener for Dad's collection, Kim said, "Pity, look at these purses. They are a good price."

I joined Kim at the racks. They were available in every color, all made from Italian leather. It took a while to choose the perfect ones for me and my girls. Kim got one, too.

I said, "What are you getting for R.A.?"

"I think I'll get him this leather wallet."

I nodded. "Great idea. I'll get one for Mike. Do you think Mom would like this apron? It has Italian spices and pasta on the front."

"Definitely. If you get that, I'll buy Mom and Dad some olive oil."

"But Sophia said we might get some bottles free from the Grecos."

Kim shrugged. "I don't want to count on it just in case we don't. We fly out early tomorrow morning, you know."

I said, "I'll get some too." We loaded up on the small bottles.

In the next shop, I found T-shirts for only five Euros. The one I liked had 'Sti Cazzi' printed in big letters. It sounded like 'still crazy' to me, but I asked the young man, "What does Sti Cazzi mean?"

He smirked and tried to explain. "Eet means 'Whatever' or 'I don't care.' Sometimes is used when surprised."

That sounded like fun, so I bought matching shirts for my girls and all my closest friends—and one for me.


Back at the villa, we still had a few hours to kill before going to the event. Martina served us our very last pasta meal and I savored every bite of the rich dish.

In my room, I laid out all the loot I had bought on the bed, then put sticky notes on each gift, so I could keep track of who they went to. I packed them in the bottom of my suitcase.

I called Ren's phone and when she answered I said, "You're awake! On a Saturday morning, no less."

She yawned. "Yes. I'm at Jennifer's and Ree is at Caitlyn's, but Shelly wants us back at their house by ten so we can go to the Big

Jack's Cadillacs' Sweetheart Roundup. Oh, and Shelly is the judge for the beauty pageant, so that should be interesting."

"Are you entering the pageant?"

"Mom! You couldn't pay me to sign up to prance around on stage." As Ren started to wake up, she spoke faster. "Oh, and there is a big ice storm coming, so they are moving the corny Sweetheart Roundup inside the showroom. Should be such fun - not."

"If the roads are bad, please don't get behind the wheel of a car."

"I promise I won't. Hey, is your big event tonight? Are you nervous? Do you have to do anything? Have you gotten to get a photo taken with Francesca?"

I tried to keep the questions straight and said, "Yes, it's in a few hours! I'm very nervous even though I don't think I have any responsibilities. And no, Francesca isn't the easiest person to get to know." That was an understatement.

I traced the design of my bed cover with my finger and said, "I just wanted to catch you before we leave. I'll call Ree next. Have fun at your Sweetheart Roundup—whatever that is."

My conversation with Ree was similar except she was trying to braid Caitlyn's hair and they giggled the whole time over the speakerphone.

When I hung up, anxiety hit, and I crossed the hall to Kim's room. "Kim, let's fly home now. I can't do this. I'm going to be so embarrassed when Francesca sings my stupid jingle."

She turned from the bathroom mirror where she was brushing her hair and put her hands on her hips. "No. We came here for one thing, and we are not missing it."

I closed my eyes. "You don't think I have to go on stage to do anything, do you?"

"No, it's not on your schedule. Just relax and enjoy the evening. And remember, you finally get to see the Macchina Forte!"

I brightened. "Oh yeah. I do! Okay, so that will be cool."

She said, "You know, we're leaving tomorrow morning, and we haven't given out any of our gift bags. Let's make a list of who to give them to. I know a few for sure: Sophia, Aldo, and Martina. How many did we buy?"

"I think five or six?"

We went back to my room where I dug around in my backpack. I found the goodies I was looking for. "Yep. Six bags. Let's go ahead and fill them."

Kim divided up the tootsie rolls evenly amongst the bags while I put a Tulsa Golden Driller magnet and deck of Oklahoma playing cards in each. They weren't very full. I said, "They look a little skimpy. I'm sure glad we didn't get the bigger bags."

She said, "It's the thought that counts. They aren't expecting anything, right?"

I nodded and then found a pack of thank you cards I had packed. We both wrote messages inside each card with our addresses and phone numbers and added them to the bags.

Kim and I dressed in our "happy" outfits of jeans and sweaters since the forecast at 7:00 p.m. was for clear skies with temps in the 50s. It seemed mild for February, especially since we were missing an ice storm back in Tulsa.

I started to put my phone in my pocket and gasped, "Oh no! I forgot to charge my phone. The battery is at 10 percent because of all the pictures I took today. How can I take photos tonight?"

Kim said, "I have plenty of charge on mine. I'll take pics."

I frowned, then whined, "But, I want to take my own pictures."

She paused for a minute. "Didn't you say you brought your new Polaroid camera? Bring that."

"Great idea! I knew I packed it for a reason." I had indeed brought the camera Mike had given me. For the event, I would have to take my backpack instead of my purse to hold the bulky camera and extra film packets, but it was nice to have a backup when my phone died.

Aldo met us out front with his adorable wide grin. "Bonjorno!"

"Bonjorno, Aldo." Since we didn't know if we would see him in the morning, we handed him a tote bag. I said, "Here is a little gift to thank you." He took it with his giant hands, making the small bag look even tinier. He pulled out the items one at a time. When his face scrunched looking at the Tulsa Golden Driller magnet, I said, "The big man is a statue in our town. You remind me of him."

Kim pointed. "Those are called Tootsie Rolls. You'll like them."

He unwrapped one and popped it in his mouth then smiled. "You are so good to Aldo. Grazie mille."

Kim said, "Let's get a selfie!"

We flanked the big man, one on each side. She held out her arm and snapped a photo of the three of us wearing goofy grins.

"May I see?" When Kim showed him her phone, Aldo laughed. "I like-a that."

I said, "I'll get one with my instant camera for you to keep."

We repeated the process with the Polaroid and watched the photo slowly appear. I gave it to Aldo, who said, "I treasure thees."

He put the picture in his little bag, and we set off for the raceway.

# Travel Tip #13
*Pack a portable phone charger.*

We barely recognized the stadium this time. Cars, trailers, and buses were starting to fill the parking lot. Aldo let us off at the same place he had earlier. As I got out, I said, "You get to come too, don't you?"

"I will find a place after I put the car away."

"Good. We'll try to save a seat for you down in front."

"No need. I am fine."

We went inside the stadium and saw every seat had a program and an Italian flag lying on it. Goodie!

As we approached the stage, I said, "Kim, that Sophia is amazing. Look. Our primo seats are roped off just for us."

I held my head high as I moved the tape as if we were special guests. Kim sighed as we sat down. "Enjoy the special treatment because tomorrow we go back to real life."

I nodded and for the first time noticed a covered car-shaped lump on the stage. "That must be the Macchina Forte! I wonder who was the lucky one who got to drive it onto the stage?"

"Carlo, maybe?"

We watched as people arrived and found their seats. The noise level rose as the huge stadium filled.

From the other entrance, a wheelchair was being pushed in by a man in scrubs. I nudged Kim. "Look, it's Rosa." When Carlo saw her, he ran to help navigate the wheelchair around the other chairs. He kissed his wife on her head. When he sat beside her, she took his hand. I was glad he was nicer to Rosa than he had been to me.

Kim sighed. "I'm happy she could come. And there, behind her are Isabella and Mario with Sophia."

I sat up straight and watched the trio approach the stage. Sophia steadied the frail Mario as he walked but Isabella needed no help making her way to a seat. Tonight, she was striking in her dark pantsuit with her white hair styled in a bob. I marveled at the spry matriarch and leaned into Kim. "Just think, Isabella single-handedly started a car company which grew into a multi-million-dollar corporation. I sure wish I had a few more days to get to know her."

Anna entered wearing a beautiful white coat with a matching beret. Her charismatic husband, Giacomo, followed wearing a dark tailored suit. He helped Anna to her seat on the other side of the podium from where her parents and sister sat. Positioned right in front of us I watched him pat her leg as if to say it would all be fine. Surely the confident woman wasn't nervous. They were a beautiful couple.

I took a photo of the group on the stage, then noticed my phone battery was only at five percent. Dang.

Kim said, "Who do you think the empty seat beside Anna is for? Francesca? That might not be a good idea after what went on this morning. And where is she anyway?"

I looked up. "I haven't seen her yet and it's making me nervous. Where did Sophia go? And where is Xander? Shouldn't he be on the stage?" I scanned the area but didn't see any sign of the three people in question. I did spot our friendly driver standing by the exit. "Hey Kim, I'm going to go ask Aldo if he wants to sit with us since we have extra seats here."

"Okay but get back quickly. It's almost seven."

I ran up the steps and over to Aldo. "Do you want to join us? We have a seat for you down front."

"No, Bella. I must stand here for problems."

I narrowed my eyes. "Okay." What problems did he expect?

I started to turn back when I saw a flash of bright purple outside of the stadium. It was Francesca wearing a strange bright purple jumpsuit with feathers on her sleeves. As she walked alongside Sophia, a sudden rush of relief flooded me. They were both here.  But why were they walking the wrong way? Where were they going?

I excused myself from Aldo and walked along the edge of the seats and looked down to see where the two were headed. I had to climb up the bleachers to keep them in view but lost sight of them when they went through a side door underneath me.

I looked out over the audience. The view was so cool I took a photo of the whole stadium including the stage, but as soon as I took it, my phone died. I would have to use the Polaroid from now on and put the phone in my back pocket. I ran back down the aluminum steps to my seat and told Kim who I had seen.

She said, "Well, Francesca is known for pulling some crazy stunts at her concerts. Maybe she has a trick up her sleeve."

I pulled up my big instant camera, ready for whatever stunt might happen. Without notice, the music blared so loud from the speakers I had to cover my ears. Once I got used to the volume, I recognized the song as one of Francesca's biggest hits. Ree loved the song and had played the album it came from a million times, so I danced in my chair and sang along with the chorus.

*Don't you tell me no!*
*I'm flying in tonight to see you*
*and I hope to hold you tight.*

The crowd sang and cheered, but when they went wild, we turned. Everyone was looking up. There above us was what looked to be a large purple bird soaring through the sky. I quickly saw that it was Francesca flying above us toward the stage. I couldn't even see the wires suspended above her. Francesca's feathers ruffled in the wind as she rode down with her arms outstretched. I snapped a photo with my Polaroid but had to wait for the print to shoot out before I could take another picture. When I tried to catch her as she neared the stage, the darned flash hadn't charged yet. Note to self – don't use a Polaroid camera for action shots. I said, "Kim, did you get that?"

"I think so, but your big head might have been in my way."

Once Francesca landed on the stage, I could clearly see she was wearing a purple mask, too. What a sight! Who knew we would get the full Francesca effect? My girls would be so jealous.

Two workers dressed in black held up a cloth hiding the superstar and moments later, Francesca emerged without her mask and wearing a short, sparkly purple dress. She sashayed to the microphone and instantly a loud, fast march sounded over the speakers. The audience stood and started clapping to the beat. After the long instrumental introduction, she began singing in a loud voice. The entire crowd joined in singing and clapping to the song. Kim and I stared wide-eyed at the spectacle. It was sure different from when *The Star-Spangled Banner* was sung in the United States. I took another photo, so I could show Ree how close we were to her idol.

The song ended and people cheered. Francesca bowed and headed over to us to sit down. When she neared the empty seat, Anna popped up and brushed past her with an eyebrow raised.

Anna stepped up to the microphone and welcomed everyone just as she had the night of the gala. As she introduced each person on stage, they either stood or waved when their name was called. When she said Francesca's name, the prima donna stood and held her arms out to the audience, which caused her fans to go nuts again.

We were close enough to Anna to see her close her eyes and purse her lips, apparently unimpressed by anything Francesca did.

Once Francesca was seated again, Anna resumed speaking. I tried to read my program, but it was difficult to see in the low light. I dug in my backpack, found my reading glasses, and then attempted to figure out who was up next. Maybe Isabella?

When Anna finished, everyone clapped. She held out her hand for her mother to come to the microphone, and then she sat between Giacomo and Francesca.

I listened to Signora Greco speak, not even caring that I couldn't understand her words. Her calm, slow melodic tone proved Italian was a beautiful language when not spoken in a rush. And what an exquisite woman Isabella Greco was. I picked up my big camera and clicked a photo of her, forgetting how loud it was when the motor whirred and shot out the photo. People around me stared, but thankfully Signora Greco didn't seem to notice.

My stomach churned as I anticipated my jingle being sung, but I was also excited to finally see the Macchina Forte. I was distracted by some movement in my peripheral vision and turned to see Anna and Francesca elbowing each other. It brought back memories of me with Kim and Kay in the back of the station wagon as kids. I nudged Kim, whose eyes were glued to the founder of Greco Motors. She elbowed me back, proving my point.

I whispered, "Look at Anna and Francesca."

She was annoyed to be disturbed but turned to the two and scrunched her nose. "What are they doing?"

"Dunno, but now they're whispering something to each other."

Their whispers became loud stage whispers, and we could tell they weren't complimenting each other. That was for sure. Giacomo tried to quiet Anna by touching her arm, but she shook him off.

When Isabella finished her speech, the audience clapped. She gave a graceful nod before returning to her seat.

As Giacomo walked to the podium for his turn, Anna didn't watch her husband. She spat more Italian at Francesca and the diva's reply was even louder. Giacomo boomed into the microphone as if to distract the crowd from the disturbance on stage. By now, the dueling women had gotten the attention of the rest of the Greco family as well as some of the crowd. It all came to a head when Francesca stood spat at Anna and stormed down the big ramp and off the stage.

Oh my gosh! What were they fighting about? How crazy to cause such a scene at such a public event.

Kim whispered, "Is she actually leaving?"

I froze. "Well, she'd better not. She has to sing my jingle."

At the microphone, Giacomo tried to smooth over the disruption by telling a joke, or so I assumed since the audience chuckled.

In a panic, I quietly snuck up the steps and over to the edge of the risers where Aldo stood. I explained to the big man, "I have to get Francesca to come back to the stage and sing my jingle."

"She does not look like she wants to go back."

I said, "She has to." I ran down the steps to the parking lot and found Francesca leaning against a post with her chest heaving. She had tears in her eyes as she frantically typed something into her phone.

I approached her slowly. "Are you okay?"

She looked up at me and said something terse in Italian, nodding her head in the direction of the stage.

"Did Anna do something to you?"

She rolled her eyes and let off a string of what I could only guess were Italian expletives. Then I distinctly heard her say under her breath in English, "A very bad man."

A limo drove up next to us and I said, "Who is a bad man?"

As Francesca walked towards the limo, my heart leaped in my throat. I urged, "Wait. Don't go! You need to sing my jingle."

She turned and looked apologetic. "I can't. I just can't." Then she got in the vehicle.

I was stunned. She couldn't leave. I took a few steps toward the car and as she shut the door, I yelled, "No! Please don't go!"

The long Greco limousine drove away and disappeared along with my chance of ever getting to hear my jingle performed.


As I slowly ascended the steps, I could hear Giacomo rambling on through the speakers. Aldo said in a soft, voice, "She did not come?"

I shook my head and made my way to our row and stepped past Kim to my seat.

She looked worried. "Did you find Francesca? Where is she?"

I whispered. "She's gone. Left for good. Now my song will never be heard by anyone." I frowned. "Maybe it is for the best. It's stupid anyway." I let out a sigh.

"I'm sure it isn't, Pity."

I raised my head and saw members of the Greco family in subtle conversations or typing on their phones. They were probably trying to decide what to do since Francesca flew the coop.

A few moments later, Sophia appeared in our row with wide eyes. She leaned across Kim and said, "Pityco, you must to sing the jingle."

I wasn't sure if it was shock or terror, but whatever it was, I knew her request was impossible. "Sophia, I can't. I just can't." My words echoed those Francesca had spoken mere moments earlier, but for very different reasons. I shook my head. "I am not a singer. I only sing for my students – never in front of an audience."

Seriously, how could I stand up in front of thousands of strangers and perform a stupid jingle? That was not part of the plan.

"Eet is in the folder and we must have someone sing, and you are only the one to know eet."

Oh, brother. I looked at Kim who nodded. "Come on, Pity. You can do it, can't you?"

Shaking my head rapidly, I said, "I haven't even thought about the words or tune in weeks. I'm not sure I even remember it." I took a quick look at the enormous crowd of people and gulped.

I turned to Sophia. "Is it really so important? Can we just skip it and move on to the unveiling?"

Then I remembered the Grecos had spent a fortune flying us here. They took such good care of us, and Sophia had been a doll. Why couldn't I do this one thing for them?"

Sophia said softly, "Please." She looked so hopeful. Could I do it? When I looked up at the stage, Anna, Carlo, and Rosa were watching us and waiting for my response. It wasn't until I saw the kind eyes of Isabella pleading with me that I relented. "Okay."

Sophia gave the thumbs up and everyone on stage visibly relaxed.

My sister patted my shoulder. "You can do it." But she had a doubtful expression. Great. Even she didn't think I could do it.

Sophia motioned for me to go with her. I'm not sure my eyes could get any wider. Surely it wasn't time yet. I had so many questions. I said, "I'm not ready."

She nodded. It is OK. We talk how to do eet."

Kim grabbed my hand as I passed her. "Good luck. You'll do great. I know you will." This time she looked more confident, so I felt a little bit better. "Oh, and I'll film you and take pictures."

"OK, but if I totally flub you have to delete everything." I handed her my Polaroid and followed Sophia.

Sophia led me to a corridor under the bleachers to a little room where there was a bathroom. She asked if I needed it. I did. When I came out, she handed me a bottle of water, and I said, "I think I'd rather have a bottle of wine right now."

"Pitico, you are funny. I'm-a sure you will be good."

I asked, "Will there be a music accompaniment, or will I have to sing it a cappella?" I wasn't sure which I would prefer. On the one hand, instrumental music might cover up mistakes. On the other hand, I hadn't heard it yet and didn't know what to expect.

She answered, "We have the music Francesca was to use."

"Okay, but I really need time to practice the song by myself."

She nodded. "I will leave you and come when we are ready."

"Thank you, Sophia."

You would think I could remember the jingle since I had created it, but no. My phone was dead so I couldn't even see the lyrics I had saved in my notes. Once she left, I found a pen beside a fruit basket on the table. The tiny card next to it had a hand-written note which read, 'Francesca, Mi Amore,' and signed 'G.'

Get to work, Pity. Stop lollygagging around and find some paper and something to write with. I resorted to looking in the trash for a piece of paper. Luckily, I found a wadded-up envelope and I sat on the lone couch and jotted down the jingle as it came to me. I wrote big, so I could have the paper as a crutch without using my reading glasses. I took them off to make sure I could read the words.

I had barely finished writing when Sophia knocked on the door. She peeked inside. "Are-a you ready?"

I gulped, nodded, and then caught sight of my jeans. "Sophia, I'm not dressed to perform."

"You look good."

I took a deep breath and followed her around to the side of the stage where we remained hidden. I shivered, but then oddly began to sweat. I hoped I wouldn't have a heart attack with my pulse beating so rapidly. I couldn't hear anything except my heartbeat and said, "I might be sick."

She put her hand on my face and said, "I think you are shy."

I wasn't sure anyone had ever used the word shy to describe me, but right now I was more nervous, anxious, uneasy, apprehensive, or any other synonym for afraid.

She said, "Maybe breathe big."

I did as she suggested and blew air out of my lungs a few times, blowing the air out slowly. It did seem to help.


When Anna spoke Francesca's name, my ears pricked up. Was she here? Was she going to sing my song after all? Oh, thank God!

Sophia said, "It's time."

"But she announced Francesca's name. Is she…"

Anna then said, "Pity Kole…"

I frowned and followed Sophia up the ramp to the stage where my mouth went dry as soon as I saw the enormous crowd. They were undoubtedly disappointed that some stupid stranger would be singing instead of Francesca, so I gave an apologetic shrug. When I reached the microphone, I took a deep breath and said, "Hello." Unfortunately, my voice boomed way too loud. I jumped back at the sound and heard a few snickers from the audience. Great.

I spread out the envelope on the lectern, but it was upside down. There was something written on it in such bold handwriting even I could read it. It had the letter X then something in Italian.

I had no time to waste as I was standing in front of thousands of people waiting for me to do something. The music started and I flipped the envelope over to my writing. The accompaniment had been performed by actual musicians rather than a keyboard but was faster than I expected. Oddly, it felt like a march. These Italians must really like that style. I was glad it was in the key of F just as I had written it, so I could sing the whole song without straining. I stood a good distance from the microphone and as the introduction came to the end, I quickly found Kim in the front row and used her as my focal point. I opened my mouth and started singing the jingle:

*"Lightning fast. Hear it echo.*
*The newest ride from Signora Greco*
*Full of style, sleek and sporty*
*Front of the pack - Macchina Forte*
*It's here. It's cool - Macchina Forte*
*Breaks every rule - Macchina Forte*
*New car, new you...*
*Macchina Forte*

I did it. I survived singing the jingle! But for some reason, the accompaniment continued and led back to the introduction, so I had to start singing it again. This time, I relaxed and became more confident. When the music started a third time, I had no choice but to go again. This time I moved with the music and snapped my fingers. People clapped along and even shouted out the name each time I sang Macchina Forte.

Oh my gosh! Seriously, a fourth time? Was this recording on a never-ending loop? I took a deep breath and sang it again. By this time, the crowd sang along with the lyrics. Even Kim smiled and sang while holding her phone up recording me. This was actually fun!

*It's here. It's cool - Macchina Forte*
*Breaks every rule - Macchina Forte*
*New car, new you... Macchina Forte!"*

Finally, there was a definite ending with a loud drum stinger. I was so relieved it was finally over that I gave a bow. When people cheered and stood, I felt giddy. I couldn't believe they liked my silly jingle.

I stuffed the envelope into my pocket and turned to find Signora Greco clapping and smiling at me. Wow. I was on cloud nine and I grinned and nodded to her before returning to my seat.

Kim hugged me. "That was great, Pity. I'm really proud of you."

"So, the jingle wasn't too stupid?" I took a drink of water.

"No. I loved it. And you were a natural up there. I'm not sure Francesca could have done a better job."

Upon hearing her ridiculous statement, I spit water onto my lap and looked at her in astonishment. "No way."

"Way." She nodded.

It was Carlos' turn to go to the microphone. He spoke for a while, mentioning the name Macchina Forte almost as many times as I sang it. I leaned into Kim. "Just uncover the danged car already. I'm dying to see what I've been imagining for two months."

Moments later, the whole Greco family gathered around the car. Rosa's wheelchair was positioned in front and everyone else stood behind it. The two men in black stood at the front and back.

Carlo was so proud. His voice lilted, and his face had a big smile. He counted backward in Italian, or that's what it sounded like. When he got to Uno, the men pulled the black cover from the car.

The audience gasped at the sight, but we had the best view of all. Right there in front of us was the most beautiful sports car I had ever seen. Its smooth shape looked futuristic yet vintage at the same time. "Look, Kim. It's the same cherry red I drooled over in the factory."

I picked up my Polaroid and took a photo of the incredible car. I tried to look through the dark-tinted windows to find out if it had my favorite color of interior too, but it was too dark to see. Forget it, Pity. Even if it did, I could never afford a car like that.

Neither Kim nor I were interested in cars, but we were both enthralled She said, "I think you hit the nail on the head with your description in the jingle. How did you know it would be so sleek?"

I shrugged. "I didn't. I just knew it was a sports car." I studied the lines and saw they truly were sleek - so much so that they sloped down in the front and back. The entire car was so low to the ground, how could it keep from scraping the road?

Standing at the podium, Carlo looked like a proud papa showing off his baby for the first time. Rosa touched it as if she wanted to drive it. Mario just stared forward and held on to Anna's hand. But Isabella glowed and seemed pleased with the audience's reaction. When she nodded her approval to Carlo, he beamed even more.

My photo didn't begin to show the luscious color of the car, but I was happy to capture the moment. I stuck the picture in my backpack along with the others.

Back behind the Macchina Forte, Giacomo gave a nod of approval. What was his role in the company? I knew he was rich, but did he have a job there? I didn't think he was an important cog in the making of the car, but what did I know?

As the thunderous applause continued, Signora Greco walked to Carlo and patted him on the shoulder. He stepped aside and she spoke into the microphone. Carlo moved to the Macchina Forte beside one of the men in black and lifted his head in pride.

Since I couldn't understand a thing Isabella said, I watched the group surrounding the car. Using my camera like a pair of binoculars, I watched through the viewfinder. I noticed a quick movement from the man next to him and Carlo grabbed his stomach. In surprise, I jerked my finger and accidentally took a photo. I put my camera down to get a better look at the man and Carlo.

What had happened? Did that man just punch Carlo? That would be weird. But if not, why was Carlo doubled over? Maybe he had a stomachache. What bad timing to get sick during his time to shine.

I looked down at the developing photo in my hand and could see the outline of the two men begin to appear. Then, as I stared, the image cleared. What was the shiny thing in the man's hand?

I sucked in my breath when I recognized the object. It was a bloody knife!

# Travel Tip #14
*Be aware of your surroundings.*

Had I just witnessed a stabbing? My mouth went dry. Why wasn't anyone screaming? I tore my eyes from the photograph and looked at the live scene. From my vantage point, I could see Carlo holding his stomach in pain, but maybe to others he seemed to be looking in the car window.

Without turning my head away, I said, "Kim! Did you see that?

She nodded. "Of course. It's such a cool car." She was still smiling at the Macchina Forte, oblivious to what had just happened.

I was still stunned but sat up straight when the man who had stabbed Carlo, turned and hurried down the ramp. Wait! The guy couldn't get away! I crammed the latest photo in my front pocket, jumped up from my seat and clambered onto the stage, not caring what anyone thought. Carlo was still doubled over, but up close I could see the blood oozing between his fingers.

I rushed to the microphone and my voice reverberated throughout the stadium, "Somebody please get a doctor for Carlo!"

Everyone stared at me as if I had gone mad. Rosa turned her wheelchair to face her husband and screamed when she saw blood spreading across his white shirt. All hell broke loose when Carlo collapsed onto the stage floor. Giacomo ran to help his brother-in-law up into a seat while a few strangers, hopefully, one of them a doctor, joined them on the stage. Anna promptly fainted. Isabella rushed to help Anna into a chair. Poor old Mario just ambled back to his chair, seemingly unaware of the chaos.

My focus turned to the man who approached the bottom of the ramp. I instantly knew I had to follow him. I mean, nobody on stage could help, with Rosa in a wheelchair and people tending to Carlo. At the microphone, I yelled, "Aldo! Catch him!" I pointed toward the steps beside him and hoped he noticed the man's quick departure.

Without thinking of any consequences, I ran to the other side of the newly unveiled car and pulled on the door handle. When the door lifted instead of out, I leaped back in surprise then jumped inside the Macchina Forte and pulled the door down. The last thing I heard before it shut was my sister yelling, "Pity, what are you…"

Once inside the small and silent interior, I quickly scanned the dashboard of the brand-new sports car for a key. To answer my earlier question, yes, the interior was indeed my favorite creamy taupe color, but I didn't have time to think of the interior now.

The key was in plain view in a cubby, and I found a red button labeled *iniziare*. It was in the spot where most cars have a start button. I hoped it would cause the engine to start and not lift off the ground like in some futuristic movie, or like I had done myself just two days earlier. I pushed the button. The car started all right. The lights came on and the engine revved loud enough to get the shocked attention of everyone onstage. Immediately, Isabella, Rosa, Anna, and Giacomo stretched their hands out to me. Their faces were contorted in alarm, but I ignored them. I had to go.

Since I was used to driving a manual transmission car at home, it was second nature for me to push the clutch and shift into first gear. There was, however, one major difference between driving the Macchina Forte and my Volkswagen Beetle. When I pushed my foot on this accelerator, I rocketed off the stage and down the ramp like Mario Andretti.

When I got to the bottom of the ramp, I stomped on the brake and fishtailed to the right to avoid hitting the cars parked in front. I quickly zoomed up to Aldo, who was standing at the bottom of the stairs with a look of bewilderment on his face. I stopped the car and motioned for him to get in.

He lifted the passenger door and stuffed his enormous body into the passenger seat.

I was out of breath, but shouted, "Where did the man in black go?"

"That way on a Motociclo. I could not-a catch him." He shook his head in surprise. "Why are you in Macchina Forte?"

As I sped out of the parking lot looking for the motorcycle, I answered, "He stabbed Carlo. We must catch him!"

When Aldo heard that, his face changed from curious to angry. He spat out what sounded like a curse word, then pointed. "There he is!"

I could see the escapee's lone headlight appear around the back of a van. When the stagehand-turned-motorcyclist headed out of the parking lot, I followed. Who knew a motorcycle could go so fast? I was sure glad my nephew, Alex, made me play his Gran Turismo video game because it was sure coming in handy. I zipped around corners as cautiously as possible. I sure didn't want to crash this expensive car. In the video game, you always get another chance, but there were no second chances tonight.

I had no business driving this incredible machine. Aldo should be driving since it's what he does for a living. But there was no time for us to stop and change drivers, plus I was on the guy's tail now.

Aldo said, "Go right to save time."

Excitement pulsed through my veins as I whipped around the corner. This car responded by hugging the road like a dream. We drove down a dark alley and turned onto a main street ending up right behind the motorcycle, just like in a *Fast and Furious* movie. My breathing was unsteady, and my knuckles had turned white as I strained to follow close in the busy Saturday night traffic.

I knew the Macchina Forte could overpower a motorcycle, but I wasn't adept enough at driving it to even try something like that. "Aldo, how can we make him stop?"

He said, "We can herd him like a sheep-a dog. Pass on the left and eet will make him go right. We take him to the Tiber."

I twisted my mouth. "I'm not sure taking him to visit a zoo is a good idea right now."

He laughed, "No tiger. Tiber River. I know a place to trap him."

My body was stiff from the tension. I whined, "I'm too nervous. Can you drive now? Maybe we can switch places? The traffic has slowed down now."

He pointed to himself. "Have you seen how big I am?"

I sighed, "Oh yeah. I guess not." He was right. It would be logistically impossible to trade seats in this car. How in the world did they manage it in those movie chase scenes? Darned movie magic.

Aldo encouraged me. "You can do the drive. You have good control. I will tell you and help to steer."

I took a deep breath and continued weaving through Rome in the dark following Aldo's plan. It worked, and I was able to come up on the left of the motorcycle, forcing the man to go where we wanted. Now and then, he would turn and glare at us. That's when I noticed he wasn't wearing a helmet. Idiot. But rather than worry about him getting hurt, I was afraid he might pull a gun on us like in the movies. Thankfully, he kept both of his hands on his handlebars.

When the runaway suddenly wove his cycle through cars and onto the sidewalk, I freaked out. He turned down a tiny alley, trying to ditch us and I yelled, "We lost him!" But Aldo knew the city so well, he directed me down a side street and we found him again.

I sighed to be behind the madman again. Since we were traveling at a fast but steady pace, I asked, "Do you know that guy? Why would he stab Carlo?"

Aldo shook his head. "It was too dark to see his face."

When the guy in question changed lanes, I followed and said, "Well, I sure hope Carlo is okay. It is so weird that one Greco died and two other family members have been injured."

Traffic sped up and our fugitive made a quick turn to the left and entered a side street. There was too much oncoming traffic for me to follow him, so I frantically asked, "What should I do? Where do I go?"

"Go now!"

I almost choked as I watched the cars zooming toward us, but there was a tiny opening before they arrived, so I gunned it, cringed, and closed my eyes for a second, hoping we wouldn't get hit.

We made it, and I let out a whoosh of air. "Whew. Now what?"

Aldo guided me around a block and there right in front of us was the motorcycle. He said, "Stay near and make-a him turn." When we approached the rider again, I came really close to hitting him. Of course, that could have stopped the chase, but I wanted to avoid an accident since the man wasn't wearing a helmet.

My hands gripped the steering wheel so hard they were going numb. I followed Aldo's directions and inched closer to the mystery man, nearly sideswiping his leg several times. Finally, I managed to herd him into the right lane and onto a dark highway.

"Good! We will be at Tiber soon."

Panic hit. What would we do after we stopped him? I hadn't thought this through. Why was I so impulsive? Everyone at home told me to stay out of trouble, but here I was racing through Rome in a stolen sports car. Hopefully, Aldo had a plan, because, as usual, I was flying by the seat of my pants with no idea of what I was doing.

Wait. Couldn't we call the police, so they could arrest him? I blurted out, "Should we call the police so they can meet us there?"

He shook his head. "No time. I will get him."

As we made a turn onto a desolate road, I panicked yet again. Even in the dark, I could tell the landscape had changed drastically. There were more trees, no streetlights, and virtually no traffic except the one taillight we followed. Not convinced the plan would work, I just had to have faith at this point.

After driving on the dark road for a while, Aldo said abruptly, "Make him go there."

I could see a dirt road off to the right and sped up into position to force the motorcyclist to turn. I started to feel more confident in my herding ability but didn't want to get cocky.

I held my breath as I drove beside him and turned the wheel slightly to the right to move him over. But just as I did, the guy anticipated my move and put on his brakes. I saw the headlight in the rearview mirror and yelled. "Aldo! What do I do?"

"Stop-a and go back."

I stepped on the brake and the car came to a stop. I stammered, "Uhh. Do you want me to turn the car around or go in reverse?"

He didn't answer but put his hand on the gear shift knob. I pushed in the clutch, and he yanked it in reverse and yelled, "Gas!"

I pushed down on the accelerator and thankfully Aldo took the wheel, steering backward as expertly as a stunt driver. I held my breath and watched through the mirror as we caught up with the man who was turning his bike around. When I heard a crunch, I took my foot off the pedal and hit the brakes. I gasped, "Did we hit him?"

"He's fine. I will get him now." Aldo lifted his door and pulled himself out of the cramped space.

I tried to turn around in my seat to watch, but it was impossible to see anything in the dark. I opened my door and poked my head out. With the dim light from my taillights, I could barely see two figures wrestling on the ground as they shouted at each other in Italian.

I figured few people would be a match for Aldo, so I hoped he would subdue the subject soon. When the shouting stopped, I saw a big shadow moving towards me. As it neared, I recognized the shadow as Aldo carrying a limp body over his shoulders.

My breath caught for a second then I yelled, "Is he dead?"

"No, just what you Americans say…napping?" Aldo heaved the man into the seat next to me and said, "You can drive a *motociclio,* yes?"

I shook my head. "No. I cannot."

"Then you must drive him in Macchina Forte to polizia."

When the man's head lolled to one side, I cringed and asked, "Why don't we just call the police to come get him?"

"No phone here."

I assumed he meant no signal and stammered, "But I can't drive with a stabber in the car."

"He probably won't wake up."

I gulped. "Probably?"

"I have tied his hands. You are fine."

Aldo slammed the passenger door down. He lifted the motorcycle from the ground, straddled it, revved it up, then shouted, "Follow me!"

I hesitated, then pulled my door down and stared at the lifeless body only inches away. Trembling, I put the Macchina Forte in drive and set out for a torturous ride.

The only upside was that it was easier to follow Aldo than it had been to follow the maniac next to me. Aldo wasn't trying to lose me. But all I could think was that I'd rather be anywhere but here; like going on another boring date with Kenny, or catering to uppity clients at my second job, or even being reprimanded by Dr. Love in the principal's office. I'd be happy to be any place but here since I was certain this guy was going to wake up and kill me.

How would Kim explain my death to our family? 'Well, you know Pity. She just had to go all psycho detective and chase a maniac – again. But at least now we know she was right; the guy actually was a murderer." She would sigh and add, "I'll sure miss my crazy sister.'

I shook my head. When would I ever learn to stay out of trouble?

My eyes flicked from the dark road to the man slumped next to me. With a little bit of moonlight, I could see cuts on his face from their fight. He seemed rather young, maybe in his twenties. There were words tattooed on his neck that I couldn't read in the dark. I sure didn't recognize the guy as someone I had ever met before.

When we reached the edge of town, I figured we had to be close to a police station, and hoped we could stop soon. I had been holding my breath for miles, so I took a deep cleansing breath and relaxed my shoulders. However, I tensed up immediately when the guy stirred. Crap. If he woke up, what would I do? I ran through some possible scenarios in my head, but all seemed to end in disaster.

Just as I was scanning the modern dashboard for an eject button to use on either him or me, I heard a groan. I looked over and was shocked to see my scary passenger staring at me with wild eyes.

He gave a soft growl but when he discovered his hands were tied behind his back, he fumed. Then, without warning, he lunged and butted my shoulder with the crown of his head.

I snapped, "Hey, that hurt!" As a reflex, I elbowed him hard in the nose.

He jerked away in surprise, and I winced to see blood trickle onto his shirt. On a normal day, I would feel bad for him, but in this instance, I worried the blood might ruin the gorgeous taupe upholstery, and worse, that I made him angry enough to break free and strangle me. What to do? Think, Pity. Think!

I honked my horn, but Aldo couldn't hear me with the roar of his motorcycle engine, so I opted for another plan. I punched the gas and surged forward so fast that our heads whipped back against the headrests. I zoomed up beside Aldo and pointed at the now wide-awake would-be murderer, whose face was strained in terror due to my wild driving. Aldo nodded at me and promptly sped through a red light, turning left in the middle of the intersection.

I followed Aldo. At this point, I wasn't even worried about the police stopping me. It would be a blessing if they showed up. I cursed myself for not charging my phone since by now surely, we had service. Forgetting for a second that my passenger was an attempted murderer, I stupidly asked, "Do you use 9-1-1 in Italy?"

He didn't answer and I remembered who I was talking to. I tried another question. "Why did you stab Carlo?"

"No. I cannot tell."

"Well, you know we are on our way to the police station now, don't you? They will make you talk."

I could sense him trying to process what I just said. After a while he pleaded, "I cannot go to jail."

I said, "Well, too bad buddy. You stabbed someone and that's where you are going."

"He will kill me. I have failed him twice."

"Who will kill you? Is it something to do with the Grecos?"

Sweat beaded on the young man's forehead. It was warm in the vehicle, but not hot. He demanded, "I will not go to polizia."

I was trying to work out his fear of the police when suddenly cold air whooshed around me. I looked over and saw the guy leaning partway out of his open window with his hands still tied behind his back. What? How had he managed to roll down the window? The guy must be very flexible.

The mother in me was afraid he would fall out of the car and onto the pavement, so with one hand I grabbed his shoe. He kicked at me to get loose and caused me to jerk the steering wheel into oncoming traffic. I quickly put both hands back on the wheel and swerved back to my lane. I yelled, "What's wrong with you? You're going to kill us both or fall out of the car!" He didn't seem to care and inched further out of the opening.

I hated to stop abruptly with so much traffic around, but I had to slow down in case my passenger indeed tried to jump out. Just as I lifted my foot to move it to the brake, the idiot put his own foot on my shoulder. In a swift movement, he kicked off from my shoulder and plunged out the window as if he were diving headfirst into a swimming pool.

I was in a stupor as I watched him disappear through the window with one of his shoelaces exiting the car last. It was as if time stood still. Then the horrible sound of cars screeching and honking snapped me back into the moment. Had he been hit by a car?

I slammed on the brakes, pulled to the side of the street, and stopped next to a swanky olive oil store. As I tried to catch my breath, I began to sweat, and my heart started pounding faster than it was healthy. I was too petrified to look back at the man.

Aldo must have seen the commotion because he quickly drove up beside me on the motorcycle. He lifted my door and helped me out. "Are you okay?"

I leaned against the car and nodded, but absent-mindedly rubbed the shoulder that had been used as a springboard. I was shivering from adrenaline and the frigid February air. I didn't want to see what happened to the man in his crazy attempt to flee the authorities. "Aldo, did he get hit by a car?" I cringed while waiting for his reply.

"I do not know. I'll be back."

The way big Aldo said, 'I'll be back,' made me think he would be a great Terminator if they ever did an Italian remake. Stop thinking of dumb things, Pity. This is a tragic situation.

I finally forced myself to look down the street and found a crowd had formed around one area between cars. Most everyone had their cell phones out either calling for help or taking photos and videos. So, there were gawkers and rubberneckers all over the world.

Aldo was easy to find since he towered above everyone in the street. He leaned down, then up again. What was the verdict? Oh, for heavens' sake, just go over there and see for yourself, Pity.

I looked both ways before stepping into the street, which was pointless since all the cars were at a standstill. I tried to see between the crowd who had gathered. Never having been good with the sight of blood, I was nervous. The chandelier accident had nearly put me over the edge. As I continued to walk, a siren blared. Good.

As the emergency vehicles approached, the onlookers parted enough for me to see the body lying spread eagle on the dark ground. The mystery man was dressed in black, but colorful lights lit up his body, making the scene macabre. I inched forward and was relieved there was no visible injury except for the scratches he received from his scuffle with Aldo. Strangely enough, the only blood I could see was the dry stuff around his nose from my elbowing him.

Aldo moved toward me. "He is alive but not awake."

Medics rushed in and the bystanders moved back to let them tend to the crazy stabber. Upon seeing the first police officer, I intercepted him and said, "You are definitely going to want to talk to us, but we'll wait over here until you're ready."

The young, uniformed officer cocked his head and Aldo interpreted what I had said. He nodded and we made our way back to the Macchina Forte.

As we waited, I leaned my head against Aldo's shoulder. "Thank you for coming along with me on my wild ride. You saved my life."

"You are one crazy American," and he patted me on the head.

# Travel Tip #15
*Enlist a travel agent to help with the unexpected delays.*

Once photos were taken and the tattooed guy was loaded onto a gurney, the ambulance left. We watched as the polizia interviewed several witnesses and then directed traffic to move again. The officer finally came to us, and I was happy to hear the young guy would probably survive.

We gave the officer a brief description of what had precipitated the accident. He made a lot of funny faces as if the story was unbelievable and directed us to go to the police station. This time I followed Aldo while driving the luxury car again. During the leisurely drive, I had time to reflect on the whole situation. Aldo was right. I was crazy and probably needed my head examined.

I parked outside the police station and handed the Macchina Forte keys to Aldo. An officer started talking to him, so I trudged up the steps, completely exhausted. What time was it anyway? I pulled my phone from my pocket, but of course, it was still dead. I had to call Kim and tell her I was OK.

Once inside, I dragged myself to a desk manned by an older woman in a gray uniform. I started to ask if I could use her phone, but I wasn't sure how to make a phone call in Italy, so I came up with a better idea. I held out my iPhone, pointed to the port, and asked, "Do you have a phone charger?"

As the woman searched a drawer, I noticed her name tag read Di Caprio. Was she related to Leo? I considered asking, but she surprised me by pulling a cord from her desk. She took my phone, plugged it into the European socket on the wall, and motioned me to sit in the chair next to it. Now that the pressure was off, I sat and took a deep breath trying to relax, but my hands still shook.

The woman must have noticed my drained state, for she came back and handed me a bottle of water. I gushed, "Grazie," and took a big swig. I couldn't believe how thirsty I was. How long had I been on that wild ride? I lifted my phone and pushed the button to turn it on. Within moments, it came back to life. The time was 10 o'clock. I also had fifteen missed calls from my sister. While reading an especially frantic text wondering where I was, her face appeared on my screen. I answered her call, "Hey, Kim. What's up?"

"Pity, what in the world? Where are you?"

"Well, I'm at a police station somewhere in Rome."

She gasped, "They arrested you for stealing the Machina Forte?"

"No. But, I was on the wildest, craziest ride ever."

Just then, the door opened, and Aldo entered with a few officers. He walked toward me. I spoke into the phone, "Kim, hold on a sec."

I held the phone in my lap and asked, "Is the guy still alive? Do they know who he is?"

"He is alive but in comma. We don't know who he is."

I was glad to hear he was alive but couldn't help picturing him lying in a comma instead of a coma. The officer motioned for Aldo to follow him, so I got back on the phone. "Sorry about that, Kim. Are you still at the raceway?"

"No. After Carlo was taken away in an ambulance, they made everyone go home. Sophia drove me back to the villa."

"How is Carlo?" I crossed my fingers that he survived.

"I don't know, but I've been worried sick about you. Why didn't you answer your phone?"

"I would have, but if you recall, my phone died."

"Oh, yeah."

"Besides, I couldn't answer while chasing a madman."

"Did you catch the guy? I want details. Will you be back soon?"

I paused when the front door opened again and then answered, "Well, sort of. It's a long story. But it may be a while before I can get back. Those detectives from the chandelier night just arrived."

"Well, make sure they know we have to be at the airport by eight tomorrow morning. Oh, and Sophia will drive us there."

"I'll tell them. I'm so sorry to have worried you. I'll get back to the villa as soon as I can, but you go ahead and go to sleep."

"Don't worry about me. Just be careful!"

The two detectives we had met before took us into a room and this time they introduced themselves. Inspector Marino was the older man and Detective Valentino was the young woman. I tried using my mnemonic device to help me remember them. With the inspector's short haircut, I could picture him wearing a Marine uniform to remember Marino. Valentino was easy enough since we had met her on Valentine's Day.

Aldo spoke in Italian to the two detectives and, when he finished, I told them everything I knew, but in English. Then I handed them the Polaroid print, feeling a bit proud that my finger had jerked the shutter at the perfect moment.

Marino studied the photo, raised an eyebrow, and gave a tiny nod of approval. "We will keep this evidence." He handed it to Valentino.

I looked at my phone. It was already eleven o'clock. I said, "Well, I need to get back to the villa. My flight is early tomorrow morning."

Valentino shook her head. "That-a will not work. You must stay in the country for more questions to be answered."

I stammered, "But I don't know anything else about stabbing. We told you everything. We were just bringing the man to you, and he jumped out of my window." I went on to explain my situation, "My sister and I have tickets to fly home to Oklahoma tomorrow. We can't stay any longer. You see, I'm a teacher, and I only got a few days off. And my daughter's birthday is Monday and my other daughter's swim meet is…" I shut up when Inspector Marino closed his eyes and shook his head slowly at me.

I pleaded with Aldo to do something, but he shrugged apologetically.

It looked like I was destined to be stuck in Italy a little longer.


As Aldo drove me back to the villa he said, "I have talked to Signora Greco and she wants for me to keep Machina Forte safe until tomorrow."

I cringed. "Is she upset with me for taking the car?"

"No. She is happy that the man was caught and sees that you had good meanings. I will wash her and keep her in garage tonight."

Once I worked out that Aldo was talking about washing the car and not Isabella Greco, I scanned the seats looking for any stains on the upholstery, but it was too dark to see much. "You might want to check for blood stains." I decided not to go into detail about how I had given the guy a bloody nose.

After stopping in front of the villa, Aldo lifted my door and helped me out. "It was a long day, Miss Pity."

"Thank you for keeping me safe." I reached up and kissed him on the cheek. I wasn't sure, but I think he blushed. "Now get some sleep, Aldo."

"Arrivederci, bella."


The villa's dark hallways looked ominous as I made my way through to my room. Not wanting to wake Kim, I wrote her a note to tell her my trip home was postponed:

*Kim, I made it back very late. I'm so sorry, but the police are making me stay until the investigation is over. I don't know how long it will be, so I think you should go ahead and fly home. I promise to keep in touch. I hope you have a safe flight. I love you! – Pity.*

I slipped the paper under her door, drank more water, plugged in my phone, and climbed into bed fully clothed.

Morning came, and I was tired, dirty, wrinkled, and my shoulder hurt after being used as a launch pad. I took a quick bath/shower and put on the only clean jeans and shirt I had left. Physically, I felt much better, but I was depressed that I had to remain in Rome for who knew how long. And staying without Kim was a real bummer. Why must I always get involved in things that aren't my business? I should have just remained an innocent bystander. But no, leave it to me to steal a car and go after a possible killer.

I was sad that there was no goodbye note on the floor inside my room. Maybe Kim was in too much of a hurry to wake me or write a note. Or maybe she was really angry with me. Who knew? There was no point in going to her room since she was gone, so I made my way down to the dining area for coffee and food. It had been ages since I had eaten anything, and I was starving.

I heard voices as I neared. Wait! Was that Kim? I entered the room and there she was sitting with Sophia. I squealed, "Kim, you are going to miss your flight!"

She smirked. "Yep. I sure am." She jumped up and gave me a hug. "I'm not letting you stay here alone." She pulled away and smiled. "Sophia took care of canceling our flights and will reschedule as soon as you are free to leave."

Tears filled my eyes. I wouldn't be alone after all.

She said, "And I already told R.A., Mom, Dad, and your girls that there has been a complication. I said we would be home a little late but not to worry. I told them you would call soon."

All my worries were now erased. "You are the best, Kim!" I turned to Sophia and said, "Thank you so very much for taking care of her and handling our flights. I'm so sorry to cause so many problems. Is it OK to stay here while we wait? If not, we can find an Airbnb or something."

Sophia, dressed in a cute black and white striped dress, assured me it was fine. "You deed the Greco family a big-a favor to find-a the bad man. You must stay here as our guests. Maybe you can fly out tomorrow."

"Sophia, how is Carlo?"

"He lost much blood but is going to be OK."

I sighed. "That's really good."

She said, "Pitico, the polizia will come this morning at eleven to talk to you and Aldo more."

I nodded as Martina walked in with a huge smile and handed me a cup of cappuccino. She asked, "Food?"

I nodded. "Si! I'm starving."

Kim said, "Guess what? They rescheduled their wedding for Monday evening. It's all arranged."

After Martina left, I said, "Oh, how sweet. I'd be smiling too if I was marrying someone like Luca in one day!" We all laughed.

I nodded and Kim pleaded, "Tell us what happened last night."

The two girls stared as I recapped our late-night adventure between bites of pastries and cheeses.

Kim's eyes were huge after hearing the bizarre punchline of how the guy exited the car, but asked, "Did he say why he stabbed Carlo?"

I shook my head. "He just said he couldn't go to jail because someone would kill him, then poof he was gone through the window." I shrugged. "Oh, and Aldo was amazing. I'm pretty sure he saved my life."

Sophia said, "Aldo ees a good man." She sighed. "But poor Grecos. They have lost Matteo, then Rosa was injuryed, and Carlo gets a knife in him." She shook her head. "Hard to think."

Something ignited in me. How had I missed it? After already suspecting the other two incidents were related, why hadn't I added the stabbing to the mix? My detective skills were slipping, and I needed to focus.

Kim warned, "Pity, you've got that look in your eyes. I can see your wheels turning. Don't even think about trying to solve another mystery. The guy has been caught, and we need to go home."

I turned to her. "But what if they are all connected? What was his motive? And who was he scared of?" I twisted my mouth wondering if it was Xander? I was sure scared of him.

She said, "Well, the guy could be in a coma for weeks and we can't wait around to ask him. We're already a day late."

I ignored my sister and asked the question that had been bugging me. "Sophia, have you talked to Xander? I'm surprised I didn't see him at the unveiling last night."

She shook her head and knitted her brows. "He was there before the start to help, but then no…thing. I try a call, but his phone went just to mail."

That was odd unless maybe he was involved in the stabber's plan somehow. I tried to sound reassuring since Sophia seemed concerned for her ex and said, "Maybe he'll call you soon."

Kim and Sophia nodded.


Back in my room with a full tummy, I was still anxious with so many questions whirring around in my head. To settle another problem, I emailed Melanie at school and told her I was detained in Rome and would need a substitute for at least tomorrow. It was sure to cause an uproar from Dr. Love, but what was I to do?

Next, I called my girls and just as I anticipated, they were not happy with me. Ree was the first to speak. "Mom, I knew it! You're going to miss my birthday!"

"I am so sorry, Marie. I didn't plan this. If I leave tomorrow, I should be there in time for part of your birthday, due to the time change, but I will be there for your karaoke party." How awful that I had messed things up, but I couldn't think of how to make it better now. I said, "Maybe your dad can do something special with you until I get there."

Ren jumped in and said, "Ha! Not if Shelly has any say. He's not even planning on going to the state swim meet Saturday because Shelly says the humidity at the aquatic center makes her hair frizzy."

Oh, brother. Shelly was unbelievable. I didn't want to bash their dad's fiancé, so I said, "Well, I'll be there rooting for you even if my hair looks like I stuck my finger in an electrical socket."

Ren said, "You better be. So, what happened last night that is keeping you there?"

Ree said, "Yeah, I hope it's a good reason."

I gave the girls a brief rundown.

Ren said, "You witnessed a stabbing?"

I nodded, then remembered they couldn't see me. "I did."

Ree squealed, "I can't believe you actually drove the fancy car off of the stage without permission. You're a nut."

I could picture the girls shaking their heads. "I know. The culprit is in a coma now and hopefully, when he wakes up, we'll learn his motive. But the investigators have to ask me more questions."

Ren said, "Hey, how did your jingle go over?"

I smiled that she remembered why I had come to Italy in the first place. I had almost forgotten myself. Was that all just last night?

Before I could answer, Ree piped up, "Oh yeah, was it amazing to hear Francesca sing it?"

"Uh…well, that's another story. Francesca didn't sing it…I did." I described to both girls my debut performance singing in front of thousands. "It was a crazy night for sure."

Ren said, "That is crazy. Well, good for you, Mom. How cool that people liked it so much that they sang along."

Ree said, "Yeah, but I'm sad that Francesca wasn't there for you. Maybe I don't love her quite as much now."

Great. Now I had upset Ree about her favorite singer. And I never even managed to get a photo with the woman either. "I love you girls and hope to get home very soon."

I hung up but had forgotten to ask about the sweetheart roundup and what else the girls had been doing. Oh, well, I'd find out later. I called my parents and Mike to fill them in on the delay. I lay back on the bed. What a crazy, busy trip this was. Since there was nothing scheduled today except talking to detectives, I hoped we could relax a little until we were allowed to go home.

Kim peeked in my door to make sure I wasn't sleeping. "Come on in." When she sat on my bed, I said, "I can't believe you decided to stick with me even after what I did."

"I know. I must be crazy." She handed me my backpack with my camera and the little Italian flag. She said, "You kind of left last night without this stuff."

"Thanks!" I waved my little flag and then froze. "You mean I was driving like a wild woman all over Rome without a driver's license? Yikes"

She said, "I guess so."

"I looked through my bag. Have you seen my glasses?"

"No. Aren't they in your bag?"

"Shoot. I had them on before I sang my jingle. Oh, maybe I left them in the little weird room under the bleachers at the raceway."

"Oh well, they were just readers. You can use mine."

"But Ren bought them for me for Christmas. She'll be crushed if I lose them."

"I guess you could call and see if they are still there."

"Good idea. I'll see if Sophia can help me."

Kim cocked her head. "Now, you aren't under house arrest, right? We can go do something after you talk to the police?"

"I don't know why not. There's a lot we haven't seen in Rome. Surely the Grecos won't mind if we leave for a while. We can just get an Uber."

I looked at the developed photos I'd taken with my Polaroid and studied the whole family on stage. I pondered aloud, "I still wonder why Xander wasn't there. He's usually lurking somewhere. Do you think he was involved in the stabbing?"

She looked at me in surprise. "Why? He's probably just in hiding. He doesn't seem to like people or crowds."

I shrugged. "You're right. He's probably on our plane right now, happy that two goofy Americans aren't bothering him."

She added, "And not sitting on his lap stroking his face." She warned me, "Please don't tell R.A. about that."

"Oh, come on. He'll think it's hilarious."

We both turned when someone knocked. "Come in?"

Luca entered with fresh towels. "Hello, Ms. Kole and Ms. Ross."

I was still amazed his English was so perfect. And why did he have to wear such tight-fitting clothes? I forced myself to look away so I wouldn't sweat. "Hi, Luca."

He put the towels in the bathroom and picked up my dirty jeans from the floor. "May I wash these for you?"

I was embarrassed to have left them there but said, "Um, sure. Thank you but let me check the pockets first." It was a habit I'd learned years ago after washing permission slips, money, and, worse, finding shredded Kleenex stuck to knit shirts.

I stood and took the jeans from him. "Are you excited about your wedding tomorrow?"

"Oh, yes." His face brightened so much it looked like it might burst. "I love my Martina so much. And we want many bambinos."

Kim smiled. "I'm sure it will be a beautiful wedding."

"Eef you are still here, you should come. We would like that."

I said, "Dang. We'll be gone by then but thank you so much for the invitation." I found a few euro coins and some paper in my pocket and put them on the bedside table. I handed my jeans back to the dark-haired hunk who glowed with happiness.

He picked up the rest of my laundry and said, "I'll get yours now, Miss Kim." He headed to the door.

I piped up. "Oh, Luca, do you know the name of the raceway we went to last night?"

"Yes. It was Roma Superstrada"

I unlocked my phone and held it out. "Would you mind calling to ask if they found eyeglasses in a little room under the bleachers?"

He shrugged and took my phone from me. "No problem." He searched for the number and made a call. After a while, he handed the phone back to me shaking his head. "Nobody answers now. There is a big race this afternoon. You can try again."

"OK. Thank you so much."

As he shut the door behind him, I marveled, "If only I could take him, Martina, and Aldo home with me, my life would be perfect."

"Your life already is pretty perfect – well, if you didn't have such a terrible principal."

I nodded. "But wouldn't it be nice to have someone to clean, cook, and drive us around?"

"Stop dreaming and let's go downstairs to face reality."

# Travel Tip #16
*Visit areas away from tourist traps.*

Detectives Marino and Valentino sat with Aldo at a table in the dining area. When we entered, they stood and dismissed Aldo. Guess they didn't want us to influence each other's answers. Fine. I had nothing to hide. I nodded to Aldo and sat in his empty seat while Kim took a chair as my moral support sister. Marino wore the same wrinkled suit from last night, and Valentino was dressed in a stodgy-looking pantsuit, making her look far too old for her age.

I introduced my sister to the two officers using their names and gave her a smug look. She raised her eyebrows, seemingly impressed I had remembered their names.

Martina appeared with bread, olive oil, and glasses of red wine, which I found odd. Maybe drinking wine at 11 a.m. on a Sunday morning was normal here. I would have to ask Mike if he ever interrogated someone officially while drinking alcohol.

At least the warm red wine might calm my nerves. I raised my glass to Kim, and we each took a sip. She leaned over and whispered, "Don't drink too much or you may say something stupid."

I nodded. I didn't want to prolong our stay further.

After I answered all the same questions as I had last night, I asked rather impatiently, "Have you found out who that guy is?"

Marino nodded. "We asked the Grecos. They identified him as Tony Benetti. He does odd jobs for them sometimes. He was working that night to help on stage. We don't know more."

I asked, "Does he have a criminal record?"

Valentino shook her head.

I let the new information sink in. "Was he at the Gala?"

Marino said, "We have no record of him being there."

I cleared my throat. "Are you interviewing all the family members? And if so, have you spoken to Xander Greco?"

While waiting for a response, I decided Valentino might want to consider clothes shopping with Sophia. She broke my train of thought by answering, "We are looking into all possibilities."

Marino gave an irritated sigh. "We will speak with everyone involved, but it is not your concern, Ms. Kole. Remember who is doing the interview here."

I nodded. "Yes, sir."

Another question popped into my mind and then out of my mouth. "Was an autopsy done on Matteo? If so, what did they find?"

Again, the two detectives looked at each other as if wondering whether to involve me in their investigation. But maybe because I was already semi-involved, Marino nodded and said, "We are still waiting for the toxicology report."

I nodded. It might confirm that the bright young man had truly been murdered. Satisfied that I had gotten all the information I could from the two, I asked, "Is there anything more you need from me, or can we go back to Oklahoma?"

The two turned heads together and whispered in Italian, which was rather silly. If they spoke out loud in Italian, I still wouldn't have a clue what they were saying.

Marino faced me and said, "We will let you know later today if you are free to go."

As Kim and I left the room, Kim said, "It sounded like you were the interviewer with all of your questions."

I shrugged. "Well, I got some intel and at least put a bug in Marino's ear to find Xander. And maybe he will keep us informed about Tony Bennett."

"His name isn't Tony Bennett, it's Tony Benetti."

"Oh, that's right. I got carried away with word associations."

When I saw Aldo standing at the villa's entry I stopped and said, "I hope you got some sleep last night."

He shrugged. "A bit."

Kim said, "Thank you for taking care of Pity last night. She can be a handful."

He smiled and gave us a big laugh. "She is funny lady."

I "So funny. At least we know the name of the motorcycle rider. Tony Benetti."

He nodded. "When he wakes, he will need a good avvocato."

I scrunched my nose. Was eating avocados some Italian remedy? I glanced at Kim who looked just as confused as me.

Before we could ask about it, Aldo said, "Today, I must take Macchina Forte to Signora Greco. If you need a ride, you can take the Greco Correre. Just-a use the navigatora to find-a your way."

Kim's mouth dropped open, and I almost choked. "You would let me drive one of the cars after last night?"

"But that is why I say you can use it. But please, no racing today. You have no Italian license and already are watched by polizia."

He dropped keys into my hand, and, with his adorable jovial voice, said, "It is silver Greco out front. Arrivederci, bellas."

Kim and I stared at each other and broke out in fits of laughter as we walked toward our rooms.

When she could speak again, Kim said, "Unbelievable. So where should we go in our Greco Correre?"

"Ah, let's just 'Rome' around."

She rolled her eyes. "You are no comedian." But I was pretty sure she was laughing inside from my hilarious pun.

While Kim was gone, I put the spare euros from my bedside table in my pocket, figuring they wouldn't spend themselves. I picked up the paper from the table. It was the envelope on which I'd written my lyrics. What a nice memento. I put it in my suitcase along with brochures from the places we toured, a wine bottle label, the Italian flag and the program from the unveiling. As I crammed it in, the envelope crumpled so I took it out to straighten it. I read the other side again with the big X. What did that mean and why would someone write it on an envelope? I stuck it in my purse and got ready for a day of exploring in our very own Greco car.

The Corerre was a small sedan. Thanks to the factory tour, I could now tell R.A. that I knew what a sedan was. I familiarized myself with the dashboard and buttons.

Kim asked, "Do you think you can drive this thing?"

"It should be a breeze after driving the Macchina Forte. That car was so powerful, if I barely touched the gas pedal it took off like a rocket." I sighed at the memory, "But it hugged the road like a dream even in turns. When I'm rich and famous, I'll buy one."

"Well, I hope you are rich and famous someday then. This thing smells brand new, Pity. What does the odometer say?"

"Hm. Only 2,500 miles. Wow, this family sure has a lot of new cars. I'll bet they change vehicles like we change underwear."

Kim made a face. "I sure hope you change your undies more often than every 2,500 miles and I'll bet those are kilometers instead of miles."

I shrugged, not knowing about the difference, but I did check the gas gauge. It was full, which was good since I had no idea what kind of fuel it took. "Let's get this party started." I pushed the iniziare button and the car came to life.

When I pulled out of the parking spot, Kim asked, "Hey, where are we going anyway?"

"I don't know…wait. Can you look up directions for the Roma Superstrada? Let's go back there so I can find my glasses."

"They aren't going to just let us in so we can poke around in some secret room."

"Well, I've got to at least try."

Kim shook her head but typed the raceway name into her phone as I handled the curves down the long driveway. We made our way across town to the raceway entrance.

I said, "Wow, this place is crazy crowded. Hope we can find a parking spot."

We drove up and down the rows and Kim said, "There's one."

I parked and as soon as we got out, we heard the unmistakable roar of racecar engines. We took a photo of the location, and the parking spot so we could find the car again. We made our way over to a surly-looking woman sitting inside a ticket booth.

"Hello. Is it OK if we go inside for a minute to look for my eyeglasses I left here last night? I promise we'll be right back." In case she didn't speak English, I pantomimed the whole question.

I wasn't sure if the woman understood my words or my charades, but she grabbed a box marked *perso e trovato.* It must have been the lost and found box because it contained a red sweater, several water bottles, a hat, and a few phones. How in the world did anyone live without their phone?

Since I didn't see my glasses I asked, "Did anyone check the little room under the bleachers?"

She shook her head. "No room."

Did she mean they didn't check the room, or that there wasn't a room there? I knew there was a room and begged her with folded hands and an earnest, "per favore," but the woman shook her head. She pointed to the ticket price posted above her head – 30 euros. It must be a special race to cost so much. The glasses probably only cost $5. I looked at Kim.

She cocked her head. "Let's just go to the store when we get home, buy the exact same glasses, and Ren will be none the wiser."

For some reason, I continued pantomiming to Kim. "But I would know." Past her, I saw two young men ticket-takers chatting at the entrance. They were out of view of the grumpy lady, and I pointed. "Hey, we can talk to them."

"Give it up, Pity. Let's go see more of the city."

I grabbed her hand and pleaded, "If they don't let us in, I promise I'll leave, okay?"

She sighed and reluctantly followed me.

As we walked, I scoped out the situation. The two guys looked to be in their early twenties. They held scanners but leaned against a wall smoking cigarettes. What else was there to do when the races were well underway and there were no other latecomers in sight?

I approached the guys, who held their hands out for our tickets.

I shrugged and asked, "Hi. Do you speak English?"

They nodded so I started to explain as sweetly as I could, "Is there any way you can help me out? Can you let us in for just a minute to see if I can find the glasses I left there last night? That lady…" I gave a pout and pointed to the woman in the booth, "won't let us in."

They chuckled and nodded, suggesting they knew full well she was a stickler for rules. When my poor girl routine didn't work and the guys went back to smoking, I went for something more drastic. "You see, I left in a hurry last night because there was a stabbing and I had to chase the bad guy."

That got their attention and the taller of the two said, "Non c'e modo! That was-a you?"

The other guy pointed at me. "You drove the Macchina Forte from the stage?"

I nodded meekly. How did they know about that? Before I could ask them, they got their phones out and took selfies with me.

Kim stood off to the side snickering as the young men treated me like I was a movie star. I was kind of glad when she snapped a photo because I wanted to remember this funny moment.

The guys looked toward the ticket lady and when they saw she wasn't looking, they ushered us through the entrance and into the stands. I turned back and whispered, "Thank you."

The crowd was super loud in the stadium, but not as loud as the cars. I had to put my fingers in my ears, so I wouldn't go deaf. We stood to the side and watched the racecars for a few minutes. I tried to get my bearings, but it was all so different from last night. Besides the unbearable noise, the stage was missing, and the ramps were gone, so I wasn't sure where the little room might be.

"Kim, I think we have to go to the bottom row of the stands."

She followed me down the steps as I searched for an opening or passageway that looked familiar. Far to the right, there were steps leading further down, so we went that way. I was stopped by a man in a uniform who spouted something in Italian. I tried to explain what we were doing, but he didn't seem to care and pointed for us to leave. We turned around and started to the opposite side of the stands, covering our ears every time the cars came by.

Kim shouted, "He probably knows who you are and was afraid you would drive off in one of the race cars and join the race."

I laughed and said, "Not me. What's the fun of driving around in a circle? I don't understand this sport at all."

As we made it to the steps on the other side, I braced myself to be denied admittance again. But this time, I just walked right past a man as if I knew what I was doing, and we weren't stopped.

I pulled Kim onto a ramp leading underground. I yelled for her to hear me. "See? I told you there was a place under the bleachers."

She yelled back. "It's kinda creepy. I can't believe we're doing this all for a cheap pair of readers."

"But it's exciting, right?"

"I guess. But remember, I wasn't looking for excitement in Rome. I was looking for art and history."

"I promise after this, the rest of the day is yours, sista." A few steps later, I found the familiar door. "Here it is!"

When I turned the handle, I was surprised to find it unlocked. "See. There is a little room under the bleachers." We walked in and flipped on the light. When I shut the door, the sound was muted dramatically, and it verged on being peaceful.

The fruit basket for Francesca was still on the table where it had been last night, so I figured my glasses would still be somewhere too. I rushed over to the couch. "Here they are! I knew I'd find them."

Kim stood by the door. "Good. Let's get out of here."

I stopped by the basket thinking it would be sad for all the beautiful fruit to go to waste. I picked up a pear and took a bite. I moaned, "You must try one of these!" I popped a grape in my mouth. "And the grapes are delicious, too."

She rolled her eyes but joined me at the basket. She ate a few grapes and said, "Not bad." We giggled a bit as we tried strawberries, blueberries, and melon too.

Kim picked up the note that went with the flowers and read aloud, "To Francesca, Mi Amore. G, or is it a C?"

I nodded as I crammed more fruit in my mouth. "I know why I'm so hungry – we haven't had lunch. I do feel kind of bad Francesca didn't get any of this fruit from her 'Amore.'"

"But wasn't her date named Marco? Why isn't it signed M?"

I looked at the card again and recognized the bold handwriting. "I don't know. Hey, look." I pulled the envelope from my purse and showed her both samples. "Is this the same handwriting? Who writes in calligraphy anyway?"

Kim examined them. "They do match." She looked up the words starting with X on her translate app. "It means "X marks the spot."

I ate another grape. "Weird. I guess we can go." I stuck the little card and envelope in my purse and turned to leave. I whispered, "Did you hear that?"

"Yes. I heard you say, 'I guess we can go.'"

"No. It sounds like someone is pounding." I cocked my head so I could hear better and slowly walked to the back of the room. The sound grew louder as I approached the wall.

Kim said, "Maybe it's the crowd stomping their feet above us."

I looked up and strained my ears. "No. The thumping above is different from this mysterious sound." I rubbed my hands along the wall as if a magical door might swing open, but there wasn't one, so I put my ear to the wall. "Someone's calling out. Listen, Kim."

She joined me and sucked in a breath. "I hear it! It's muffled so I can't understand the words."

"I'm going around to see if I can find the person. I'll be back."

I returned to the loud corridor, but found no door next to ours, nor a perpendicular hallway to reach a place behind us. I joined Kim again and said, "I couldn't find a way to get back there. I think someone is in trouble. I pounded hard on the wall and yelled, "Ciao."

The pounding continued and a muted voice shouted, "Aiutami!"

I said, "What do you think that means?"

Before she could look it up in the app, I said, "It sounds like a man's voice." I yelled, enunciating every word. "Do You Need Help?"

We listened closely. Even though muffled, we heard, "Yes. Help!"

My eyes widened and Kim's grew even wider. I put my hands on the wall and shouted, "Stay there! We'll get you out." I turned to Kim. "Let's go find him."

We ran out of the room, but checked to make sure I had my glasses in my purse before catching up with Kim. "Which way should we go?"

She huffed as we left the corridor and climbed the stairs, "Let's get security to help us. There's one there."

"Good idea."

When we reached the uniformed officer, we explained that there was a man trapped someplace underneath us. The man was distracted by watching the race and continued to stare at the track. Apparently, it was the last lap, and someone was getting ready to cross the finish line. The crowd was on their feet screaming. I looked at the cars but didn't get what was so exciting. The security guard literally brushed us aside.

I said as loud as I could, "Gee, Kim, it's a good thing there isn't an emergency like someone being trapped!" I grabbed her hand and pulled her to another officer who looked equally enthralled by the race. This was ridiculous. I pulled out my phone, found the business card for Detective Marino and dialed his number. We moved to the side, out of the way of crazed fans.

A woman answered, "Pronto."

That was a weird thing to say, but I hurried anyway. "Hi, I'm trying to reach Detective Marino. I'm at the Roma Superstrada and someone is trapped underneath the stadium. Please send help."

She said, "Un Minuto." Good, she was going to get Marino or someone who spoke English. But unbelievably, in the background, I heard the same announcer whom I heard live. I listened in stereo as he yelled something about the winner. Was she watching the stupid race on TV instead of responding to my call? I was about to hang up when she came back. "You're at the raceway? Did you just see that finish?"

"No! I am not watching the race. We have an actual emergency." I recounted my story with as many details as I could and then said, "We're going to try to find the guy. Please tell Marino and send help."

I hung up and shook my head at the gall. I huffed to my sister, "I will never, ever, ever understand why people are sports fanatics."

We poked in every bathroom, concession stand, and hallway we found, trying to find the mysterious room. After exhausting every opening on the lower level, Kim said, "Remember when Francesca flew in from up there? Maybe there's another entrance."

That sparked a memory of Francesca walking with Sophia to a door at the rear of the stadium. "Thanks, Kim. You gave me an idea."

We went back out to where the young men stood. I showed them my glasses so they could see I hadn't lied, then told them about the situation. "Is there another entrance with an elevator? We think some guy is stuck in a room below and we must get him out."

Their ears perked up, and the taller one said, "Just around that corner, there is a door. You will find a lift." He pointed to the place where I had seen Francesca and Sophia disappear.

We said, "Thank you!"

I added, "Oh, and if the polizia arrive, tell them where we are."

The guys gave each other high fives, happy to be involved.

Just as we started to leave, the ticket Nazi appeared like a bad penny and rattled off a long string of Italian expletives to the boys while waving her hands at us.

Our guys replied and the exchange was rapid-fire. Then the woman just shook her head and walked away.

I was flummoxed. "What did you say to her?"

The tall boy said, "I just reminded her my papa manages the raceway and she can be fired if she isn't nice to guests."

Ahh. So that was how the young fellas knew about me and the episode with the Macchina Forte.

"Well, thank you." We turned and rushed to the side door and stepped inside an elevator. I was tempted to push the up button to find the place where Francesca took off on her flight, but focused on my task and pushed the button for the lowest level. When the elevator came to a stop, the door opened onto an empty hallway with several doors. We could still hear the noise from the spectators above us.

Kim said, "See if any of the doors are unlocked!"

The first one I tried was unlocked, so we entered. The door shut behind us, but the room was empty. When I tried the handle to leave, it wouldn't open. Kim tried the knob too, but it seemed to be locked from the outside. We too, were now trapped inside. What in the world?

We pounded on the door, but of course, nobody could hear us. When we heard knocking coming from the room beside us, we realized we were stuck in the room beside the man we had come to rescue.

I ran to the wall and yelled, "Hey, are you there?"

This time his voice was much clearer as if the wall was paper thin. He said, "Where are you? Get me out!"

How stupid we were to get locked in, and according to Kim's face, she was embarrassed too. She answered for us both, "We were coming to help you, but we got locked inside the room next door."

We heard the man growl, so I quickly said, "But don't worry, we called the police, and they should come save us soon." Kim nodded her head in agreement. I sure hoped this was the case. I checked my phone but there was no service in this underground cave.

As we stood staring at the wall separating us from the mysterious man, I noticed some loose screws in a panel. "Hey Kim, do you have a tool or something we could use to unscrew those?"

She took a closer look and said, "I'll check."

Thankfully, our space was well-lit and had couches, so it wasn't exactly like a dungeon. We sat down and rummaged through our purses for anything that could help us get to our fellow prisoner. I found a bottle of water, hair clips, mascara, a baggie of cashews, lipstick, a poncho, sunglasses, my wallet, and my glasses and then I saw it. I said, "Here's the letter opener I got for Dad."

"Good, because all I found was tweezers."

I ran over to the wall and painstakingly removed two screws.

Kim spoke up so our neighbor would hear what we were doing, "We are trying to loosen the screws on this panel…" She knocked on it so he knew which one, "so we can reach you."

He shouted, "Stand away."

We looked at each other and stepped back from the wall. There was a loud thump, and the wall moved a bit. We jumped back further and in a sudden burst, the whole left side of the panel broke free. We covered our eyes. When we looked up, a cloud of debris and dust dissipated, and a giant Goliath-looking man loomed over us.

Kim and I exclaimed simultaneously, "It's you!"

# Travel Tip #17
*Be prepared to change plans.*

I sputtered, "Xander! What are you doing here?" Yep. The man standing in the makeshift doorway was our giant airline grump.

The large man was covered in a light layer of dust from his demolition work. He had dried blood on the side of his pallid face, and he was breathing heavily.

Kim said, "Are you alright? Do you need water?"

He nodded. "Yes."

We both grabbed our bottles and handed them to him as he stepped into our room. He gulped the remaining water from one bottle and then quickly drained the second one. I found it sad that the big, confident man needed something so basic. I handed him the pack of cashews and he ripped it open as if he hadn't eaten in forever.

Once he had finished off the nuts, I said, "How did you end up in there?"

He took a deep breath, then shook his head. When he didn't answer immediately, I ushered him to a couch.

He put his head in his hands and mumbled, "That bastard hit me and locked me inside."

I raised my eyebrows. "Who?"

"Let me rest." He leaned his head back against the back of the couch and closed his eyes as if relishing the food, water, and a comfortable place to sit.

While he rested, I stepped through the demolished wall and checked out the room where Xander had been imprisoned. I looked around the room, which was difficult because it was dark. Once my eyes acclimated, I saw there was no bulb in the ceiling fixture. With no window or chair, his room was truly like a dungeon. With the light from our room, I saw what looked like a plastic water bottle glinting in the corner, so I headed over to it. That's when I noticed a dried puddle of blood lying next to the bottle. I skirted around the gore and snatched the full bottle, wondering why he hadn't drunk it.

I took the water back over to Xander and held it out to him. "You had a bottle of water in the room all along. Why didn't you drink this?"

He slowly opened one eye and said, "Poison."

I gasped and dropped the bottle as if the liquid would seep through the plastic into my skin.

Kim stared at the bottle rolling towards her feet and said, "How do you know it is poison?"

At this point, Xander realized we weren't going to leave him alone. He opened both eyes, sat up straight, and said, "Would you trust water left by someone who lured you into a room, knocked you out and locked the door?"

She scrunched her face. "Probably not?"

I was fascinated with his story and that the man knew how to speak more than three words in a row. I was even more shocked he spoke without growling. What happened to Mr. Grumpy Pants? He was actually answering our questions. Maybe it was the cashews? Or maybe being alone for so long, he re-evaluated his life. Or maybe he just figured we would never give up and gave in.

He continued. "When I noticed the lid was not sealed, I smelled the water and identified the sweet odor as antifreeze."

I leaned in. "And is that poisonous?"

He nodded. "Oh, yes. I've been around cars all my life. Mother taught us it would kill our dogs if they drank it."

Oh boy, now I might find the answer to my big question. "And your mother is?"

He cocked his head and squinted as if I should already know. "I am the oldest son of Isabella Greco."

My eyes brightened with the confirmation. I didn't mention he had no resemblance to his siblings, but I looked closely at him and said, "I think you have her eyes."

I wasn't sure, but I might have seen a flicker of a smile.

Kim said, "So have you been trapped in there since before the unveiling last night?"

He nodded and winced as if the movement really hurt.

I shook my head in disbelief. "Who locked you in there?"

"It was one of the hired workers. He wanted help carrying large speakers. It is common to ask me to help, so I followed him."

I nodded, realizing a man of his size probably would get roped into carrying heavy things. "Did you get a good look at the guy?"

He shrugged. "He was young and small."

My mouth flew open. "I wonder if it was the guy who stabbed Carlo!"

Xander's eyebrows flew up. "Carlo was stabbed?"

I said, "Oh, that's right you missed the whole ceremony." I nodded. "It ended with Carlo getting stabbed, but don't worry, he's going to be alright."

Kim added, "It was crazy. Pity is the only one who noticed. She called for help and then jumped into the Macchina Forte and chased the guy."

He turned to me in amazement. "Did you catch him?"

I nodded, and, after I gave him the CliffsNotes version of the evening, I asked, "So did the guy who locked you in have a tattoo on his neck?"

He squinted, then remembered, "Yes. It was a Sti Cazzi tattoo."

I said, "It has to be him." Then I brightened. "Did you say, 'Sti Cazzi?' How funny. I just bought a bunch of T-shirts with that very saying printed on them."

He scrunched up his face. "You did? Why?"

I nodded. "Yep. They were cheap and cute. I got them for friends and my daughters."

"Really?" He gave a chuckle. "Do you know what Sti Cazzi means?"

"Well at first, I thought it meant still crazy, but the seller said you use it like, 'Whatever.' Or 'So what?'" I looked at his confused face and asked, "Why? What does it mean?"

"It literally means…these dicks."

I choked on my own spit, and Kim started laughing so hard she couldn't stop."

I was horrified, but managed to ask, "Why in the world would they even sell shirts with those words?"

He chuckled. "Oh, people use it like, 'So what?' 'I don't give a *blank*' or sometimes, 'You're *blanking* kidding me.'"

I shook my head and sighed at my ignorance, "Oh, well, I guess I can use the shirts for rags."

He rolled his head around his shoulders and said, "Did you say the policia are coming?"

Kim stopped snickering and said, "I hope they get here soon. I need to go to the bathroom."

I realized that our cellmate had been here without a bathroom for a long time and changed the subject, "So we know the name of your assailant. It's Tony Benetti. Have you ever heard of him?"

"No." Xander shook his head and then touched it with his hand as if it hurt to move. "It's good I was too tall for him to get a good hit on my head or he might have crushed my skull. I was out cold for a long time. When I awoke, I pounded but nobody heard me... until you did today."

Kim said, "Do you think the poisoned water was an attempt to finish you off in case you woke up?"

He nodded.

I suggested, "Xander, have you ever considered maybe Matteo didn't have a medical episode? And maybe the chandelier incident wasn't an accident?"

He took a deep breath and nodded. "Matteo was young, healthy, and strong. I came back to Rome to find the truth about his death. I believe someone was trying to topple the Greco line."

"But why? Do you know of any reason why this Tony guy would want to hurt your family?"

He shook his head slowly. "I have no idea."

I said, "I think someone may have put him up to it. He told me he was afraid for his life. It was just before he jumped out of the Macchina Forte."

We all sat up when we heard voices coming from the hallway. I ran to the door and pounded. "Help! We're in here!"

After a moment, the door opened, and I was face to face with Detective Marino.

He said, "You again?"

I shrugged. "It's a long story."

Behind him were several police officers and medics. The two young men we met at the gate stood in the back, straining their necks to see inside the room.

Kim rushed up and whooshed out a thank you to the group.

I said, "Yes, thanks," then pointed to Xander. "He needs medical attention and definitely food and water. He's been trapped for almost 24 hours."

Xander growled something in Italian and lumbered toward the door, apparently ready to leave.

In a forceful voice, Marino said, "Senor Greco…per favore…" then something else in Italian.

Xander groaned, rolled his eyes, and reluctantly sat back down. I was glad we weren't the only people who annoyed the man. A woman in a white uniform rushed to him and started inspecting his head wound while another followed, carrying first aid bags.

In the doorway, the ticket-taker guys were now taking cell phone pictures. I sidled up to them and spoke softly, "Thanks for your help, but you might not want to post any photos of him…" I pointed to Xander, "if you know what's good for you."

They nodded and kept snapping, but less conspicuously.

As Marino and a few other officers questioned Xander, a man dressed in a stylish gray suit stormed into the room.

The tall ticket-taker greeted him as "Papa" and rattled off a whole string of Italian words to explain what happened. The father inspected the door handles of both rooms, then bellowed something before noticing the wall had been torn down. He stepped through the broken doorway and then came back, roaring something at Xander and the police.

Kim and I stood to the side while Marino tried to calm the man down. Xander completely ignored the raving manager.

Once the explanation was made, the raceway manager snapped at us in perfect English, "Why did you tear down my wall?"

I stammered, "Uh, well. We were locked in and since Mr. Greco was trapped, we needed to help him."

Kim added, "And he was very thirsty."

The angry man shouted, "Someone must pay for this damage. He stomped over to our door and inspected the handle. His lock was tampered with, but you were not locked in. You must push this button to exit." He pointed to a button on the side of the door jam and shook his head while saying, "Dumb Americans."

I blanched at his tone of voice and felt ignorant for not knowing how to open a door. But how was I to know that trick? I was getting perturbed by his rude behavior, and I exploded, "Well, I think you should be more concerned for this man who spent the night stuck in one of your rooms with no water or bathroom. It certainly wasn't his fault. There is no way to call for help with no cell service down here. This place is a fire trap with no escape and no stairway. You should be apologizing instead of yelling at us."

The man seemed taken aback by my rant. His shoulders slumped when he realized I was right. "It was tampered with, but I do not know how." He walked past us and said something to Xander.

Then, as he came back toward us, he said, "I'm sorry for your inconvenience. We will sort this out with the police. Come, boys."

Kim leaned over and said, "Wow. You sure told him."

After Marino took our statements and we were all set free, literally, Xander rode the elevator up with us. We all stood in awkward silence until he cleared his throat and said an unprecedented, "Thank you."

True to my word, I made Kim plan the rest of the day. We started by simply wandering the streets of Rome on a gorgeous, clear Sunday afternoon. After we had a wonderful pizza lunch, we shopped a little and bought a beautiful vase for Martina and Luca as a wedding present. The shop lady even gift-wrapped it for us. We then sat and enjoyed the beautifully ornate Trevi Fountain and climbed the Spanish Steps.

Later, as we walked across the Ponte Sant'Angelo, we looked down at the Tiber River and I smirked at a memory and confessed, "Hey Kim, right in the middle of our car/motorcycle chase, Aldo said let's go to the Tiber. I thought he wanted to go to a zoo to see a tiger."

She shook her head with a snort. "How many times have we been tricked by crazy Italian words? I'm looking up avocado now." She leaned against the bridge and typed into her phone. She laughed. "Oh, Pity. Aldo was actually saying that Tony Benetti needed to get a good 'avvocato.'" She emphasized the t and explained, "It means lawyer."

I chuckled. "And I was planning to eat guacamole if I ever came out of a coma."

I was proud of myself for being able to drive in Rome, but credited my success to Kim, my navigator. As we made our way back to the villa, I said, "I'm sure glad you stayed here with me instead of flying home like a normal person would."

She shrugged. "I guess I'm not normal. It has been exciting, but I'm ready to go home. I hope Sophia gets us a flight out tomorrow."

I nodded. "Me too or Ree may never forgive me."

As we drove up the curvy drive to our Italian home away from home, there were two police cars and several unfamiliar Grecos parked in the drive. I said, "They must be having more interviews today." I maneuvered around the extra vehicles and safely parked the car, then pocketed the keys to return to Aldo.

When we opened the familiar ornate door, voices came from the dining room, so we headed that way. The scene looked like a Greco family reunion. Isabella sat at the head of the table with a much cleaner-looking Xander next to her. Mario stirred a cup of coffee from the seat next to him. Anna sat on the other side of the table beside Giacomo, and, surprisingly, Rosa was there with crutches leaning against the wall. I hoped her presence meant Carlo was doing better.

The only people who looked out of place were Marino and Valentino, who sat taking notes.

All heads turned to us, and Sophia, who had been hidden in the corner, rushed up and whispered, "The Grecos are having a meeting."

We nodded and stepped back into the hallway. She said, "Your plane is to fly in the morning. You are good-a to go. The tickets lay on your beds."

Kim and I looked at each other and smiled. I would make it home for Ree's birthday.

I whispered, "Thank you so much, Sophia. You are the best!"

"Eet is just-a my job."

I couldn't help but ask, "So what is your job?"

She smiled her adorable, dimpled smile. "I am assistant to the Signora and do any jobs she may want. But she doesn't need me so much right now and asked to take care of you two."

I smirked, "Well, you are a very good babysitter. Is there any news on Tony Benetti? Or Carlo?"

She shook her head. "The bad man has not opened his eyes, but Carlo gets stronger and will heal."

The meeting must have adjourned because, one by one, the Grecos trickled out of the room. First came Isabella who reached out and took my hand along with one of Kim's. She said, "I cannot express my gratitude for finding my son. I would be lost without Xander."

Kim said, "We're just glad he's alright."

Isabella had tears in her eyes. "And thank you for capturing the man who injured him and Carlo."

Kim nodded toward me, "That was all Pity and Aldo."

I lifted my shoulder, not knowing what to say. Signora squeezed my hand gently, then released it and ushered her feeble husband to the door. Xander took me by surprise by carrying a pink purse. Then I saw Rosa struggling to walk with her crutches behind him. He nodded to us and helped his sister out of the villa. Sophia smiled as she followed them outside.

It was like we were in a receiving line of sorts because Anna and Giacomo walked up to us next. She said to me in perfect English, "I wasn't sure about you at first, but I am glad you won the contest. You helped the family a great deal."

Did this woman, who had barely looked at me before, just compliment me? I gulped before saying, "Thank you."

Her husband gave me a flirty smile and said, "By the way, since your jingle was so popular at the unveiling, we just voted to use it in future commercials. We will pay you, of course."

I was gob smacked. My jingle would be heard by others, and I would be paid. I almost choked. "Really?"

Kim nudged me. "That's so cool!"

Giacomo continued, "We will discuss the compensation terms and get back to you."

The handsome couple nodded and left me speechless. I was on cloud nine. "Kim, imagine, even if I only get ten dollars, that makes me a professional songwriter or at least a professional jingle writer!"

She smirked. "They'll probably give you more than that."

"I really don't care how much." As I stood there in a stupor, I was distracted by shouting coming from outside.

We rushed to the door to see what was happening but couldn't see much through the cathedral glass window. There was a flash of bright red, then other figures moving around. We hated to open the door, so I said, "Let's go to the window in the dining room."

We rushed into the dining room, forgetting the two detectives were still there. They raised their eyebrows as we barged in. I shrugged. "Just want to see what's happening outside."

They joined us at the window where the four of us witnessed Anna pointing her finger in the face of Francesca. The singer wore a cherry red jumpsuit, and her contorted face was about the same color. The two women leaned in nose-to-nose as if a fight might break out.

I whispered to Kim, "What is Francesca doing here?"

"She's probably the next to be interviewed."

I nodded and watched Giacomo as he jumped between the two women and held them apart. Inspector Marino sprinted to the door and rushed outside to intervene. Of course, I couldn't tell what anyone was saying, but it was clear the two women were furious.

After a bit, Giacomo managed to escort his wife to a light green sports car, and they drove away while Inspector Marino brought Francesca inside the dining room. She had calmed somewhat but breathed heavily and said something under her breath as she plunked down into a chair.

Sometimes, I felt like I was in another world, not understanding anything. Wait. I was in another world – Italy.

Valentino looked a bit flustered, maybe from being in such proximity to the superstar. She said, "You two must leave."

I hated to go, figuring this was the last time I would see Francesca, but the expression on the detective's face told me to scram. When Valentino walked us to the door, I said, "Can you just tell me if any of the Grecos knew Tony Benetti?"

She gave an annoyed sigh, but answered, "None of them knew him. He was only a hired worker for the event…maybe he had problems with their success. That happens sometimes. Jealousy is a sickness."

That was it? They were chocking a murder attempt up to jealousy? If it were up to me, I sure wouldn't give up on the investigation, since he told me someone put him up to it. But alas, it wasn't my problem and I needed to get home.

Valentino nodded her head, like, 'Move it!' so we scooted into the hallway again. I certainly wouldn't miss either of those detectives.

We made our way back to our rooms, and I found sweet surprises on my bed: My airline ticket, two bottles of Greco olive oil, and two bottles of Greco wine all wrapped in bubble wrap. Luca had even stacked our clean laundry.

Smiling, I ran to Kim's room and was happy to find she too got the gifts. I said, "Sophia is incredible."

She nodded. "Unbelievable!"

Sitting in the only unoccupied space on her bed, I checked the flight times on her ticket and cringed. It would take 21 hours to get home with layovers in London and Dallas. I said, "Even with 2 stops, because of the eight-hour time difference, we should still arrive by 10:30 p.m. on Ree's birthday."

Kim nodded. "That's good! Don't forget we need to give away the gift bags before we leave. I wish we had something more to give them after all this." She waved her hand across her stash.

"I know." I shrugged and changed the subject. "So…do you think Francesca would let me take her picture after she finishes talking to the detectives?"

"I doubt she's in the mood to pose for a shot. At least you got a picture of her flying over the stage, right?"

I nodded. At least that was something. We spent the rest of the afternoon packing. I ordered a flower bouquet to be delivered to Ree on her birthday.

At six o'clock, we went downstairs for dinner where Martina brought us our antipasti. I decided I would use that new Italian word from now on when I spoke of appetizers. Kim handed Martina the small canvas bag. Her eyes lit up as she took it. "Per me?"

We nodded and she looked inside and smiled. Then I gave her the gift box containing the vase. "This is for you and Luca. For your wedding."

She came around the table and gave us each a hug. She took the box and said, "Voi dolce regazza."

After she left, I said, "I think she was happy because dolce means sweet – at least it does in music."

Kim nodded. "Another hint was her smile and hugs."

We enjoyed a wonderful final real Italian pasta dinner. As we stood to leave, Martina rushed back in and handed us each a small box. I peeked inside and found those delicious pastries I had wanted to take home to the girls. How nice.

We headed back to our rooms where I slept soundly.

# Travel Tip #18
*Don't let anything delay your flight home.*

Sophia met us downstairs bright and early as planned. She wore a pink wool coat, which somehow made her eyes look even darker. "Are-a you ready to go back home to Okalomia?"

I stifled a giggle at her pronunciation and said, "Yes. We are very ready to go home. We have a little something to thank you for all your kindness. You have been wonderful."

Kim handed her the bag and the little pixie squealed with delight. After explaining what each item was, Kim said, "Please keep in touch."

I added, "Yes. Let us know what happens with the investigation. I need to know why that Tony guy hurt Xander and Carlo."

She nodded and said seriously. "I weel do that. Oh, I almost am forgetting. Here is letter for you from Greco Motors."

I shrugged and put the envelope in my purse. "Sophia, if you ever come to the States, please visit us."

We gave her goodbye hugs but when I realized we would never see the sweet gal again there was a strange tug at my heart.

When we walked outside, I perked up. "Allo, Aldo!" I gave him a big hug. "Here are the keys to the Greco Correre. I liked it almost as much as the Macchina Forte."

He nodded. "Is a good car. Shall we go?" He packed us up in the car, and we took our last drive through Rome. I sighed, thinking of all the memories Kim and I would have of our time in the amazing city.

Standing on the curb of the passenger drop-off, the giant man handed us our luggage. I said, "Please come visit us in America."

"I would like that, but my wife and six bambinos may be a lot for you to handle."

I was stunned. Aldo had a family? Why had I never asked him anything about himself?

Kim said, "No worries, we can make room for all of you."

I nodded. "Yes. Bring them all! Thank you so much for everything you did for us. We will really miss you."

As we turned to go, tears welled up in my eyes. How could I feel so strongly about people I had only met four days ago?

We checked in at the ticket counter, dropped off our big bags, and made it through security without a hitch. "Kim, we have two hours to kill. What do you want to do?"

She thought for a second. "Let's find our gate, and then we can look around.  I have some extra Euros to spend."

I nodded. We checked the numbers on our tickets and found our gate. Lo and behold, who was sitting there with headphones on, but Xander.

Kim said, "Oh my gosh, he really is on our flight again? I hope he isn't sitting next to us this time."

I giggled, turned around, and pulled her arm so we were suddenly walking the opposite way. "Let's not poke the bear."

After spending most of our remaining Euros on expensive airport souvenirs, I said, "Let's go get a coffee."

As we sipped our last cups of real Italian espresso in an airport restaurant, I said, "Ooh, I should read the letter I got from the Grecos." I pulled the envelope from my purse and ripped it open with my finger, wishing I had Dad's souvenir letter opener handy. After I unfolded it, I gasped, "It's a check for two thousand dollars!"

"Whoa. Let me see." Kim looked over my shoulder. "Good job, sis! It's signed by Giacomo Rossi. What beautiful handwriting – looks almost like calligraphy. What are you going to do with the money?"

"Well, first of all, I'm going to stop chiding myself for buying the overpriced Colosseum keychain in that gift shop." I pointed across from us. "But I'll put most of the money in the bank and make sure to do something special with part of it."

Feeling like I was on top of the world, I smiled. I could sure use a cushion in my bank account. Teenage daughters were expensive, and Todd was not overly generous in helping out with his daughters.

Kim said, "Well, while you gloat, I'm going to use the bathroom. Watch my stuff."

"OK, but hurry because we need to get to our gate. We board pretty soon."

She walked off, leaving me alone and yes, I did gloat. I was ecstatic. Not only did I get this unforgettable trip, but I also got paid.

While she was gone, I decided to recap the last four days by looking at my pictures. I opened my iPhone photos and found the first ones taken around the villa. Then came the set from the car factory, which made me roll my eyes. While I was suspended in the air, why hadn't I taken photos from that flying car? Then people would have to believe me.

When I got to the Gala pics, I slowed and took in all the gorgeous dresses. That night, I was so embarrassed about my shoes and busy drinking wine, I didn't get a good look at the gowns. Now I'm glad I took so many pictures.

I scrolled through slowly and did a double take when I caught a glimpse of a waiter who looked like Tony the stabber. I enlarged the photo to look for a tattoo, but with his shirt collar buttoned up I couldn't see if he had one. I willed him to turn around, so I could see his face better, but alas it was a still shot.

He stood talking to a tall man whose face I couldn't see. They were both looking up. Were they looking at the chandelier?

The next photos were aimed at the other side of the room. Then came my terrible selfie with Francesca scowling in the background. Dang. It was the closest I had got to a photo with her.

Next, I found a blurry picture I had taken from the dance floor. After that shot, I must have switched to Live photos because the rest of the images moved when I touched the screen.

In the corner of one of the images, the tall man stood beyond a group of people again with the man who might be Tony Benetti. I held down the Live photo, to watch one-and-a-half seconds of movement to see if I could spot his tattoo. There it was on his neck! It was definitely him. When the taller man beside him turned around, I saw it was Giacomo, Anna's charismatic husband!

I blinked. Wait. He told the inspectors he didn't know the guy, but in this photo his hand was clearly on the young man's shoulder.

I scrolled through more pictures until I got to the video I had taken after the chandelier accident. I stopped the video when I saw Giacomo standing behind the family table. I enlarged the video and saw him whispering in Tony Benetti's ear. He handed the young waiter an envelope just like the one I had gotten from him. I hadn't noticed the men before because the video's focus had been on Isabella in the foreground. I saved the cropped section as a new video clip.

Oh my gosh! Was Giacomo behind all of the attempted murders?

Kim appeared and said, "If you go to that bathroom, don't use the first stall, there is no toilet paper. I had to use Kleenex from my purse."

I stuttered. "It was G, Giacomo!"

"What?"

I pulled her over and showed her the photos and the video clip. "Look, it's Tony Benetti, and he's with Anna's husband, Giacomo."

Kim's face blanched. "But he said he didn't know the guy. That doesn't make sense."

"Well, obviously he lied about that. I think he might have hired Tony to do his deeds."

She shook her head. "Why would he want to hurt someone from his wife's family?"

"I don't know, but we need to call Marino." I dug through my purse, found his business card again and dialed. I wasn't sure if it was the strong coffee or adrenaline, but my heart was beating super-fast. While it rang, I asked Kim, "Do you remember Giacomo's last name?"

She said, "I think it's Rossi."

I nodded at Kim just as the inspector answered with, "Pronto."

I practically yelled, "It's Giacomo Rossi. He's the one who hired Tony Benetti to kill the Grecos. I have pictures of them together at the Gala."

I could hear a slow sigh, and then Marino spoke with irritation. "I thought you left Italy."

Great. He wasn't even listening. I slowed down, repeated my statement, and added, "You must stop Giacomo from hurting anyone else."

"That is not likely. Signor Rossi is a respected Roman citizen. He is also the financial manager at Greco Motors and a member of the family. A photo at a party is no proof, for he knows everyone. I'm sure you are mistaken."

I stammered, "But…"

Marino said, "Ms. Kole, have a safe flight back to America."

The phone went dead. I sighed and turned to Kim. "Well, Marino doesn't believe me. Says Giacomo is an outstanding member of society, but I'm just sure of his involvement." I looked at the back of the inspector's business card where I found his email address "You know what? I'm e-mailing him the photos anyway." I uploaded the incriminating shots and video. "Maybe he'll look at them and maybe he won't. What more can I do?"

Kim said, "Well…we could show the photos to Xander."

"Good idea!"

We gathered our belongings and rushed to our gate but didn't see the big man anywhere. Then I noticed there were hardly any people waiting around the gate. I asked Kim, "Where is everyone? Have they already boarded the plane? Don't tell me we are going to miss our flight!" My anxiety level bumped up a notch.

She said, "Let's ask the gate agent."

We rushed up to the man behind the counter. Where Kim asked, "Did they already board the plane to London?"

The agent shook his head and smiled. "No. The flight is delayed a few hours. Go get some food if you want."

Glad we hadn't missed the plane, I said, "Whew! Grazie."

Kim shook her head. "Now what?"

"I guess we'll look for Xander and have an early lunch."

She said, "Ok, but first I'll call R.A. and tell him we are delayed. Want me to have him tell your girls?"

I nodded, still stunned that the charming husband of Anna Greco could be the one who planned the horrible deeds. I sat down in a seat beside a woman who had a bag with the statue of David pictured on the side. Dang, did we miss seeing David? Or maybe he's in another city. I started to ask the woman but told myself to forget about David and get back on track.

My nerves were jangling. Was there anything else I could do to stop Giacomo? I didn't have Anna's number and, really, would I want to be the one to tell her that her husband might be a murderer?

I had a flashback of Giacomo kissing my hand when we met, and I shivered. And he even signed my check. Ick. I opened my purse and pulled out the envelope. As much as I wanted the money, I worried it was blood money. I stared at his signature. It was so distinctive and familiar. I rummaged through my purse and found the other envelope I had kept and compared the writing. They were definitely written by the same hand. My eyes widened when it registered that Giacomo must have written the Italian 'X Marks the spot.' But why? Because he was having Xander locked away? I shook my head but when I studied the little card from the fruit basket, the proverbial light bulb clicked on.

Kim disconnected her call and returned to me. "So, R.A. said he'll keep tabs on the flight, and he'll be there to pick us up whenever we land…Pity? Are you okay?"

I barely heard her because my brain was working overtime trying to connect the dots. I finally said, "Remember how angry Anna was at Francesca?" I looked up to see Kim nod, then continued. "I think this is why."

Holding all three samples of Giacomo's handwriting out for her to see, I said, "Not only did he write X marks the spot, but Giacomo is the G on the love note for Francesca! And when Francesca told me, 'He's a very bad man.' Giacomo must have been that bad man."

Kim nodded slowly as she processed the details. "So, Anna must have found out something was going on between her husband and Francesca, and that's what they've been fighting about?"

Just then, my phone rang from an Italian number. I grabbed it. "Hello?"

In a breathy voice, Marino said, "Signora Kole, you were correct. We had polizia stationed at the hospital to make sure Benetti wouldn't escape if he woke from his coma. But when a doctor left Benetti's room, the alarms rang…."

An obnoxiously loud announcement came over the airport speakers telling us something in Italian. It was so loud I couldn't hear Marino. "Hold on a second. I can't hear you."

The announcement ended, and he started again, but the announcer now came on in English! "Please do not leave baggage unattended. Unattended baggage may be confiscated."

When the announcer finally shut up, I said, "I'm sorry, Inspector Marino. There was a loud announcement. Can you repeat what you said after 'when the alarms went off'?"

He gave a frustrated sigh and repeated, "When the alarm went off at the hospital, nurses entered the room. One of our officers went to ask the doctor about Benetti's health, and he recognized Signor Rossi, who was disguised as a doctor. When confronted about it, Giacomo panicked and ran down the stairs and out the doors. We think he might have gone there to finish off Benetti. There was a syringe on the floor which they are testing now. But…Giacomo Rossi got away."

My eyes grew wider with each statement he made. "Oh no! Is Tony Benetti okay?"

Marino said with a more somber tone, "I do not know. They are working on him right now. I saw your photos and believe it is more proof of his involvement. We have put a call out for his arrest."

"Thank you for telling me. Let me know if you find out more."

When I hung up, I relayed the news to Kim.

She scrunched up her face. "So, he tried to poison Tony Benetti?"

I shrugged. "Kinda like how Benetti tried to poison Xander. I guess this time it was to get rid of the witness. Just awful."

She shook her head. "You did it again, Pity. You knew there was something fishy. Well, I'm even more anxious to get out of Rome now that there's a killer on the loose."

I nodded. "I know. Let's just get something to eat and fly home."


We found a restaurant where we could sit and discuss all the craziness. I took a bite of my final Italian pasta. It couldn't match Martina's pesto sauce. "Do you think Giacomo wanted to get rid of all the other siblings, so his wife, Anna, could take over?"

Kim said, "Maybe. He did spare her from the chandelier crash. But if he loved her, why did he have a fling with Francesca?"

I shook my head. "And why stab Carlo unless he wanted Carlos' job too? It's just all so confusing. Guess we'll have to wait to find out once we get home. I'm done with it. Hey, watch my stuff, I'm running to the bathroom, then we can pay up and go back to the gate."

As I washed my hands, I studied my reflection in the mirror. Had I aged over the long weekend, or was I just tired? So much for a relaxing trip. I was ready to go home to my babies.

On my way back, I decided to stop in just one more shop. I mean, assuming I cashed Giacomo's check, I would have money to spare. Kim would be fine at the table for a few more minutes. I saw several items featuring the David statue and asked the cashier, "Where is David?" I held up an apron to make sure she knew which David I was talking about.

The woman replied, "He is in Florence, but many replicas exist around the country."

"Ahh….Florence," I said. I would just have to see him on another trip. I giggled. As if I could ever afford to come back to Europe. I bought a magnet with the beautiful David statue and some Italian candied almonds and then hurried off to join Kim.

As I walked, I looked up to the top of the escalator. What was on the upper level? More shops? As the long, moving stairway carried people downward, a couple caught my eye. The tall man and woman both wore black coats and sunglasses. They looked like spies in those getups. The man carried a backpack, and she had her hood pulled up. The couple seemed to be arguing with one another as she struggled to move away from the man who stood one step above her. Upon closer inspection, I saw the man's hand was gripping her arm. What a jerk trying to control her.

As I looked at the man's face, my eyes widened. It was Giacomo Rossi! How had he gotten here so fast? Where was he going? When the woman jerked to the side, her hood fell back, revealing her face. It was Francesca! Were they running away together?

I hid behind a pillar and stood still as they descended toward me. I was pretty well hidden as I gaped at the two, but Francesca saw me and mouthed two words, which were easy to lip-read: "Help me!"

Was Giacomo holding the superstar hostage? Was he planning to fly away with her somewhere without her permission? How could that work? Okay Pity, think. How could I possibly help the singer get away from the murderer? I was confident Giacomo hadn't seen me but was nervous since I was no match for him. What to do?

I followed them through the terminal until I reached the restaurant where I had left Kim. I rushed up to our table.

Upon seeing me, she tapped her watch and stood up. "About time. We need to go."

I slammed my hand on the table and gasped, "Giacomo is here!" I strained my neck to make sure the two were still in sight. "He's got Francesca. She is being held against her will. I'm sorry, but I've gotta follow them. Please find Xander."

Scooting through the crowd of passengers, I tried to catch up with the kidnapper and his famous hostage, but navigating the concourse was more like going through an obstacle course. I had to jump over rolling suitcases and skirt around children who pulled tiny bags on wheels. I was almost run over by a man pushing two wheelchairs, but I finally caught sight of them not far ahead of me. Giacomo was fairly easy to spot, since he was so tall.

I hopped onto a moving sidewalk, hoping to catch up with them but it moved so slowly I could have walked faster. I had read the rules; Stand on the right, walk on the left, so I started speed walking, passing people until I reached two ladies who stood side by side taking up the whole width of the conveyor.

"Excuse me," I said, but they didn't move aside. Duh, I needed to say it in Italian. "Mi scusi." Still nothing, so I tried the only other version I knew, French. "Pardon." Finally, the two looked back. I motioned that I needed to get by, and they let me pass. Jeez.

Moments later, I exited the people-mover and ran until I was close behind the couple. I could tell Francesca was in trouble by her body language. She glanced around for help, but Giacomo's hand was still clamped onto her arm. The place was so crowded I didn't know what to do. Wait! That was it. The place was crowded!

I went with my idea and pointed, then yelled in a loud and excited voice, "Look! It's Francesca! Right there in the black coat! She's here to sign autographs!"

Several people looked at me to see where I was gesturing. A teenage girl screamed and ran in the singer's direction, yelling, "Francesca, I love you!"

Other passengers caught on to what was happening and rushed toward the couple. One girl pointed to a Francesca shirt she wore and yelled, "Can you sign my shirt?" Soon a crowd formed around the superstar.

By this time, Giacomo had released Francesca's arm and slowly walked backward. He adjusted his backpack on his shoulder. I tried to see where he went but was distracted when Francesca took her sunglasses off and her eyes met mine. She mouthed "Thank you!"

I sighed, relieved to know she was away from that monster, but suddenly a cold hand grabbed my wrist!

# Travel Tip #19
*Make sure to thank your hosts in some way.*

When I turned back, I was face to face with Giacomo, who leaned down and breathed into my ear, "You're going to pay for your little trick. And don't even try to get away."

I was frozen with fright as he pulled me through the crowd. I stumbled after him, twisting my arm to free his grip. I tried to get Francesca's attention, but she was leaning down, signing an autograph. When I called out for help, nobody could hear me with all the crazed fans shouting "Francesca!"

One comforting thought was that he probably didn't have a weapon. I mean he must have gone through security, so they would have caught it. It was just me and Giacomo. I could handle this maybe.

Without warning, he yanked my arm, but I tripped and fell to the ground. Suddenly, my body was lifted into the seat of a nearby electric passenger cart. It was one of those golf carts used to take people with mobility issues to their gates. When my hands were free from his grasp, I tried to jump out of the cart, but Giacomo grabbed my shirt and pulled me back into the cart. I started hitting him with all my might, but he caught my arms and somehow managed to zip-tie my wrists together. Something sharp poked my waistline. Was it a knife? That scared me more than the zip ties, and I froze.

To add to my misery, he used another zip tie and connected both of my wrists to the steering wheel of the cart! Dang. Now what to do?

A policeman walked by, and I pleaded, "Help me!" But he didn't see or hear me with the Francesca ruckus. Besides, the guy had more important things on his mind. I watched the officer smile and hold up his phone to take photos of the superstar. Oh, brother.

Giacomo growled, "You like to take exciting rides, no? Let's go." He stomped on the pedal and the cart took off faster than I thought a little electric vehicle could go. Since my body was off kilter, I was forced to lean across the seat with his backpack lodged between us. Something in it had sharp corners. My hands jerked with every turn of the steering wheel and the plastic ties dug into my skin. I started to cry from pain and anger, but he continued to beep the horn and expertly navigate through the concourse without hitting anyone.

I huffed to my captor, "I know you hired Benetti to kill the Grecos. The police know too! You can't possibly get away."

"You think not?" He gave a maniacal laugh. "I have a way."

Since my feet were not tied, I kicked at Giacomo as he drove, but I couldn't get leverage with my arms still attached to the steering wheel. As frustrated as I was and as much as I hurt, I felt horrible when a woman walking with a cane held up her hand for a ride. As we passed her by, I yelled a weak, "Help?" but Giacomo was still beeping the horn, so nobody heard me.

In a flash, Giacomo turned right, and just like on my favorite amusement park ride, the Scrambler, I slid over, crashing hard into the backpack sandwiched between us. Giacomo put his right arm around my shoulder and held me tight. I closed my eyes in pain. It was the same shoulder his accomplice had bruised by kicking me just two days earlier. When I opened my eyes, I was shocked to find we were heading toward a ramp. I braced myself as we rode down the slope heading for a rubber strip curtain. I closed my eyes as we went right through the flaps and out onto the tarmac!

Where was he going? We passed a truck pulling two carts full of luggage headed for the planes. Was that mom's blue suitcase with my music note luggage tag? I cringed as we drove between two buses stopped to pick up passengers. When Giacomo nearly hit a woman with a walker, a uniformed man with a whistle held out his hands to make us stop, but we kept going. Maybe that stunt would at least get the attention of airport security.

I screamed for help again, but my voice didn't carry very far with the roar of all the engines. As we rode farther away from the terminal and closer to the airplanes, I pondered my fate. Was someone going to rescue me or was I destined to be zip-tied forever and carted off to Timbuktu by a maniac? What was Kim doing? Had she found Xander?

I twisted my head to try and get a good look at my captor. Under his coat, Giacomo was still wearing scrubs from when he had impersonated a doctor just hours earlier. As we zipped along, I tried to find some sort of weakness in the guy, some Achilles heel that might help me escape. When we turned a corner, I saw his coat sleeve had slid up, and his bare arm, still wrapped around me, was vulnerable. I moved my head down and bit as hard as I could on his forearm.

He screeched and yanked his arm away from me. The quick movement caused us to turn hard and he slowed the cart down. "You crazy caga!"

His arm was dripping blood. Wow, I must have some strong teeth. Since we were going slower, I could jump out if I could just break the zip ties. What was it they did in movies when they jumped from a moving vehicle? Stop, drop, and roll? No. That's for a fire. Forget it. Jumping was off the table since I was still fastened to the steering wheel.

I looked up from my awkward and uncomfortably bent position to see us approach a giant Stivale Airways plane. A bus next to it was unloading passengers, so they could board. Oh no! Was that our flight? Well, I guess missing the plane was the least of my problems.

Suddenly, I heard someone yell, "Jump, Pity." Was that Kim? Was she here on the tarmac? I craned my neck but didn't see her.

Then I heard another voice shout, "Just jump off the damn cart!"

Apparently, no one knew I was attached to the steering wheel. I screamed, "I can't. Help me!"

The golf cart started to accelerate. Giacomo growled, "Nobody can help you now. You are going with me."

Just then, Xander appeared alongside the cart. He reached over, grabbed his brother-in-law, and tugged at him. When he did that, Giacomo jerked the wheel which caused me even more pain.

Xander grabbed him again, which had to have been difficult to do while running alongside the moving vehicle. This time, he managed to pull my kidnapper out of the cart. Yay, I was free - almost.

Somehow, I managed to straighten my misshaped body up, so it was in closer range of my hands. I wrenched my neck around to see where the two guys were, but the cart was moving way too fast. Wait. Why wasn't the cart slowing down? Didn't someone have to press the pedal down to make one of these things go? I wasn't doing it since both of my feet were still on the passenger side. I looked down and saw Giacomo's backpack lying on the accelerator pedal. It must have fallen from the seat when Xander pulled Giacomo out of the cart.

I scooted my feet over and tried to push the backpack off the gas pedal, but it was too heavy. What was in the bag, bricks?

I heard screaming and looked up. My mouth went dry when I saw I had driven onto the actual runway. I almost fainted when I spotted my even bigger problem. An airplane was aimed right at me as it came in for a landing!

I instinctively slammed my foot on the brake, but I must have scooted part of the backpack under the pedal because the brake wouldn't engage.

I heard another scream and realized this time it came from my mouth. I yanked the steering wheel to the right and managed to get out of the flight path. Unfortunately, the zip tie got caught on my belt buckle and I couldn't straighten the wheel out again. I kept turning to the right, making donuts on the runway.

A joy ride like this might have been fun in an empty parking lot with friends in the car, but not so much with a giant airliner heading right for me. I was in really big trouble!

The roar of the jet was deafening, but as I circled around a second time, I saw all kinds of emergency vehicles racing toward me. Their arrival was appreciated, but it didn't exactly calm my nerves since the plane was about to land on top of me.

What should I do? They never covered this scenario in high school drivers' training class or even in the video game. And where was the adrenaline rush that helped people to lift cars when they were in danger? For heaven's sake, I couldn't even move a backpack or unhook a plastic tie from my pants.

As the plane's wheels almost touched the ground in front of me, I closed my eyes and waited for contact. At least it would be over quickly. I begged forgiveness from my family and braced for the crash. When the sounds changed from a roar to an even louder tone, I opened my eyes to see the plane's nose pointing upward. It was climbing back into the sky.

Oh, thank heavens! The pilot must have seen me or had been directed by air traffic controllers to abort the landing. Ahh, I may not die just yet after all.

Would I ever be freed from playing ring-around-the-runway? And what else was happening outside of my twirly world? Had Xander subdued Giacomo or had the killer gotten loose? Even though the plane's thunderous noise had receded, my ears were ringing from the earlier cacophony. Then I heard someone calling, "Stop the cart now!" through what sounded like a megaphone. I tried to focus my eyes on who was speaking, but I was too dizzy from my never-ending merry-go-round ride. I closed my eyes to keep from throwing up.

Were they crazy? Did someone actually think I was driving on the runway just for fun? I yelled as loud as I could, "I can't stop it!"

A few moments later, the cart bumped. Had I hit something? My eyes flew open to find Xander sitting next to me in the passenger seat. He easily lifted the backpack from the accelerator pedal and out from under the brake and we immediately slowed down. He shook his head and said, "Now I see why you were making rings. Let's get you out of here." He pulled out a knife from his pocket and slit the horrible zip ties, freeing my hands at last.

I rubbed my battered wrists as Xander steered the cart out of the path of the aircraft and slowed to a stop. Police officers, medics, and airport personnel rushed over to us. I squeaked, "I didn't mean to cause a problem."

When I heard my sister's voice say, "Pity, are you alright?" I burst into tears as the stress of the whole event finally hit me.

She hurried over to me, helped me out of the cart, and hugged me while cooing, "It's ok. You're safe now."

I sobbed, "He tied me to the steering wheel. I couldn't…My belt…I couldn't…It was awful. The airplane almost…"

Kim interrupted my gibberish and looked me over, saying, "It's going to be fine. They'll fix you up. Giacomo is being held by police." She handed me a tissue and turned to Xander. "Thank you so much, Xander. You are a lifesaver."

I looked at him for the first time since he jumped onboard my runaway vehicle. I sniffed, "Yes. You really are."

Once my cuts were cleaned and bandaged by medics, the three of us were led inside the terminal to a small office. I was dizzy and Kim had to help me walk straight. She led me to a chair where I tried to catch my breath.

After a few moments, I looked up at Kim and Xander. "How did you ever find me?"

Kim used her hands to help explain, "Well, after you told me to get Xander, I went to our gate and the agents were scanning passengers' tickets to ride the shuttle bus to the plane. Since I still couldn't see Xander, I figured he was on the bus or plane, so I followed the group. I saw him on the bus, pushed my way over to him and relayed what you told me about Giacomo and Francesa. When I showed him the photos of Giacomo with Tony Benetti, he freaked."

We both glanced at Xander, who seemed to be fuming now as he was reminded of all Giacomo had done.

She continued, "When we reached the plane, we started to ride the bus back to find you, but just then a golf cart buzzed by with Giacomo driving. I didn't even see you at first."

I nodded. "Good thing you saw him, or I'd still be going 'round in circles." I blew out a big breath. "Xander, do you know what was up with Giacomo and Francesca?"

He threw his head back and closed his eyes. I was sure he would stay silent, but instead, he focused on me and said, "They dated each other before he married my sister, so Anna has always been jealous of Francesca. Everyone was sure it was over, but I guess Giacomo couldn't get over her."

Well, that certainly explained the tension between the two women, but why had he kidnapped Francesca? Such drama. Then I remembered the papers in my purse and pulled them out. "Is this Giacomo's handwriting?" I handed Xander the envelope and the card and watched his face as he looked them over.

The big man shook his head and scoffed, "X marks the spot. That is what the guy yelled to me as he locked the door."

Xander held up the card that went with the fruit basket and nodded, "At the gala, Francesca told me Giacomo was still pursuing her, but she wasn't interested in him at all anymore."

I said, "So, once he was discovered in Tony's hospital room, maybe he just snapped and decided to take Francesca and leave?"

The other two shrugged.

Kim asked, "Well, why did Tony stab Carlo?"

The door opened, interrupting Xander's explanation. Several uniformed men came in and pelted questions at us. It took a lot of translations for me to explain my story. The airport officers tried to comprehend the whole escapade, but they seemed especially confused when I told them how Giacomo had switched prisoners. Thankfully, our friendly detectives arrived, and the questioning moved faster. Marino and Valentino were already familiar with my antics, so they weren't surprised or confused at all.

I was relieved when the two familiar detectives assured me that Giacomo Rossi was safely tucked away in police custody. The Greco family had been informed of the situation and Francesca was safe.

Marino asked, "Did you realize Mr. Rossi's backpack was filled with cash he had embezzled from Greco Motors?"

All three of us shook our heads in surprise.

Valentino added, "Along with some gold bricks."

I knew it. There *were* bricks in the backpack. No wonder I couldn't budge it.

Marino said, "It is a good thing Rossi was captured because he had a private plane waiting for him at the end of the runway. Who knows where he was headed with the Grecos' money?"

"And me!" I said.

He shrugged, "Yes, and you, too." He hesitated and then turned to Xander. "Signor Greco, I should also inform you we got the toxicology report confirming Matteo had the same poison in his system as was in the water bottle left for you. We believe that is what caused the crash that killed him."

In the silence that followed, we let the revelation sink in. Young Matteo Greco had indeed been murdered.

Xander put his head in his hands. "I knew it."

Kim turned to me and asked, "Pity, are you ok? You look pale."

I nodded. "I just want to get on our plane and go home. I ache so much; I feel like my whole body is broken."

Kim said, "Well, our airplane is long gone. I'll go see about changing the flight and get you something for your pain."

My sister got permission from the authorities to leave the room and left Xander and me to answer more questions.

Kim came back in and handed me ibuprofen and a bottle of water. She then showed me our new tickets and said with a frown, "We couldn't fly out today, so we'll go tomorrow. I'm sorry you'll miss Ree's birthday."

I nodded. "It's ok. It's my fault for trying to protect a superstar."

Finally, after signing a few documents and discussing the kidnappings at length, the detectives drove Kim and me back to the villa. On the now familiar drive, Marino said, "So, are you two ever going to leave Italy?"

What I wanted to say was, 'Well, if I didn't have to do your job, I'd already be home by now.' But instead, I said, "I sure hope so. Please tell me I'm finished with interviews."

Valentino spoke this time, "We may have a question or two, but there is no need to detain you further."

Kim smiled at me and whispered, "Now, it's up to you to stay out of trouble, so we can get home."

I nodded as we pulled up to the villa. "Thanks for the ride, officers. Hope we never see you again…just kidding."

Marino shook his head but gave us a smirk. "Arrivederci, bellas."

When we entered the villa, we were almost run into by people dashing around with flowers and trays of food.

Kim said, "The wedding! It's today."

I sucked in my breath. "I forgot all about it. We can go now! How cool is that?"

Sophia rushed by and did a double take when she saw us. She stopped and said, "You did not go on the plane?"

I smiled to see the little sprite again. We gave the short version of the mess and told her our flights were rescheduled for tomorrow.

She shook her head. "Non-believable! And everybody is okay now? Francesca and Xander?"

We nodded and she let out a big sigh. "Buono. Well, your rooms can still be for you. They have not-a been clean yet."

I said, "That's fine. I hardly expect Luca to clean rooms on his wedding day. What time is the service? We are so excited to go."

"Eet will begins at seven."

Kim and I must have had the same thought at the same time because we both looked down at our outfits, frowning. Reminiscent of what Cinderella told her Fairy Godmother, I said, "But…we have nothing nice to wear because our luggage went home without us."

Sophia twisted her mouth. "I find something for you both. Pitico, long sleeves for you, no?"

I looked at my bandaged forearms and gave a grateful nod. "Please. And thank you so much."


Kim and I had several hours to clean up and relax. It was odd being back in the rooms we had said farewell to just that morning.

I lay on the bed and called Ree to wish her a happy birthday. Kim had already informed R.A., so the girls knew about yet another delay but no details of my newest perilous adventure.

When she answered, I immediately sang "Happy Birthday."

"Thanks, Mom. I got your flowers. I'm still sad you are stuck there, but they are beautiful. You know purple is my favorite color. Shelly said they smelled gross, so we had to take them to our house."

I rolled my eyes at that, but said, "Well, you can enjoy them when you go home tomorrow. Are you having a good day?"

She bubbled over with excitement as she told me what she planned to do after school. Then Ren got on the phone and said, "Mom…I don't know what you are up to over there, but please come home. It's torture staying here with Shelly."

"I'll be home tomorrow – no more messing around, I promise because I miss you girls way too much! Now off to school with you both. I'll try to call on my way to the airport in the morning – which will be around 9 tonight for you."

Next, I made calls to Mom and Dad to say their stranded daughters would be home tomorrow. I could always explain further in person. Maybe a bottle of olive oil would soften their reaction to my outlandish stories.

I then called Mike. "So did you give up on me coming home?"

He said, "Well, I did start to think maybe you ran off with some handsome young Italian."

I chuckled. "I did not, but our suitcases ran off without us."

He said, "Oh yeah? I have a buddy who works at Tulsa Airport. If the bags are there, maybe I can get them and take them to your house."

"Oh, that would be great, Mike. You are the best. I hate to have them just going round and round on the carousel waiting for us. I promise I will be back tomorrow, and boy do I have stories to tell."

"I'll bet you do. Safe travels, girl, because I miss you."

Lastly, I emailed Melanie at school again with another day's delay. I was sure digging myself in a deep hole with Dr. Love.

After we hung up, Kim joined me and said, "It's weird to be back in our rooms, huh?"

I nodded. "Yes, and this time I'm really anxious to leave. But I've been wondering how Sophia can get outfits for us. She didn't even ask for our sizes."

"Well, she can't loan us hers. We couldn't fit in her tiny dresses."

It hurt to laugh with my side still being out of whack, but I chuckled just as there was a knock at my door. "Come in!"

Two dresses walked into the room. Well, technically Sophia carried them, but she held them so high they covered her face. I rushed over to take them from her. Oh my, they were beautiful. One was a knee-length, long-sleeved, turquoise dress in a simple design and was just my size. The other was equally lovely and light blue. I handed the blue one to Kim, and she held it up. It looked like it would fit perfectly.

I said, "Sophia where did you get these?"

She smiled. "Oh, I spoke with Signora Isabella, and she said to buy something, so I have some fun on computer to order from local shop. They delivered just now."

I said, "So Signora Greco is our Fairy Godmother, and you are our Fairy God-Sister."

Apparently, the comment didn't translate for Sophia, and I said, "Good job, Sophia. They are absolutely beautiful!" I added, "Do you think Isabella will be at the wedding so we can thank her?"

She nodded. "Yes. I think she will see the marriages." She headed toward the door.

Kim said, "Thanks again, Sophia. We will see you at seven."

As soon as she left, we tried on the dresses, and I swooned. I looked better than I did on the whole trip. "Kim, you look amazing. How did she know blue was your favorite color?"

"I don't know, but now I want to kidnap her to shop for me."

I cringed, "Please don't say the word kidnap to me."

# Travel Tip #20

*If you get a chance to experience an authentic ceremony, do it.*

Kim and I had the slip-on shoes we wore to the airport and were happy to see they didn't look too bad with the new Italian-made dresses. Once we fixed ourselves up as well as we could without makeup or brushes, we headed downstairs for a real Italian wedding.

Chairs were set up in the ballroom, the same place where our initial cocktail party was held. The decorations were simple and sweet with white roses and streamers. We were met by a striking boy of about fourteen who spoke to us.

Kim said, "Non parlo Italiano."

The boy's eyes twinkled as he said, "Come this-a way, please. You are from America? The ones who caught Senor Rossi?"

I nodded. "Yes. Sort of." How did he know so much? As we followed the handsome youth with the lovely accent down the long aisle, I asked, "So, how do you know Luca and Martina?"

He turned to me and, with a captivating smile, said, "I am Lorenzo, Luca's brother."

Oh wow, he is Luca junior. Instantly I could see the similar cheekbones and smile. I nodded. "You look like him."

Lorenzo stood a little taller as he escorted us to a row halfway down. Kim went in first and I sat in the aisle seat. As guests started to arrive, I watched Sophia set up several tables on the other side of the room. She was such a hard worker.

Isabella entered, beautiful as usual. Her husband, Mario, tottered behind her looking dazed and confused. I was surprised when she stopped beside us and spoke softly. "We are indebted to you for discovering Giacomo's evil plan. Thank you both ever so much. And we are very sorry for the danger he put you in, Ms. Kole."

As I waved off her apology, my bandages started to show, so I lowered my hand quickly. I said, "We are sorry for all of your troubles and hope things settle down for Greco Motors and your family."

She gave us a warm smile and said, "Oh, they already have. Carlo will go back to the factory when he heals. Rosa is mending and will work hand in hand with Anna in finances. And my brilliant Xander will be taking the lead to run the company." She sighed. "Of course, we miss Matteo terribly. But to think, I may have lost my eldest son too if you had not found him." Then she bowed her head to us.

Before Signora Greco turned to go, I remembered to say, "Thank you for these lovely dresses." I pointed to our outfits. "We'll give them back to Sophia tonight."

She shook her head. "There is no need. They are now yours." As she walked away, I nodded to her husband who gave me a blank stare.

Kim said, "We get to keep the dresses? Wow."

Stifling a giggle about getting to keep our dresses, I turned to Kim. "I'm just happy she's not angry at me for stealing the Macchina Forte."

She nodded. "Well, you do realize you probably saved the Grecos millions of dollars by helping capture Giacomo…not to mention by figuring out who was behind Matteo's murder."

We watched Signora Isabella Greco and Mario sit in the front row along with the families of Martina and Luca.

Kim looked behind me and said, "Look."

I turned to see Xander helping Rosa hobble down the aisle. When I managed to see beyond the big man, I drew in a quick breath to find Anna following the two. The poor thing. I couldn't even imagine the emotional upheaval she must have experienced after discovering her charming husband was a murderer. And to top it off, he tried to force another woman to run away with him.

Xander helped Rosa sit in the second row. Anna sat next to her sister. I whispered to Kim, "I can't believe Anna's here."

"I know. Poor thing must be devastated." She shook her head in empathy and looked back. "Holy Moly. If you want another shock, look who just walked in."

My jaw dropped when Francesca entered the room. I barely recognized her in a sleek brown pantsuit. Her brown long hair was braided, and she wore very little makeup, a big change from the attention-getting look we were all used to. She looked fresh and classy.

I almost choked when the superstar stopped next to me. She leaned in and said, "You saved my life, and I will not forget it. At the reception tonight, please tell me what I can do for you."

She stood up straight and proceeded to stop by the Greco family. I was still stunned by her words but held my breath in anticipation of a big blowout when Anna saw her. But, in a huge plot twist, Anna stood, hugged Francesca, and offered the star the seat next to her.

Kim's mouth was open. "I wouldn't believe it if I didn't see it."

Still stunned, I replied, "Maybe Anna finally heard the story about the fruit basket, the kidnapping, and the fact that Francesca wasn't trying to steal Giacomo from her, but she was yet another victim."

After all those surprises, we got a few more. Once Sophia finished fiddling around with food and decorations, she winked at us as she passed by. She made her way down the aisle and sat beside Xander, who put his arm around her. Aww…now that was cool!

The last surprise before the wedding, was when we saw our large friend, Aldo, enter. He ushered his big family into the row across from us. His wife was a portly woman with a huge smile. She carried a chunky baby on her hip. Five more adorable children took up the rest of the row. When Aldo saw us, he laughed and said, "See, you don't-a want thees whole bambinos at your houses in Okaloma."

I shook my head, "Oh yes, we do. We want them all."

When the wedding began, we were mesmerized by the ceremony. Martina's white dress was simple and had a lovely train. Luca practically swooned when he saw her. The service was fascinating. Of course, we couldn't understand anything they said, but we enjoyed watching an Italian wedding.

Once the gorgeous newlyweds walked back down the aisle, people cheered, and the lively reception began. We stood and nodded hellos to people we didn't know and joined in to help move the chairs over to the tables on the side of the large room.

Before we joined the receiving line, Sophia handed us each a little net pouch. When we stared at our bags, she said, "It is confetti."

The bag felt a little bit heavy to contain confetti, but I asked, "When do we throw it at them?

Sophia looked horrified. "Why would you throw at the couple? This is your gift, candies. For luck."

Embarrassed, I stammered, "Oh, I'm sorry. But in America the word confetti meant tiny papers."

We went to the end of the receiving line and hugged Martina and patted Luca on the shoulder.

Martina smiled at us, then whispered something to Luca and he nodded. "We are so glad you could join us in our wedding. Please enjoy lots of food, wine, and dancing."

And that's just what we did. We danced and ate our final Italian antipasti, pasta, and wine. Gee, how many times did I think I was eating my final Italian pasta? As much as I loved the food, I hoped it was really the last time because I wanted to go home.

After laughing and visiting with the Grecos, Sophia, the newlyweds, their families, and Aldo's whole crew, we finally said our goodbyes and returned to our rooms. Sitting on my bed, I shook my head. "What a lovely wedding. I can't believe all the delicious food at the reception."

Kim held her stomach. "I know. I think I may have gained ten pounds with all the pasta, bread and cheese. And the wedding cake was so good."

I echoed, "So good." I wondered if Martina had made her own wedding cake. I brightened, "I was glad the gift bags were in my backpack so I could come get them and give the rest away."

She nodded. "Well, I understand giving them to Xander and Isabella, but I was surprised when you gave the last bag to Francesca."

I shrugged. "She deserved it for what she went through. She must have liked it because right afterward, she let us take selfies with her." I sighed. "Ree will be thrilled when she sees the photo." I added, "Oh, I forgot to tell you…Mike said he would check to see if our luggage arrived in Tulsa. If so, he'll retrieve them for us."

Kim nodded. "That's great."

I sighed with a frown. "Just think, if it wasn't for me getting involved, he could retrieve us too."

"It's OK, Pity. We got to see an amazing Italian wedding."

After Kim said goodnight, I sent a message to Ren and Ree telling them Mike may drop our suitcases by the house. If he did, they could go ahead and open Mom's big blue suitcase. I said there were sticky notes on the souvenirs with the names of who they went to.

I turned my phone off and took a few more ibuprofen. After tossing and turning my battered body, I finally found a comfortable position and fell asleep.

The next morning, bright and early, we said our goodbyes again and Aldo drove us to the airport, where we checked in and went through security. I called the girls and told them we were at the airport, and I refused to be distracted, detained, or delayed anymore. Ree was glad but bubbled over telling me about her birthday.

After hanging up, we spent about an hour people-watching before boarding the bus and heading to the plane. I looked at the tarmac and imagined how crazy I must have looked going round and round.

As we walked up the steps to the plane, flight attendants in their green and red suits welcomed us. One man with an adorable accent pointed us to seats in the second row. I turned and said, "Those can't be our seats. We fly coach in the back."

"He took my ticket and said, "Non. You are first-a class."

I stared at my sister. "Kim, did you pay for the upgrade when you rebooked us?"

She rolled her eyes at me. "What do you think?"

Of course, she hadn't. Neither of us would consider paying for first-class seats. I sat down in the crazy seat which resembled an odd bed. So weird. I asked Kim, "How did we get these seats then?"

Kim shrugged just as Xander appeared. He stopped by us and smirked. "Now you won't wake me for any reason."

"Did you upgrade us?"

He said, "No. It was Mother. She is glad for what you did."

Another passenger tried to get by and Xander sat in the seat across from us. I couldn't help but ask him, "Why are you going back to America when you will be working here?"

"I must tie up strings from a job in Dallas. Then I will come back."

We nodded, and I said, "I'm glad you will be working with Greco Motors again. If you talk to Signora Greco, please tell her thank you for this special treatment... and tell Sophia how much we love her."

Before he settled in his pod, I saw a twinkle in his eye.

A flight attendant welcomed us with champagne and doted on us the whole flight. I put my feet up in the special compartment across from my seat and leaned over to Kim. "Are you enjoying this one-in-a-lifetime deluxe treatment?" I guessed she was because her eyes were closed, and a huge smile was planted on her face.

We changed planes in London and were thrilled to find we had first-class seats on our long flight to Dallas too. Before heading to our gate, we caught Xander.

I said, "I'm sure you are sick of us, but we really appreciate all you did for us. We wish you well."

He grunted. "You were a pain in the ass." Then he shrugged. "But you came in handy. Sophia and I are getting back together, and I believe we owe it to you two." He winked at us.

Jointly, Kim and I squealed, "That's wonderful!"

We gave him hugs and wore smiles all the way through customs.

...

When we landed in Tulsa, I gave a big sigh and said, "Let's go home, sister."

Kim nodded and we headed to baggage claim. But in an unexpected twist, a big group stood in a clump to meet us. Our parents, my girls, R.A. and Alex, Mike, Lin, and even my teacher buddies were all there. They held a painted banner obviously made by Jules. It read, "Welcome home...finally."

The scene was so sweet, I beamed...until they lowered the banner. Oh no! All the gals wore the "Sti Cazzi" T-shirts I had bought. Apparently, the girls had read the sticky notes and handed them out.

Kim and I broke out in laughter and had trouble stopping. Rather than explain the embarrassing T-shirt blunder to everyone, we just embraced our family and friends, happy to be back. Tears of laughter and joy filled my eyes.

A few people from our plane stared at us, as they passed by. Did they think we were famous like Francesca? But when one lady shook her head and scoffed her disgust and mumbled, "Sti Cazzi." Kim and I started giggling again.

We thanked everyone for greeting us and I gave Mike an especially nice hug and kiss on the way to the parking lot.

When we got home, I saw a vase of beautiful flowers and asked the girls, "Who got flowers?"

Ren said, "You did–on Valentine's Day. I forgot to tell you."

I opened the card, anticipating a note from Mike, but shook my head and let the girls read it.

Ree read aloud, "To my darling Valentine. You bring out the best in me. I long to be with you again. Forever yours, Kenny." She looked up and said, "Unbelievable."

Ren said, "I'm beginning to think he will be around forever."

I unpacked my bags and hung out with my girls. They loved the leather purses and other souvenirs.

Ree was so happy with the selfie of me standing with Francesca, she said she planned to show it off at school. After I Airdropped it to her, she brightened, "Hey Mom, did Francesca happen to give you tickets to her concert in Dallas tomorrow night?"

I frowned. "No, honey. We'll have to catch her another time."

I was so jetlagged that I fell in bed exhausted. The girls came into my room and Ren pointed to her shirt. "OK, Mom, what is the deal with the T-shirts? Why did you laugh so hard when you saw them?"

I sat up and explained, "So…after I bought them, I learned Sti Cazzi translates literally to…" I cringed. "Well, it means these dicks."

There was silence as the girls scrunched their noses.

Ree asked, "Why did you buy shirts that say that?"

"Well, the guy who sold them to me told me it meant "whatever" or "no way." Later, when I learned their true meaning, I was horrified and figured I would just use the shirts as rags. But I forgot to take off the name tags and now everyone has one." I shrugged. "Guess I should tell them, so they don't wear them in public."

Ren looked down at the huge letters printed on her shirt. "I think it's funny. I might even wear mine to school and see if I get in trouble."

Ree said, "Well, I'm not going to because there's a new boy in my class from Italy. He would know."

I nodded. "Yes. He would. Now leave, so I can go to la la land."

The next morning, I wanted nothing more than to go back to sleep, but I heaved my groggy self out of bed and got ready to face Dr.

Dreadful at school. When I entered Arrowstar Elementary, there he was, standing sentry beside his office tapping his toe. He whined, "I see the prodigal teacher has returned."

"Hello, Dr. Love. I hope you got my messages saying I was detained in Italy."

He raised an eyebrow. "I did, but it seems unlikely you were unable to leave. My guess is you just wanted to extend your vacation further."

Of course, he didn't believe me. But anticipating his negative response, I held out Marino's business card. "If you need proof of why I was delayed, please contact the polizia in Rome. Inspectors Marino or Valentino will be happy to verify why I needed to stay longer." I worried that if he did call them, they might tell him they were thrilled when I did leave.

Dr. Love twisted his mouth and took the card. "Well, you must discuss your absences with human resources." He lifted his chin and continued, "I'm sure you have been wondering about your schedule change. Here is your copy. It goes into effect tomorrow."

I considered running away but before I could, he shoved the paper at me. Rather than give him the satisfaction of watching my reaction to its content, I gave a weak attempt at a nod and walked out.

As I left his office, several teachers and students greeted me with smiles and said, "Welcome back." I wondered how much of my Italian adventure was common knowledge.

I was nervous to look at the wall to see if the mural had been desecrated with the school rules, but when I reached it, the adorable children's book characters were still there, bigger than life. Whew.

My classroom looked good. I read the substitutes' notes and adjusted my plans to add what the subs hadn't completed. Then I scooted over to the art room to find my friends. When I entered, they yelled, "Welcome back, Pity!"

I slapped my hand over my eyes because all three were wearing their Sti Cazzi shirts again. I had forgotten to warn them not to wear their rude shirts in public. I said, "No, no, no!"

Once I told them the meaning of the words, Jana looked horrified, Jules laughed and Becca said, "It's now officially my favorite shirt!"

After my morning classes, I finally pulled the new schedule out of my bag and read it. It was worse than I expected, and my pulse raced. What was he thinking? Before I blew a gasket, I called Jeff from the teachers' association. "Hi Jeff, Pity Kole here at Arrowstar."

He sighed. "What did Dr. Love do now? I just had a pow wow with parents over the mural being painted over."

"I'm emailing you a screenshot of my new schedule that goes into effect tomorrow morning. I need your help ASAP."

He said, "I just got it. Oh, my this is bad. How does he think he can get away with this? I'll take care of it."

"You are a lifesaver! And I was detained in Italy for two more days than expected and hope I'm not in trouble with Human Resources?"

"I'm sure they'll work with you. I'll transfer you and get back to you soon about the other problem."

All was good with my added days. I just needed to use sick days since it was unavoidable.

After school, Melanie called and said I was needed in the office. I couldn't tell from her tone of voice if I was in trouble or not, but I grabbed my stuff and headed that way.

Melanie's lips were clamped shut and her eyes were wide as if she had a juicy secret. She nodded for me to go into the office. I took a tentative step in and saw our district's superintendent standing beside Dr. Love's desk. I tapped on the door, and he motioned me in.

I croaked out, "Hello Dr. Mccalister and Dr. Love."

When I saw our principal, I almost laughed. He was shrunk down in his chair with his head bent down, resembling a schoolboy who had been caught writing on the bathroom stall.

"Ms. Kole, Dr. Love has something to tell you."

Dr. Love stood, cleared his throat without looking at me, said, "Ms. Kole, I have rescinded your schedule change."

I let out a sigh of relief, but Dr. McCallister said, "And?"

My principal took a deep breath. "And I'm sorry."

The superintendent said, "Please elaborate."

Dr. Love looked at me and said, "I'm sorry that I have made your past year rough by giving you unfair treatment. I will attempt to do better. I hope you will accept my apology."

At this, my chin started to drop, but I kept it in place, so I didn't look too shocked, but I truly was speechless. Dr. Love was admitting to treating me badly? I looked at the two men and finally said, "Thank you for your apology. I would appreciate working hand in hand with you from now on, Dr. Love."

Dr. McCallister said, "Thank you Ms. Kole, you may go."

After I slipped out the door and shut it behind me, I made a silent scream to Melanie. I whispered, "He apologized to me."

She made sure nobody was listening and whispered, "It was either that or be reassigned to an office, but you didn't hear that from me."

I said, "Mum's the word," and I locked my lips with a fake key.

I felt as though a weight had been lifted from my shoulders as I drove home. Maybe my nightmare was over, and I could even have my fifth-grade musical without a fight.

# Travel Tip #21
*Once you get home, keep the memories close forever.*

I had a dinner date planned with Mike that night but was still suffering from jetlag, so I took a quick nap when I got home. I sure didn't want to fall asleep on our date. I awoke refreshed and put on the new dress Sophia and Isabella bought for me.

"Mom, you look amazing!" Ree said when I entered the room.

I twirled and said, "Oh, it's just a little something I picked up in Rome." Then I told them how I got the gorgeous dress.

Ren said, "You are the luckiest unlucky person I know."

The doorbell rang and I found Mike standing on the doorstep holding a gift bag. When he looked at me, his big blue eyes widened.

He whistled, and said, "I practiced saying 'buongiorno, bella,' but I think 'Mamma Mia!' is more appropriate."

I laughed, jumped up on my toes, and gave him a big kiss. "You are a sight for sore eyes, Mike Potter.

He stepped inside, saw the flowers, and frowned. "Are those from your new Italian lover?"

I groaned, "No. They're from my old American stalker."

He nodded. "Kenny is trying to keep me on my toes. Who knows? He may wear you down and someday you'll choose him over me."

I scoffed, "Umm…that's a hard no. But if you're lucky I'll tell you about the Christmas present he sent me." I sidled up to Mike, raised my eyebrows, and grabbed his bag from his grasp. "So, what's this?"

"Just a little welcome home gift."

I led him into the living room where we sat on the couch. I removed the tissue paper and pulled out a beautiful striped, hand-knit throw in pinks and reds. I gasped. "Mike! You made this for me?"

He nodded. "Hope you like it."

"Oh my gosh! I love it." I wrapped myself up in it and said, "It's so soft. Can I wear it to dinner?"

He chuckled and said, "I'd rather you not cover up your gorgeous dress, but if that's what you want…"

After some serious, yet fun persuading by Mike, I opted not to take the blanket on our date. We drove for a romantic dinner at the restaurant I wanted to go to more than any other: Goldie's Patio Grill.

As we sat side by side in the cracked vinyl booth he said, "Are you sure you didn't want to go somewhere nicer than a hamburger joint? You look like a million dollars - I mean a million euros."

"I know it's probably an odd choice since I was gone less than a week, but all I've wanted since arriving home is a good cheeseburger and a beer. In Rome, I had so much pasta and red wine, that I thought I might turn into a giant bowl of spaghetti."

After we ordered food, I pulled a small bag from my purse and handed it to him. "Something for the special man in my life."

He took out the brown leather wallet. "Oooh, that's nice."

I said, "It even has a euro in it for good luck."

"But I've already got my lucky charm with me." He leaned over and kissed me. "But thank you. I love it."

We munched on pickles, and I told him about my adventures. He shook his head. "I can't believe you made it home in one piece."

I shrugged. "But if you ever need help in a car chase, you know who to call." I winked. "But I will never get in a golf cart again."

Our Goldies Specials arrived and between bites, I asked, "So what's new with you?"

"Well, just regular police stuff at work. But my sister wants to meet this crazy girlfriend of mine, so if you are free Sunday for lunch, she would like to have you and the girls over to her house."

"I finally get to meet Sally, Scott, and little Jesse? Ooh, I can take her a bottle of Italian wine I brought back."

He held up a finger. "Well, maybe you should hold off on that because she just announced she's two months pregnant!" His face lit up. How cool that he loved his family so much.

I gave a happy pout. "Aww. That's wonderful news. I'll bet they're thrilled. I'll take them olive oil instead and a little Pinocchio for Jesse."

He nodded. "That would be perfect."

. . .

The rest of the week at school was great, with no drama from our leader. I was so happy about it that I dropped off a bottle of Italian wine for Jeff at his office.

He said, "Thank you, but I didn't really do anything. There were so many formal complaints from teachers and parents about Dr. Love that Dr. McCallister wanted to fix it once and for all. He interviewed a few people and discovered you had been his main target.

I said, "Well, I'm thrilled now. We'll just see how long it lasts."

Life was crazy at our house on Saturday with Ren nervous about the state swim meet and Ree excited about her birthday party. That morning at the pool, the whole family, minus her dad and Shelly, cheered Ren on. Mike sat between me and my parents while Ree and Caitlyn explained what was happening to Kim and R.A. Ren's relay team came in third in the 200-medley relay. Later, she swam a personal best in the 100-meter backstroke. We were all happy she did so well.

After the congratulatory hoopla, Ren left with Jennifer, Chris, and the rest of the team to their favorite after-meet pizza spot. Mom and Dad went home, but the rest of us drove to Okie Karaoke where we met Ree's friends.

A teenage boy wearing an Okie Karaoke T-shirt took us to our private karaoke room and handed out menus. We ordered pizza and pitchers of pop. I reminded him we had preordered cupcakes.

All the adults sat in the corner away from the giggling teens, while Ree opened birthday presents from her friends.

The boy served pizzas to both tables. His voice cracked when he asked if we needed anything else. Mike said, "No, sir. We're fine."

While we ate pizza and watched the kids, Lin said, "What a crazy trip. Were you really driving around in circles on the airport tarmac?"

I nodded as I took a sip of Coke.

She added, "I'm sure glad you told me what that shirt meant before I wore it to work."

Kim said, "You should have seen the reaction of our Italian friend when Pity told him she bought so many of the shirts."

I looked at Kim. "Friend? Are you talking about Xander?"

"We saved his life. He saved yours. I think he qualifies as a friend."

"Hm. I guess so."

One of Ree's friends asked me where the bathroom was. As I pointed to the door, I noticed her cute kitty T-shirt and turned to my brother-in-law. "Hey, R.A., did you ever name that cat?"

He gave his adorable smile that made his eyes crinkle and said, "I sure did. I named her Atticus."

When the name registered, I clapped my hands together and said, "Because you found her in our attic!"

Kim hugged his arm and glowed. "And also, because To Kill a Mockingbird is my favorite book." How creative and sweet.

A well-dressed man appeared, replacing the teen worker. This apparent manager asked in a deep voice with a slight British accent, "Are you ready for the fun to begin?"

I shrugged. "I'm not sure we're ready to hear them sing, but they are more than ready to start. So, yes."

The man walked to Ree's group and said something to them that caused the girls to chant, "Birthday girl! Birthday girl!"

Ree smiled and stepped up onto the tiny stage. She asked the guy, "Can you play 'Don't Cha Tell Me No' by Francesca?"

I nudged Kim and said, "Can you believe we saw her sing this song live in Rome?"

Kim was as giddy as I was. I held up my phone so I could record my youngest daughter singing one of her favorite songs. When the introduction ended, Ree started out singing quietly, but when it came to the chorus, she belted out the lyrics with her sweet voice, *"Don't you tell me no, I'm flying in tonight to see you and I hope to hold you tight."* Kim and I started singing along when the chorus repeated.

For some reason the music grew louder, and a recognizable voice blared over the speakers. Ree stopped singing and looked confused.

R.A. shook his head. "The dummies. They switched to the original recording with the voice on. This is supposed to be karaoke." He stood up to go correct the situation.

As he took a step, there was a flurry of pink, and the one and only Francesca stepped onto the stage. My mouth dropped open. What in the world? Was I seeing things? Everyone in the whole room was stunned.

The Italian superstar, dressed in a pantsuit covered with pink sequins, put her arm around my Marie and continued to sing. Seeing her idol standing so close, Ree went pale and looked as though she might faint, but Francesca kindly urged her to join in singing her famous song. I kept recording and beamed as my baby came to life and sang a duet with Francesca. They sounded amazing.

The party girls jumped up and down screaming. The man who had started the music stood at the door with his arms folded. In that position, I realized he wasn't the Okie Karaoke manager, but Francesca's bodyguard/driver I'd seen with her before.

I handed my phone to Mike, asked him to keep recording, and then leaned across the table to Lin. "Can you call or text Jennifer and have her bring Ren here right now – just the two of them?"

While Lin contacted her daughter, I ran to the man at the door and said, "If two teenage girls get here, please let them in."

He nodded.

I ran back to our table and gushed, "Kim, did you arrange this with Francesca?"

She shook her head vehemently. "No! I thought you must have."

I recalled back to the wedding reception when we had spoken. Had I cooked up this plan and forgotten about it? Of course not. Francesca had asked me what she could do to repay me for saving her from Giacomo. The only thing I recall asking of Francesca was for a selfie with me to give to Ree. I just told her my daughter loved her more than anything and wished she could have gone to the concert in Dallas. I may have mentioned Marie was going to sing her songs at a karaoke place on Saturday, but I was sure I didn't mention the name Okie Karaoke or even Tulsa. I did have a lot to drink, but I wasn't out of it enough to ask her for more than that.

When the song ended, Ree's happy tears streamed down her face, making my own eyes tear up. Francesca shouted out the name of another of her songs and yelled to the teens above the noise, "This time all you gals have to join us."

The young teens stared at her for only a second before jumping up to join them on stage. What an experience. As they sang another familiar Francesca song, I was distracted by movement at the door. Ren poked her head in and when she focused on the scene, her jaw dropped. She and Jennifer slipped into the room and hurried to me.

Without taking her eyes off the stage, she whispered, "Mom, what is going on? How did Francesca get here?"

"I have no idea. I'm just as surprised as you are."

The two 17-year-olds found chairs near our table and watched the group on stage in awe.

When the music stopped, Francesca motioned for me to join her. I gulped and made my way to the stage, pretty sure my face was bright red. She announced, "I wish to thank my friend, Pity, for without her, I would be on a plane to who knows where?" Our group clapped and

I heard, "Yay, Pity!" Ree's friends who had all been my former students, yelled, "Go, Mrs. Kole!" I squirmed from the attention.

The pop idol took my hand and continued, "Since I am between concerts in Dallas and St. Louis, I decided to stop by and say happy birthday to my biggest fan, Marie." She leaned over and said, "Happy Birthday!"

The girls on stage patted Ree on the shoulder. I was pretty sure she felt like a superstar herself. Francesca continued, "But I must leave right away to catch my next flight."

Everyone in our group clapped, and I gave Francesca a big hug. "Thank you so very much! But I can't figure out how you found us."

She winked. "You are not the only one with investigation skills. Plus, you gave me your little bag at the party with your town name. It was not too hard to find a 14-year-old karaoke party in Tulsa on this Saturday."

I pointed to Ren, who was now standing close to the stage. Her smile was huge and her green eyes were round. "This is my older daughter, Lauren."

Francesca looked at both of my daughters and said, "You beautiful girls have a very brave mother."

They nodded and Ren said, "And maybe a crazy one."

Ree agreed. "We can't keep her out of trouble."

I shrugged. "Francesca, as long as you are here, can the three of us get a photo with you?"

"Of course."

Ren grinned and jumped on stage. We stood in a row while Kim, Lin, and Mike closed in to take pictures of us.

Francesca said, "Maybe now we should get a group picture with everyone here." She called her bodyguard over to take a photo of our whole crew of family and friends. Mike handed him my phone and I motioned for Kim to stand on the other side of Francesca. I was happy when Francesca acknowledged my sister by saying, "Hello again,

Kim." She put her arms around our shoulders. Once R.A., Mike, Lin, Jennifer and all the girls were crowded in the small space, the bodyguard took several photos.

Before Francesca could leave, I said, "I can't thank you enough for managing to come here. None of us, especially Ree, will ever forget your kindness."

She put her hand on my arm. "It was no problem." She perked up. "Oh, by the way, I will be recording your jingle next week for the Grecos. It is very cute and will be featured in commercials for the Macchina Forte in the coming months."

My face flushed, and I gave her another hug. "That's so exciting. I can't wait to finally hear you sing it. Thanks again for everything."

The bodyguard handed my phone to me and then helped Francesca into a long coat, which almost covered all the pink. She waved to us, reached into her coat pocket for her sunglasses, and said, "I almost forgot."

She pulled a CD out of her pocket and handed it to Ree. When she looked at it, she said, "It's your newest album – and it's signed to me!" Ree rushed to Francesca and gave her a bear hug.

Francesca put her sunglasses on and looking less conspicuous, disappeared through the door leaving everyone in a stupor.

The next day, we wound down from the surprise visit from an international celebrity and relaxed around the house. Ree said, "Mom, do you think I can become a famous singer like Francesca?"

"Well, you do have a lovely voice. With a lot of hard work, a lot of luck, and being in the right place at the right time, I suppose it could happen. But for now, let's focus on your schoolwork."

That afternoon, we got to meet Mike's adorable sister, Sally, along with Jesse and Scott. Sally and I had a connection the moment we met and didn't stop talking for the rest of the visit. Mike and Scott talked about work, and the girls fell in love with little Jesse, and played with him until we went home.

Then came Monday and it was back to my normal daily tasks of teaching music to elementary kids, sparring with a terrible boss and working a second job. When some days became too stressful, I found myself longing to be back in the villa, eating incredible food, and experiencing the excitement of fancy galas and sports cars. But then I would remember how much I missed my girls while there. And I recalled I had been in mortal danger several times and became thankful for my semi-boring life.

What wasn't boring was dating Mike. In our spare time, we talked on the phone, went on dates, and became more comfortable with each other. There were no big plans other than just spending time together.

About a month after I got home, we happened to see the Macchina Forte commercial on TV. When I heard my song, I grabbed the remote and hit record. As expected, Francesca sounded fantastic singing my jingle. I replayed the clip repeatedly and found it hard to believe something I wrote was being heard around the world.

As for the money I had received from Greco Motors, it went straight into the bank. It was a good thing because not long after we heard the commercial play, our heater went out, and I had to get a new one, taking up my bank cushion. But at least I had the money, so I didn't have to take out a loan.

One evening while the girls watched reruns of *Bob's Burgers*, I sat on the couch wrapped up in the throw Mike had knitted for me and worked on lesson plans. I searched the Internet for interesting facts about *The Sound of Music* for my musical unit. I read an article that made my pulse race.

"Hey girls, can you pause the show?"

Ren reached for the remote and the animated, bunny-eared character, Louise, froze on the screen with her mouth open, no doubt amid a snarky comment.

They turned around and said, "What?"

I was hardly able to contain my excitement: "Listen to this!" I read the article aloud, "Are you creative? Do you love musicals? If so, enter now and write a children's version of *The Sound of Music*. The top prize is a trip to Salzburg, Austria, where the winning musical will be performed in the church where the real Maria and Captain Von Trapp were married!"

I looked up from my laptop and said, "Don't you think this contest is perfect for me?"

My girls yelled in unison. "Oh, no. Not again!"

# About the Author

Martha Kemm Landes is a former Oklahoma public school music teacher. Besides writing musicals for her students, she is known for writing the Oklahoma State Children's Song, <u>Oklahoma, My Native Land</u>. After moving to New Mexico in 2011, she began her transition from composing music and musicals into writing fun mysteries.

Martha lives with her author husband and two adopted dogs in Rio Rancho, New Mexico. They enjoy spending time at their cabin in the nearby Jemez Mountains and traveling the world. Last year, they visited Italy and most recently made it to their seventh continent, Antarctica!

Besides writing mystery novels and renting out the cabin, Martha's indoor activities include quilting, pickleball and learning to spin wool.

She also loves the outdoors and finds the weather perfect in New Mexico for hiking, biking, gardening, and hosting weekly movies at their large backyard movie theater.

*Scan the QR code for a quick link to Martha's website where you'll learn about fun news, giveaways, and* **Mini Morsels from Martha***.*

# What's next for Pity?

## PITY THE RELUCTANT FAN

*There's no crying in baseball…unless something goes afoul.*

When Pity is invited to go with her boyfriend on a bus tour of the East Coast Major League Baseball parks, she is reluctant to go because she doesn't like bus rides and worse, she dislikes sports. But she agrees to go along to spend quality time with Mike and explore the big cities.

Unfortunately, Mike has to leave the tour, and Pity must attend the games surrounded by extreme sports fans. After misfortune befalls people on her tour, Pity goes to bat for her new sport-loving friends and investigates the cause. In her typical style, Pity slides into trouble everywhere she goes, often causing more problems than she fixes.

Do we pity the miserable spectator, or will she hit a home run and solve the mystery?